A PENGUIN MYSTERY

JUNKYARD DOGS

Craig Johnson is the author of eight novels in the Walt Longmire mystery series, which has garnered popular and critical acclaim. *The Cold Dish* was a Dilys Award finalist and the French edition won Le Prix du Polar Nouvel Observateur/Bibliobs. *Death Without Company*, the Wyoming Historical Association's Book of the Year, won France's Le Prix 813, and *Kindness Goes Unpunished*, the third in the series, has also been published in France. *Another Man's Moccasins* was the Western Writers of America's Spur Award Winner and the Mountains & Plains Book of the Year, and *The Dark Horse*, the fifth in the series, was a *Publishers Weekly* Best Book of the Year. *Junkyard Dogs* won The Watson Award for a mystery novel with the best sidekick and *Hell Is Empty* was a *New York Times* bestseller. All are available from Penguin. The next in the series, *As the Crow Flies*, will be available in hardcover from Viking in May 2012. Craig Johnson's Walt Longmire novels have now been adapted for television in the series *Longmire*. Johnson lives in Ucross, Wyoming, population twenty-five.

Praise for *Junkyard Dogs*

"All of Johnson's trademarks are present in his sixth mystery featuring Sheriff Walt Longmire—great characters, witty banter, serious sleuthing, and a love of Wyoming bigger than a stack of derelict cars."
—*The Boston Globe*

"Great story, great people, great reading. Craig Johnson is on my 'can't miss' reading list."
—*Western Writers of America Roundup Magazine*

"[*Junkyard Dogs*] again demonstrates Johnson's biting wit and his ability to blend very human motivations, mystery, and mysticism. . . . Longmire displays his heart alongside his badge."
—*Billings Gazette*

"Johnson keeps things moving quickly . . . and gives us a snarling story lightened with bits of dark comedy."
—*Austin American-Statesman*

"Johnson inject[s] unpredictable twists that include complicated family bonds and family secrets. The breathtaking beauty of Wyoming shines in its pages."
—*Sun Sentinel*

"[Johnson's] chilly, muscular sense of place is . . . out in full force, along with page-turning plot twists. . . . Bundle up, pinch your nose, and dive in; the big sheriff won't let you down. Johnson continues to crank out top-notch literary mysteries in this series, which has proved hot with fans and critics alike since Longmire debuted in *The Cold Dish*."
—*The Portland Oregonian*

"[A] terrific mystery . . . Johnson's laconic, often laugh-out-loud style keeps the whole thing afloat amid the . . . blizzard-ridden landscape of Wyoming in February."
—*Providence Journal*

"A mystery storyteller at the level of Michael Connelly, Tony Hillerman, and James Sallis."
—*I Love a Mystery* magazine

"Longmire may be contemplating early retirement, but readers will demand that he serve out his full term of service—and run for reelection."
—*Booklist* (starred review)

"A compelling crime story and enduring hero . . . Series fans as well as newcomers will cheer the laconic Walt every step of the way."
—*Publishers Weekly*

Praise for the Walt Longmire Mystery Series

"The characters talk straight from the hip and the Wyoming landscape is its own kind of eloquence." —*The New York Times*

"Pile on thermal underwear, fire up the four-wheel drive, and head for Durant. Walt and his idiosyncratic crew are terrific company—droll, sassy, and surprisingly tenderhearted."
—*Kirkus Reviews* (starred review)

"Johnson delivers great storytelling in an intelligent mystery packed with terrific characters and an engulfing sense of place . . . capturing life in a breathtaking, unyielding landscape."
—*The Portland Oregonian*

"With five good novels behind him and more ahead, Craig Johnson is among the young luminaries of mystery fiction."
—*The Dallas Morning News*

"Walt Longmire is strong but fallible, a man whose devil-may-care stoicism masks a heightened sensitivity to the horrors he's witnessed. Unlike traditional genre novelists who obsess mainly over every hairpin plot turn, Johnson's books are also preoccupied with the mystery of his characters' psyches."
—*Los Angeles Times*

"Johnson knows the territory, both fictive and geographical, and tells us about it in prose that crackles. . . . A really good book."
—Robert B. Parker

Also by Craig Johnson:

The Cold Dish
Death Without Company
Kindness Goes Unpunished
Another Man's Moccasins
The Dark Horse
Hell Is Empty

Forthcoming from Viking:

As the Crow Files

CRAIG JOHNSON

JUNKYARD DOGS

PENGUIN BOOKS

PENGUIN BOOKS

Published by the Penguin Group

Penguin Group (USA) Inc., 375 Hudson Street, New York, New York 10014, U.S.A.

Penguin Group (Canada), 90 Eglinton Avenue East, Suite 700,
Toronto, Ontario, Canada M4P 2Y3 (a division of Pearson Penguin Canada Inc.)

Penguin Books Ltd, 80 Strand, London WC2R 0RL, England

Penguin Ireland, 25 St. Stephen's Green, Dublin 2, Ireland (a division of Penguin Books Ltd)

Penguin Books Australia Ltd, 250 Camberwell Road, Camberwell,
Victoria 3124, Australia (a division of Pearson Australia Group Pty Ltd)

Penguin Books India Pvt Ltd, 11 Community Centre,
Panchsheel Park, New Delhi–110 017, India

Penguin Group (NZ), 67 Apollo Drive, Rosedale, Auckland 0632,
New Zealand (a division of Pearson New Zealand Ltd)

Penguin Books (South Africa) (Pty) Ltd, 24 Sturdee Avenue,
Rosebank, Johannesburg 2196, South Africa

Penguin Books Ltd, Registered Offices:
80 Strand, London WC2R 0RL, England

First published in the United States of America by Viking Penguin,
a member of Penguin Group (USA) Inc. 2010
Published in Penguin Books 2011

5   7   9   10   8   6   4

Publisher's Note: This is a work of fiction. Names, characters, places, and incidents either
are the product of the author's imagination or are used fictitiously, and any resemblance to actual
persons, living or dead, business establishments, events, or locales is entirely coincidental.

THE LIBRARY OF CONGRESS HAS CATALOGED THE HARDCOVER EDITION AS FOLLOWS:
Johnson, Craig, 1961–
Junkyard dogs : a Walt Longmire mystery / Craig Johnson.
p. cm.
ISBN 978-0-670-02182-6 (hc.)
ISBN 978-0-14-311953-1 (pbk.)
1. Longmire, Walt (Fictitious character)—Fiction. 2. Sheriffs—Fiction.
3. Wyoming—Fiction. I. Title.
PS3610.O325J86 2010
813'.6—dc22   2009047237

Printed in the United States of America
Set in Dante MT
Designed by Alissa Amell

For Ned Tanen (1932–2009), friend, mentor,
and Cobra (CSX2125) co-pilot

ACKNOWLEDGMENTS

Around twenty years ago when I arrived back in Wyoming the second time, the only going retail concerns in Ucross were the Ewe-Turn Inn, a dilapidated Sinclair service station turned bar, and Sonny George's junkyard. His father's salvage operation had been transplanted to the fork of Clear and Piney Creeks, when the founding fathers of the county seat figured that the first thing you should not be confronted with when you exited the new interstate highway just outside Buffalo was a junkyard.

Sonny was a legend and a great source of car parts and home-grown philosophy. Other than derelict automobiles, the tiny corner where Wyoming routes 14 and 16 part ways had goats and dogs aplenty, and it was Sonny who was responsible for the addendum hand stenciled at the bottom of the UCROSS POPULATION 25 sign, which read DOG POPULATION 43.

He was cantankerous, so periodically people would call me and ask if I'd go over and barter with him. I would, because I liked him. He might have been obstreperous to those he considered outsiders, but he was always soft-spoken and dealt with me in an even-handed manner. There was an ongoing battle between Sonny and the Ucross Foundation, who desperately wanted to get the junkyard out of their backyard, but he held on until a massive coronary whisked him away via Flight For Life to Billings and beyond.

I sometimes stop at the corner, pull my truck over to the side, and look at the beautiful job that Ucross Land & Cattle did in cleaning the place, with the cottonwood trees and high-plains wildflowers—but I miss Sonny's junkyard. I never envisioned myself as one of those guys nursing a Rainier, sitting around the Ewe-Turn Inn, and starting all my statements with, "You know, back when . . ." Hey, things change, and the bar, like the junkyard, is gone, but I remember.

People ask where I get the stories for my novels and little do they know—I get them from the memories.

There are a few timeless models I'd like to thank for making not only this book possible, but all the others to boot. Gail Hochman, the '61, flat-floor Jaguar XKE, Series 1 of agents; Kathryn Court, the '59 Rolls Royce Silver Cloud of publishers; and Alexis Washam, the '66 Ferrari GTB/4 of editors—all of whom continue to check my oil and keep me aligned. A free windshield wash with fill-up for my good friends Maureen Donnelly, the '59 Cadillac Eldorado Biarritz of publicity czars; Ben Petrone, the '68 Hemi Dodge Charger R/T of senior publicists; and Meghan Fallon, the fuel-injected '63 split-window Corvette of publicists.

But most of all, to my wife, Judy, the '65 Shelby, MKIII 427 Cobra of my life—a true classic, and cherry.

See ya on the road,

—C.

Oh heart! Oh blood that freezes, blood that burns!
Earth's returns
For whole centuries of folly, noise and sin!
Shut them in,
With their triumphs and their glories and the rest!
Love is best.

"Love Among the Ruins," Robert Browning, 1885

JUNKYARD DOGS

1

I tried to get a straight answer from his grandson and granddaughter-in-law as to why their grandfather had been tied with a hundred feet of nylon rope to the rear bumper of the 1968 Oldsmobile Toronado.

I stared at the horn pad and rested my forehead on the rim of my steering wheel.

The old man was all right and being tended to in the EMT van behind us, but that hadn't prevented me from lowering my face in a dramatic display of bewilderment and despair. I was tired, and I wasn't sure if it was because of the young couple or the season.

"So, when you hit the brakes at the stop sign he slammed into the back of the car?"

It had been the kind of winter that tested the souls of even the hardiest; since October, we'd had nothing but blizzards, sifting snowstorms, freezing fogs, and cold snaps that had held the temperature a prisoner at ten below. We'd had relief in only one Chinook that had lasted just long enough to turn everything into a sloppy mess that then encased the county in about six inches of ice with the next freeze.

It was the kind of winter where if the cattle lay down, they weren't likely to get back up: frozen in and starved out.

I lifted my head and stared at Duane and Gina.

"Yeah, when I hit the brakes I heard this loud thump." She shrank into her stained parka with the matted, acrylic fur of the hood surrounding her face and tried not to light what I assumed was her last Kool Menthol.

We all sat in the cab of my truck with the light bar revolving to warn passing motorists of the icy roads. The roads, or more specifically the thick coating of ice on the roads, was what probably had saved Geo Stewart and, if it hadn't been for the numerous 911 calls that my dispatcher, Ruby, had fielded from passing motorists and the stop sign on state route 16, the seventy-two-year-old man would have made the most impromptu arrival into the town of Durant, Wyoming, in its history.

"I guess he slid into the back." Gina Stewart nodded the same way she had when she'd told me she'd been after cigarettes, Diet Coke, and a box of tampons from the Kum & Go, where she worked part-time.

I looked at the bubblegum-pink lipstick that stained her lone smoke. I'd warned her three times not to light up in my truck and tried to ignore the vague scent of marijuana that wafted off the pair. If she was down to her last cigarette, it smelled like they still had plenty of something else.

"He's a tough ol' fucker. That isn't the first time he's come off the roof."

We all listened to the static and random calls of northern

Wyoming law enforcement on my Motorola, and I stopped scribbling in my duty book. "The roof?"

"Yeah."

I looked at Duane, but he'd yet to utter anything more than a grunting agreement to whatever Gina had said. "Yunh-huh."

I studied the two of them and thought about resting my head on the steering wheel again. "The roof of the car?"

She shook her head inside the hood and pulled the unlit cigarette from her mouth. "Roof of the big house."

"The big house."

"Yeah."

It was quiet. I thought about the Stewart family's compound, comprising a Victorian house and a number of single- and double-wide trailers. "And what was he doing on the roof of the big house?"

She pulled the hood back from her face; the heater from my truck was just beginning to bring the temperature inside the vehicle to past the ice age. For the first time, I noticed she had enormous brown eyes and a lovely, heart-shaped face. It was spoiled by dirty-blond hair, but she was pretty in a shop-worn way.

She had learned that to captivate men you must treat them with the utmost attention. I'd only been in the cab with Gina for ten minutes, and I was already dizzy; of course, that could have been from the less-than-legal fumes floating off the two.

She looked at Duane, and so did I, figuring that the rest of the saga was his to tell.

Duane Stewart had dropped out of school at the age of fourteen with his parents' consent, because he was, in an internal combustion sense, gifted; if you had any type of motor-driven vehicle produced before 1972, Duane could fix it. He and his uncle Morris had a ramshackle mechanic's shop that was on the road to the junkyard, which was the family's other going concern.

Thickly built, he had a few pimples scattered across his face that reminded me how young he still was—early twenties at best. His eyes hunted mine, but he ducked away and cleared his throat. "Yunh-huh, we was cleanin' out the chimney."

I watched the blue and red lights from my truck that joined with the yellow ones from the EMT van behind us as they raced across the hillsides. "In February?"

He looked at his new wife again and then back to me. "Yunh-huh."

I took a breath and leaned back in my seat. "Maybe we need to start at the beginning."

The young man tipped his grease-stained cap back on his head—it read HEMI. "The chimney of the big house gets stopped up in the winter after you burn it for a few months, so we dip a mop in kerosene and force it down the flue to clean it out."

"Kerosene."

"Yunh-huh." He warmed to the story and began gesturing with his hands, the work embedded in the swirls of his fingerprints and nails. "I'd a done it, but I'm afraid of heights and Grampus's agile. He can climb out that top window on the gable end and get ahold of the gutter and swing a leg up onto the roof." He made the statement as if it should have settled everything.

It hadn't. "So, the rope—"

"It's slippery up there with the ice, so he tied it to his waist and slung it over the peak and I tied 'er off to the Classic."

It was coming all too clear now.

He nodded as he studied my face. "Yunh-huh. I was in the backyard watching Grampus when Gina come around the house and said she was going to the store and did we need anything. I told her no, and then she left."

I covered the smile that was creeping onto my face with a hand. "The Classic is the car that your grandfather was tied to—the Oldsmobile?"

"Yunh-huh. We heard the car door slam and the motor catch, and that's when Grampus and me looked at each other. It was about then that the rope went tight." His callused hand smacked the palm of his other and leapt forward. "Grampus fell over backward, and then he shot up the roof and over the other side."

"Duane, you stupid prick, how'm I supposed to know you've got Grampus tied to the back of the car?"

His neck stretched in indignation. "We . . . we do it every year." He turned back to me. "We dump snow beside the driveway, so I figure he landed on that, but with the forward momentum I don't figure he hit anything solid till he took out the mailbox at the end of the driveway."

I went ahead and rested my head on the steering wheel anyway.

Gina rejoined the conversation. "We always park the car facing forward so you can see both ways when you pull out." Then there was an accusation, just to even the score. "People drive too fast on that road, Sheriff."

Duane reached a hand out and played with the coiled cord that led to the mic clipped to my dash and then gestured toward his partner in crime. "I guess we're lucky nobody ran over him before she got stopped."

I raised my head and nodded. A local sculptor had made the first 911 call when the junkman had slid by him. "Mike Thomas says your grandfather waved as he passed him going the other way."

Gina nodded her head. "We like Mike."

They both smiled at me. I sighed and placed my pen on the aluminum clipboard. "So, what did you do then, Duane?"

"I jumped in one of the wreckers, but they ain't near as fast as that 455 in the Classic, and it's front-wheel drive so it took a while for me to catch up—especially with the roads bein' as slippery as they are, and by the time I got here that deputy of yours already had Gina pulled over."

Gina nodded. "And she used some really rude language."

I brought my face a little forward so that the young woman would know I was addressing her. "Did you hear the thump again, the second time—after Vic stopped you?"

She fingered the fur around her neck. "No, he kinda swung into the barrow ditch back there after I made the turn."

I nodded and slipped the clipboard back into the pocket of the driver's side door. The Stewarts were a drama waiting in the wings. It seemed as far back as I could remember the clan members had been involved with some form of misadventure or another, usually resulting in a visit to the Durant Memorial emergency room.

"Duane, didn't your dad die falling off a roof?" The young couple sat there unmoving, and I didn't say anything either. It wasn't like I was accusing him; I just wasn't perfectly sure. "About five years ago, wasn't it?"

Duane's eyes stayed still, and his head dropped a bit. "Nunh-uh, it was a heart attack."

I assumed that *Nunh-uh* was the opposite of *Yunh-huh* and nodded at him to encourage the rest. "After he fell off the roof."

"Yunh-huh."

I was sorry to keep at the boy since it seemed to sadden him, but I figured I had a certain amount of leeway in the interest of public safety. "He wasn't cleaning the chimney with the kerosene mop, was he?"

The young man took a deep breath. "Nunh-uh." He cleared his throat. "It was in September, and he was patching a hole. He slipped and fell—then he had the heart attack."

Charging any member of the Stewart family with reckless endangerment smacked of delivering coals to Newcastle, or to Moorcroft, for that matter. I nodded and pulled down my new hat, buttoned my sheepskin coat, and flipped the collar up to defend against the bracing February wind that was slicing down the foothills of the Bighorn Mountains.

I opened the door and lodged myself in the opening just long enough to speak to Duane one more time. "You know, Duane, maybe your family should stay off roofs."

*　　*　　*

We were in the process of enduring our second week of sub-zero temperatures for the third time; in the day it was no higher than a balmy one, and at night it plummeted to as low as forty below. Everybody was getting tired of it, and I was threatening to move to New Mexico again.

I passed the '68 Toronado, which I considered the ugliest car to ever roll out of Detroit on bias-ply tires. It was a gold-colored beast with more than a few rust patches but, as my deputies could testify, the drive train had been modified to the point that it wasn't your father's Oldsmobile anymore, and it ran like a raped ape. Ever since they'd gotten married a little less than six months ago, Duane and Gina had taken turns do-ing public service and going to driving school in attempts to keep their respective licenses.

I noticed the untied yellow rope still leading to the ditch, felt the onset of another headache, and trudged on.

I'd broken a bone in my foot back in October, and it was still giving me a little trouble. Struggling against the wind and attempting to get a good footing and a half on the ice, I lurched one of the back doors of the EMT van open. The vehicle was parked in the drive of Deer Haven Campground beside Vic's unit, and I almost knocked myself out on the ve-hicle's headliner.

Vic stood by the other door. I looked at my undersher-iff. Second-generation law enforcement, Victoria Moretti was the personification of the fact that ferocious things come in small packages. After five years in the Philadelphia police department, she'd landed in our high-altitude, currently perma-frosted neck of the woods and had slowly begun defrosting my heart. She looked like one of those women you see draped over the hoods at car shows; that is, if you've ever seen one with attitude and a seventeen-shot Glock.

Santiago Saizarbitoria—Sancho, as Vic had christened our Basque deputy—was seated on the wheel well and was watching as Cathi Kindt swabbed road debris from a few scratches and burns on Geo Stewart's ear where he'd collided with one of the chrome-tipped tailpipes of the Olds.

I looked at the assembled deputies and EMTs—it was either a slow day for civil service on the high plains or everybody was looking for a place to get inside. I put my gloved hands on my knees and leaned in for a look at the junkman. "You know, in this country we usually reserve this kind of treatment for horse thieves."

Geo smiled, red-faced and glassy-eyed. He was a ball of tendons and stringy muscle, tanned by the scorching Wyoming summers and freeze-dried by the winters into a living jerky. He had pale blue eyes, and the edge of his pupils looked like rime ice.

The aged Carhartt coveralls hung from him like shed skin with torn openings that exposed a red lining looking like a subcutaneous wound. His logging boots were double-tied, and he sported a welder's undercap in a faded floral print. A huge key ring, attached to a loop at his hip, jingled as he spoke. "Hey, Sheriff."

George "Geo" Stewart's great-grandfather was one of the original founders of Durant and said to be the first Caucasian baby born in the territory, but it was Geo's father who started the junkyard after the Second World War. When a mild amount of suburban sprawl overtook his collection of discarded automobiles and trucks in the early sixties, the county commissioners persuaded Geo the elder to take his rusting inventory and swap his in-town spread for a larger one farther east that they had acquired from Dirty Shirley, the last madam to do business in the county.

The commissioners had retained some of the land next to the junkyard and had made it the town landfill, so when Geo the elder died, Geo the younger inherited the junkyard and the part-time position of maintaining the weigh-station scales and the municipal property.

He had a knack for such things, and I only heard from him when people tried to dump without a city water bill, when they tried to skim on the amount of refuse they unloaded, or when kids got into his junkyard and tried to make off with vintage goods. "Hey, Geo, how are things up at the dump?"

His expression took on a serious quality, but he was nothing if not unfailingly polite. "With all due respect, Walt, Municipal Solid Waste Facility."

I shook my head at the old man. "Right."

"He won't go to the hospital." Cathi looked back at me. The Absaroka County sheriff's department might not have too much to do besides stay in out of the winter wind, but Cathi Kindt was another story.

I avoided the paramedic's gaze and sat next to Sancho. "Does he need to?"

She sat on the gurney next to George and folded her arms.

"He's seventy-two years old and just got dragged behind a car for two and a quarter miles."

I took off my hat and studied the inside band to gain a little time and let Cathi cool off. Mike Hodges up at H-Bar Hats in Billings had been kind enough to build me a fawn-colored one, since I'd pitched the last one into the Powder River after I decided that I was not a black hat kinda guy.

I leaned forward and looked past the irate EMT. Geo was still smiling at me, and I figured his teeth were the best part on him. "He looks pretty good, considering." The grin broadened. "How do you feel, Geo?"

He looked around the interior of the van and took in the expensive equipment. "I ain't got any of that gaddam insurance."

I figured as much. "Geo, what part of you hit the mailbox?" Everybody in the van looked at me, Cathi started to speak, and Vic covered a grin and snorted a quick laugh.

"M'shoulder." He moved it, and I could see its alien position and hear the joint grind. "Little stiff."

"Why don't we get it X-rayed?"

He shrugged with the other shoulder. "I told ya. I don't have none of that insurance."

I smiled back at him and shook my head. "It's okay, Geo, the county's got plenty of money."

"I want a raise." Vic walked along beside me as the glass doors of Durant Memorial's emergency entrance closed behind us.

"No."

We were bringing up the rear of the Municipal Solid

Waste Facility entourage. I nodded for Saizarbitoria to follow the gurney into the operating room and gestured to Duane and Gina that they should sit on the sofas by the entryway where Geo's brother, Morris, joined them. He'd evidently heard that his brother had been injured, and the gravity of the situation was partially reflected in the fact that as far as I knew, the man only came into town about three times a year.

"Hi, Morris." I waved at him, but he didn't wave back.

"You just said the county has plenty of money."

I lowered my voice in an attempt to get her to lower hers. "They do for medical services involving recalcitrant, uninsured junkmen but not for the sheriff department's payroll."

Her voice became more conversational. "I want to buy a house."

I nodded and then smiled just to let her know that she shouldn't take her current annual wage personally. "Then you should work hard and save your money."

"Fuck you."

"It's amazing the respect I seem to command from my staff, isn't it?"

Janine, who sat behind the desk, was my dispatcher Ruby's granddaughter. She looked up at us from her paperback, nodded, and scratched under her chin with the large, pink eraser of her pencil. "Amazing."

Vic leaned her back against the counter and crossed her legs at the ankles. "I'm not kidding, at least about the house. I'm tired of living in a place with wheels on it."

Ever since arriving in county, Vic had occupied a single-wide by the highway, and I'd often wondered why she hadn't taken up a more permanent residence. Perhaps my latest re-election and promise to abdicate to her in two years was having an effect. "Where is this house you want?"

"Over on Kisling. It's a little Craftsman place."

I looked past her. "The one with the red door?"

She didn't say anything for a moment. "Okay, who died there?"

I shrugged. "Nobody. I just drove by yesterday and saw a for sale sign. Do you know that the Jacobites in Scotland painted their doors red in support of the Forty-Five Rebellion and Bonnie Prince Charlie?"

"Do you know I don't give a bonnie big shit?"

Janine snickered.

Vic uncrossed her ankles and shifted from one booted foot to the other. "I've got an appointment to go over and look at it again tonight. I guess there's a bunch of people interested."

"Would you like me to go with you?"

She raised an exquisite eyebrow. "Why in the *This Old House* hell would I want you to do that?"

She had a point; my home skills were just short of negligible—I'd only gotten around to having the Mexican tile in my six-year-old log cabin installed this past fall. "It's a guy thing; even if you don't know anything about cars, you open the hood and look at the engine."

"Seven-thirty. Then I'll let you take me out to dinner."

I took the weight off my sore foot and looked down at my boots, which were covered with buckled galoshes. "That's a nice part of town. The houses around there usually go in a hurry. What do they want for it?"

"One-seventy-one, but I think I can get it for one-sixty-two. Alphonse says he'll front me the down, and then I can just pay him back when I can, sans interest."

Alphonse was Vic's uncle who had a pizza parlor in Philadelphia and, other than Vic's mother, Lena, the only non-cop Moretti. "How's the rest of the family feel about this?"

"They don't know about it." As a general rule, the machinations of the Moretti family made the Borgias' seem like Blondie and Dagwood.

Her shoulder bumped into my arm as she changed the subject. "So, your daughter and my brother are getting married this summer?"

I took a deep breath with a quick exhale. "All I know is what I get from the answering machine at home."

"At least you've got a home." She shifted her weight again, this time in not-so-simple dissatisfaction. "Mom says the end of July."

I shrugged. "Mom would know." I thought about Vic's mother, and the brief time I'd spent in Philly almost a year ago. "Did she mention whether they were thinking of doing it here or in Philadelphia?"

She looked up at me. "There was supposedly talk about some special place on the Rez—Crazy something . . ."

I thought about it. "Crazy Head Springs?"

"That's it."

"Uh-oh."

"Why uh-oh?"

"It's where I once helped raise the powwow totem; it's a

sacred place for the Cheyenne but controversial. Crazy Head was a Crow chief, but part of the break-off Kicks-in-the-Belly band."

"Like Virgil?"

"Yep, like Virgil." Virgil had been one of our holding cell lodgers who, after having been released, had gone MIA. "The Cheyenne don't like the idea of a Crow chief being exalted on their reservation. Henry took Cady along with us when she was seven, and she's always said she wanted to be married there."

Vic shook her head. "We'll see if it lasts till the summer."

"What's that supposed to mean?"

Her eyes met mine, but she diverted again. "So, has the Basquo talked to you?"

I started to yawn and covered my mouth with my hand. "About what?"

"Quitting."

I stopped in mid-yawn. "What?"

I studied her a moment more, but my eyes were drawn to an approaching lab coat flapping toward us from the hallway. I swiveled my head to meet Isaac Bloomfield, surgeon and all-around Durant Memorial physician-in-charge. As a member of the lost tribe, who must've really been lost when he settled in Wyoming, Isaac Bloomfield had set up practice in Absaroka County more than a half century ago. He had been one of the three living inmates of Dora-Mittelbau's Nordhausen when Allied troops had liberated the Nazi *Vernichtungslager*. "How's the patient?"

"Well, that's the first time we've ever had that happen."

He looked up at me through the thick lenses of his glasses, which magnified the multiple layers of skin around his eyes. "His hair has grown through his long underwear."

Vic made an unflattering noise through her nose.

"Probably more than we needed to know, Doc."

He adjusted his glasses and motioned with his almost bald head toward the double doors of the ER. "Walter, I need you to come with me." He glanced back as Vic started to follow. "Alone."

I turned to her as I followed the thin man into the inner sanctums of Durant Memorial. "Stay here. I want to know more about the house and the wedding. And Sancho."

She stuffed her hands in the pockets of her duty jacket and called after me. "I've got that appointment at seven-thirty."

The Doc walked me into the first examination room and closed the door. I glanced around and noticed we were the only ones there; that's why I'm a sheriff, because I notice things like that. "Where's the patient?"

He placed the edge of the clipboard on the counter next to a sink and studied me. "In the next room."

"Please tell me he didn't just have a heart attack." I thought about it. "You know the family has a history."

"Yes, but the patient in question suffers primarily from diabetes, not heart disease."

"All right, then." I looked at him. "What's up, Doc?"

I stood there in his disapproving silence. He slowly brought his gaze up. "You've had a rough year. A very rough year." He peered at me and tapped the examination bench. "Climb up here."

"Isaac, I don't have time . . ."

He patted the clipboard. "Neither do I. I have every intention of retiring soon and handing the responsibility for this place over to the new young man we've hired."

"Who?"

He ignored me and patted his clipboard again. "These are the mandatory examination papers for the county health plan and, if you do not sit down, I will have them cancel the coverage."

I took a deep breath and looked at him; he was studying the contents of the folder that contained a running documentary of my physical misadventures. The Doc usually dragged me in for the health insurance examination whenever he felt it was high time and long enough.

Bushwhacked.

"Ruby called you, didn't she?" He didn't say anything, so I sighed, stepped up, and sat.

He placed the file on the gurney beside me, reached out and thumbed both sides of my knee, pressing up on the cap through my jeans. "How's the knee?"

I winced. "All right, till you started monkeying around with it."

He looked up at me, all the world the likeness of some venerated Caesar and just as forgiving. "The shotgun wound to your leg has healed moderately well?"

"Yep."

"No lingering symptoms from pneumonia from drowning?"

"I didn't really drown."

His voice was sharp. "When you have to be resuscitated, you drowned."

"Okay."

"Take off your coat."

I did, and he took my left hand and examined the scar tissue. He held my upper arm and turned my forearm, rotating the elbow. "Does this hurt?"

I lied. "No."

He unsnapped my cuff, raised the sleeve of my shirt, and looked more closely at the elbow itself. "You have some swelling here, under the scar tissue."

I lied again. I didn't usually lie, but with the Doc it had become a habit. "I've always had that."

He shook his head and manipulated my shoulder. It sounded gravelly like Geo Stewart's. "The shoulder?"

"It feels great."

"It doesn't feel great to me, and it doesn't sound so good either." He frowned as he compressed the joint and lifted my arm. "How's that?"

It actually hurt like hell, so I pulled my arm loose. "Not so great, which is why I've dropped mandatory departmental saluting."

"How is your foot?"

"Fabulous."

He studied me with a look, and the only description that might apply would be askance. "You're still limping."

"I've come to consider it a character trait."

"Take off your hat."

"I don't think that's going to help with the limp."

He placed his hands on my head, adjusted the angle, and pulled my left eye down for a look; this was the part I was dreading. He released my head and got a small plastic bottle of something from the cabinet behind him. "These drops are for your eyes; would you like to do it, or would you prefer I administer them?"

"How many drops?"

He held up two fingers, and I did my part for the advancement of medical science. My vision became blurry as he studied his wristwatch and waited. After a bit, he reexamined my eyes. "Well, your pupils don't show any particular abrasion, but it's the damage to the ocular cavity that has me worried." He released me, picked up the file, and stepped back, folding his arms over the folder and his chest. "I can't make out any detachment of the retina, but it's possible that there's some trauma." He thumbed his chin and continued to look at me like a card player would an inside straight.

"I could'a been a contender, Doc."

"You could also go blind as a bat in your left eye if you get hit there again."

I froze. "What?"

"Just a little medical humor. If you're not going to take your condition seriously, why should I?" He hugged my file a little tighter. "Still having the headaches?"

"Only when I come in here."

I had made the mistake of mentioning to Ruby that I had had a few recurring headaches, which must have resulted in this examination. I started to edge my rear end off the table.

"How often?" He continued to study me without moving out of my way.

I took a breath and settled. "Every once in a while."

"What about the flashes?"

"It was a onetime thing; I just moved my head too fast." Once again, it was a lie, and I was pushing my luck because the Doc was pretty good at spotting them. After those smiling government *Gruppenführers* with black uniforms had taken him away, Isaac Bloomfield had become a walking polygraph test.

"You're sure?"

The trick to a good lie, no matter how outrageous, is sticking to it. "Yep."

He shook his head very slightly, just to let me know he knew I was lying. "Walter, I have a deal for you."

"Okay."

He started to speak but then stopped. After a moment he licked his upper lip and tried again. "I will sign these forms indicating that you are in fine shape, which you are for a young man with this many accumulated injuries." I liked it when the Doc called me a young man and tried not to dwell on the fact that he was in his eighties. "But, only on one condition."

There was always a catch with the Doc. "And that is?"

"You have Andy Hall in Sheridan do a complete examination of your left eye."

"All right."

I had started to get up again, but it was too quick of an answer and he placed a hand on my knee, the bad one, to stop me. "I will set up the appointment."

I hedged. "I can do it, just give me his number."

"No, I will make the appointment for you. What time this week is good?"

"This week?" Even with my blurred vision, I could see his large brown eyes studying me.

"Yes."

Damn. I thought about it and figured the more time I had, the more time I'd have to get out of it. "Friday?"

He produced a pen from his lab coat pocket and scribbled on the top of the forms with a flourish followed by a stabbing period. "Thursday."

"That's Valentine's Day."

He smiled, his mission accomplished. "Maybe your heart will be in it."

I pulled on my coat and put on my hat. "All right, now that you're through cutting me off at the pass, do you mind telling me how Geo Stewart is?"

"Routine dislocation of the left shoulder."

"Well, that would explain why he was waving at passing traffic with only one arm."

Isaac nodded. "I'd like to keep him here for observation, but there's something else that's come up in casual conversation that I thought you might need to know."

"Now why do I not like the sound of that?"

Isaac Bloomfield cleared his throat. "It would appear, that at the dump—"

"You mean the Municipal Solid Waste Facility?"

The Doc continued as if I hadn't interrupted. "They have found a body part."

2

"We could put it in the lost and found." I stared at him as he scratched his substantial beard. "Are you sure it's a finger, Geo? 'Cause if we drive all the way out there, and it's the end of a leftover bratwurst . . ."

"Not 'less they started puttin' fingernails on hot dogs."

I looked around the room. Neither Saizarbitoria nor Doc Bloomfield was offering much help. I sighed and chewed on the inside of my lip. "I don't suppose there's an engraved ring with the owner's name inside on that finger, is there?"

He thought about it. "Nope, just the finger."

"That was a joke, Geo."

"Oh."

I studied the old man and decided that his hat might've been a red and white floral pattern when it started out, but the accumulated grease gave it a rich patina that approached black. Curls of dirty silver escaped from underneath the cap and reached down past his predominant Adam's apple. His skin was roasted a burnt coffee from the acid of long, hard labor and more than a few lines were etched around the welled sockets of his mouth and his Caribbean blue eyes.

Whenever I saw his eyes up close, I wondered what he would look like if he ever washed or shaved. Chances were, the collective county would never know.

"Can he travel, Doc?"

The attending physician nodded and crossed his arms over his ever-present clipboard. "I suppose so. His family members are still in the waiting room."

I took a deep breath and leaned in as close to Geo as the fumes would allow. "Promise me, this time, you'll ride inside the car?"

I pulled my ten-year-old Ray-Bans from my breast pocket and steered them onto my face to give my dilated pupils a little relief. Even though the skies were gloomy, damp, and gray like a dead body, there was enough of a glare to affect my sight. It was that part of the winter that stretched out like a Russian novel—a really, really long one.

I carefully picked my way across the frozen moguls of the Durant Memorial Hospital parking lot with Santiago Saizarbi-toria trailing along behind me.

I wanted a little time with the Basquo alone.

It wasn't very far to the reserved emergency vehicle spot, but I was glad I'd remembered to put my galoshes back on. I started to open the driver's side of my truck but then remembered that my eyes were still dilated. I stepped back to look at Sancho. "Sorry, I forgot."

I walked around the front of my unit to the unfamiliar passenger side of the Bullet. When I opened the door, there was a surprise—Dog was seated in the front. He turned to look at me as if I'd lost my mind. He had Saint Bernard in him and some German shepherd with a bunch of other things, most of them domesticated except for when you had bacon— then he was part great white shark.

"Where the hell did you come from?" We stared at each other or him at me and me in his blurry, general direction. "Back."

He looked forlorn for a moment and then hopped his hundred-and-forty-five-pound frame onto the jump seat in the rear of the cab. I climbed in and turned to sort of look back at him. "Sorry, official business."

Saizarbitoria climbed in the driver's side, closed the door, strapped himself in, and turned to look at me. "You got the keys?"

"Yep." I snagged the set from my jacket pocket and handed them to him. He fired up the three-quarter-ton, and I pointed a finger south. "To the dump, James."

As he negotiated the parking lot, I fumbled with the mic on the dash and keyed the button in order to raise Ruby. "Base, this is unit one, over?"

Static. "How was your examination?"

"I'm going to get you for that. So, did Dog make his way to my truck or did you send him over with someone?"

Static. "The Ferg dropped him off on his way home. I've got a Methodist women's meeting tonight, and you're not trustworthy."

Ruby did a lot of dog-sitting for me, and it was true that I abused the privilege every once in a while.

The airwaves went dead without further comment or levity.

I glanced at the young deputy in my driver's seat and thought about what Vic had said. He looked good, considering what he'd gone through in the last few months, what with complications stemming from having a serrated kitchen knife filleting one of his kidneys in July and the birth of his first child, Antonio, in November. I'd been easing him back into full-time duty, but it did seem that his energy level was low. "So, you wanna take this show on the road?"

The Basquo smiled weakly as he rolled the steering wheel and pulled out. "Yeah."

I looked out into the frozen landscape and thought about my daughter; I thought about how she hadn't called lately, which is what I usually thought when I thought about Cady. I blamed it on the young man she was going to marry this summer, figured they had a lot to talk about. Michael Moretti was occupying Cady's time, and I was jealous.

The radio broke up my infantile reverie.

Static. "Vic just got here. Are you taking Dog to the dump?"

I keyed the mic and reached around to pat his massive head. "Sure, with twenty-three square inches of olfactory membrane, it'll be like Disneyland for him."

Static. "Don't forget about the Stewarts' dogs."

Geo had a pair of mutt wolf-dogs, Butch and Sundance, that were famous countywide as being two of the fiercest creatures this side of Cerberus. They had killed a cougar, a few coyotes, and run at least a couple of black bears off their turf—not to mention more than a few adventurous teenagers. I looked back at the now-expectant canine eyes. Mine were still swimming a slight backstroke as I keyed the mic again. "I'll keep him close."

Static. "He gets filthy, you get to wash him."

"Deal." Dog looked at me and smiled a fanged smile while I scratched under his wide chin.

I turned back and studied Saizarbitoria as he carefully drove my truck out of town, and I tried desperately to see a little bit of the wayward spark in the musketeer's eye.

Sancho steered through the foothills outside Durant—the darkening skies were absorbing what little heat there had been and giving none. It was Monday of the second week in February and people talked less because their words were snatched from their mouths and cast to Nebraska. I had an image of all the unfinished statements and conversations from Wyoming piled along the sand hills until the snow muffled them and they sank into the dark earth. Maybe they rose again in the spring like prairie flowers, but I doubted it.

As we made the turn where Geo Stewart had slid into the barrow ditch, an orange '78 Ford pickup waved us down. A mustached cowboy lowered his window as Santiago switched on the emergency lights and slowed to a gentle, sliding stop on the rinklike ice.

The Basquo pushed the button on his window, and I shouted across him. "Hey, Mike."

The sculptor shook his head and smiled. "Did you get old man Stewart untied from that Oldsmobile?"

"Yep, we did."

"I wasn't sure if somebody had cut him loose or if he'd just worn off." He draped a hand over his steering wheel and checked to make sure no one was behind him. "I dropped a load of junk off at the dump, but there wasn't anybody at the scales, so I figured you'd taken the old man to the hospital." He drew his hand across his face and chuckled. "Ozzie Dobbs was up there unloading a bunch of stuff, and I don't mind tellin' you he was just as happy to not see Geo there."

I looked through the windshield and thought about the new housing development that had planted itself on the rise that led to the foothills just west of the dump and Geo's junkyard. They didn't call it a housing development, but that's what it was, if you could call five-acre ranchettes with four-million-dollar mansions alongside a golf course a housing development.

Redhills Rancho Arroyo had been the brainchild of Ozzie Dobbs Sr., a developer from the southern part of the state, who had taken the opportunity to buy the cheap land adjacent to the dump that happened to have views of the eastern slope of the Bighorns. Ozzie Sr. had quietly passed about two and a half years ago, and the reins had gone to his son, Ozzie Jr., who had been making a public case for having the junkyard/dump moved again. Geo Stewart was having none of it.

Mike Thomas's tidy, picturesque ranch was over a couple of ridges from my cabin, and whenever Martha and I had driven by Mike's place, my late wife had looked at it wistfully. He'd sculpted it as meticulously as he did his statuary, with hand-hewn logs, crafted doors, and an artist's eye. It made me want to hate his guts, but he was too nice a guy. Geographic proximity made him an interested party in what was, southeast of town, the makings of a modern range war.

All this history clattered through my mental projector and slapped the tail end with the sculptor's voice. "Walt, those people are a hazard."

I tried to rethread the film. "Yep, but thank goodness it's mostly to themselves." I smiled back at him to let him know that my preoccupation wasn't personal. "Hey, Mike, can you show me your hands?"

He looked puzzled but held up a full complement of digits.

We continued on our way, and I remarked to Sancho with my most determined investigative face. "We call that detecting."

He didn't laugh like he used to.

We drove into the driveway of the Stewart family's big house, careful to avoid the mailbox lying in the roadway, and took the cutoff leading to the junkyard's double gates, which were across from the dump's drive-on scales.

The combination junkyard/dump was in an old gravel quarry, and the cliffs at the back of the place rose to almost a hundred feet. Even though you could see row after row of antiquated vehicles to the left and mound after mound of trash to the right, it wasn't a bad spot.

Geo's incongruous-looking office, an art-deco structure that had been salvaged from the city pool and still a startling, if peeling, turquoise with white circular windows and rounded trim, was straight ahead. If you looked hard enough, you could still see the darker paint where the letters that spelled SNACK BAR had fallen off.

The Classic was parked by the scales along with a phalanx of tow trucks, all from different decades, but no one seemed to be around.

"Pull over here and park it."

He did as I requested without comment. It was possible he was dreading the rest of the long winter even more than I was and that his words were also gone to Nebraska with the wind.

I took a sounding. "How's Marie?"

It took a moment, but the words slowly surfaced. "More tired than she was when she was pregnant."

"I bet." I had thought about telling him a few months ago how tiring it would be when the little rascal was out and about but had decided to keep that nugget of wisdom to my-self. "How's Antonio?"

He continued to look at the zigzag patterns of snow, his face away from me. "He sleeps . . . sometimes."

"It can get a little wearing."

I watched his breath on the window. "What?"

"Babies, they can get a little wearing."

He still didn't move. "Yeah."

"Have you figured out whose he is?"

He sat there until he turned his head far enough forward so that one eye drifted my way. "What?"

I leaned against my door, readjusted my old .45 so that it wasn't poking me, and looked at the Basquo. "All right, what's on your mind, Sancho."

He contemplated the Remington twelve-gauge locked onto the transmission hump, and we sat there listening to the dry rhythm of the wind gusts as they pushed against the outside of the truck. His voice sounded like it was coming out of a barrel. "I'm thinking about going back to corrections."

Santiago had started his law enforcement career in Rawlins at the state prison's maximum security wing. I'd had him for less than a year but liked him and wanted to keep him. "Why?"

It took him a moment to respond. "I think I'm better suited working in an environment where I know everybody's guilty."

I smiled. "At least judged to be guilty by a jury of their peers."

"Well then, in an environment where I can treat everybody as if they're guilty." I didn't say anything. "Look, I know you're going to try and talk me out of doing this . . ."

"No, I'm not."

"You're not?"

"Nope." I tipped my hat back and looked at him. "You decide to go, I'll give you a recommendation that'll turn the state attorney general's head, but the only thing I ask is that you give it a few weeks and not make your move too quickly. It seems to me you've got an awful lot on your plate right now and—"

"I'm giving you my two-weeks' notice as of today." He turned back to the glass.

So much for the wise ol' sheriff routine.

I closed my mouth, took a breath, and continued to inspect him for remnants of the man I'd hired fourteen months ago. It was a tough business coming to terms with your own mortality, and some people, once they are confronted with its face, never forget its features. "Okay."

We returned to the silence, and then he spoke again. "I've talked it over with Marie."

I thought about Martha and how she'd never adjusted to the life. "Okay." The word was like a bad taste.

"You still want me for the two weeks?"

I thought about all those years, all those times I'd thought about quitting. "You bet."

I cracked open my door, and even in the cold, the smell was like a wall.

I had noticed that Duane had approached the driver's side of the truck, but Sancho hadn't. When Duane tapped on the driver's side window, Santiago started, which made Duane jump back in turn, whereupon he lost his balance and fell onto the frozen ground, which was pooled with a slick of motor oil and frozen rusty water.

Sancho turned and looked at me. "Jesus."

I opened the door the rest of the way, and Dog jumped out. I gave Duane a hand up. There were tattoos on his knuckles and under his thermal hood was a T-shirt with the inscription, MESS WITH ME, AND YOU MESS WITH THE WHOLE TRAILER PARK. The humor didn't seem to match the young man's sensibilities, so someone must've bought it for him or maybe I was underestimating Duane.

"You guys here about the hand?"

I nodded. "We heard it was just a finger."

He looked nervous, but then he always looked nervous when we were around. He still smelled vaguely like marijuana. "Yunh-huh, yeah, a finger."

I heard a low growl and looked at Dog, who was sitting on my foot. He was transfixed and looking directly at the junkyard's quasi-office where, in one of the claw-scarred, Plexiglas windows, Butch and Sundance were seated at attention with only their heads showing. They were as big as Dog but not as bulky. He growled again, low enough to quake my own lungs, and I swatted at him.

"Stop it." He easily evaded my hand and looked at me, hurt at my admonishment. I threw a chin toward the two Heinz fifty-seven variety wolves. "They're behaving, so you better be good or I'll put you back in the truck."

I glanced at the two sets of eyes that studied us, aware that even if they were behaving, it didn't mean they weren't planning. There was something about the way they sat there quietly that reminded me of what my friend Henry Standing Bear says about the quiet ones being like the Cheyenne, waiting until you were in a compromised position, then moving to action. For now, they were behind closed doors, and I was just as glad.

"Are you watching the office for your grandfather?"

"Yunh-huh."

"Where's he?"

He gestured with a thick hand. "That way."

I nodded and started off. "Make sure to keep Butch and Sundance in the office, okay?"

"Okay."

Piles of garbage were heaped to the surrounding hillsides

on our right and as Double Tough, another of my deputies, would have said, the unfettered smells were bad enough to gag a maggot off a gut wagon. All in all, it looked pretty much how I was beginning to feel.

The Basquo caught up but kept a hand over his mouth and nose. "How about I stay in the truck?"

I shook my head. "Nunh-unh." I waited for a response, but there wasn't any. "If this is your last two weeks, then you're going to be the primary on this one."

He sighed, and his shoulders shrugged a little as he stuffed the small evidence kit under his arm. "It's freezing. How come we don't just drive the rest of the way in?"

"Because I've already lost two tires to scrap metal and wayward drywall screws in this place, and I'm not about to lose another."

I flipped the collar up on my coat and stuffed my gloved hands even deeper into my pockets. The high plains was a place of extremes with a people of extremes—most of my work involved the sentient and venal aspects of human nature—but even with the wet and the real, we generally didn't get body parts.

As we walked toward the hill, there was a cracking sound from the road that led to the dump's interior. Saizarbitoria looked in the direction of the noise and then back to me. "Are those shots?" There was more than a little concern in his voice.

"Yep. A .22, I'd say."

He picked up his pace, and I followed along like a one-man posse. I'd gone about three steps when I remembered Dog—he was still watching Butch and Sundance. "Hey."

He looked at me, back to them, and then followed.

I nudged him with my leg. "What're you, a tough guy?"

When we got over the hill, it was as I'd expected. Geo Stewart, Durant Memorial Hospital patient-at-large, was dispatching rats with a Savage automatic varmint rifle at an alarming rate. At least, I assumed it was rats. He turned to prop the stock on his knee so that he could remove the tiny magazine, gave us a brief nod of his head to indicate that he was aware of our presence, and then scooped a handful of rounds from his stained and tattered Carhartt. "Hey, Sheriff, long time no see."

Evidently the shoulder wasn't bothering him. "Hey, Geo."

He studied my face as we got closer. "Somethin' wrong with your eyes?"

I pushed my sunglasses farther up onto my nose, effectively covering the twin saucers of my pupils. "What are you shooting, Geo?"

He went back to thumbing .22 longs into the spring clip of the rifle's magazine. "Damnable rats, found one of 'em in the cooler trying to run off with the finger I told you about." His chest-length beard was zipped into his coat. "Adjuster came up here a few months ago and said that if I didn't do something they'd cancel the insurance. Gaddam insurance."

Sancho pulled the collar of his jacket up as a makeshift filter since the wind had shifted and we were now getting the full, odiferous impact of the surroundings. "Jesus." The Euskadi eyes leveled with the junkman's. "How do you get used to the smell?"

Geo eyed him without irony and then moved off with the words "What smell?"

★   ★   ★

It was a two-gallon Styrofoam cooler—one of the cheap ones that you can pick up at any service station in the summer season and then listen to it squeak to the point of homicidal dementia. It was sitting on the top of a toppled old avocado-colored refrigerator from the seventies. The cooler must've been relatively new, however, because it had a bar code sticker on the side.

I didn't take my hands out of my pockets. "So, is the fickle finger of fate in this?"

Geo nodded, and he, Dog, and I looked at the Basquo.

"Okay, fine." Saizarbitoria stepped up and plucked the top from the cooler, the vacuum pressure causing it to shiver as he lifted. He stood there for a moment, craning his neck for another perspective, and then closed it. "It's not a finger."

I could tell the effects of the drops were beginning to fade as I looked at Geo, who was starting to protest.

Santiago raised a hand. "It's part of a thumb."

I stepped in, and the Basquo obliged me by lifting the lid again.

The thumb was lodged in a thin skim of ice along with a little dirt and a couple of crushed Olympia beer cans. I made a show of pulling my hands from my pockets, then holding them up like a fighter pilot for review. "Not mine."

Geo went as far as to present his two thumbs, and we both turned toward Saizarbitoria, who refused to play the game.

It was fresh, and of prodigious size, almost as large as my own. Mottled with a whitish cast, the separated end was crushed and gave no impression of having been surgically removed—it was going to be hard to get a print. "Male."

Santiago nodded. "Yeah."

"What do you figure?"

The Basquo took a deep breath and immediately regretted it. "A day, maybe two, but as cold as it's been it could be longer."

I nodded. "Maybe it just froze off somebody."

He pulled an evidence bag from his kit along with a pair of plastic gloves, which he stretched with a bellows of air from his lungs. He stuffed his leather gloves in his jacket pocket and then snapped the latex ones over his hands. He set the cooler top to the side and reached in to gingerly take the digit from the filthy ice; then he placed it in the evidence bag, zipped it shut, replaced the cooler top, and wedged the entirety under his arm.

"I'll check the bar code with local merchants, interview the medicos to see if anybody had a thumb removed or was treated for any like injury. I'll also check the NCIC fingerprint bank, but it's mangled so you're going to be lucky if you get even a partial hit."

I nodded. "You gonna set a grid and check the scene?"

He looked at the darkening sky. "You've got to be kidding."

"You never know."

Sancho turned to Geo with a resigned dip of his head and spread his hands. Geo blinked like a whitetail deer and cupped the rifle in a two-palmed hammock like an Indian would have.

There was an Indian air about Geo, or maybe it was a mountain man quality. Some people live on the high plains because they can't live anywhere else, their antennae fixed to a frequency that is preset to offense. Once in a long while they venture into town and drink and argue too much. Like fine instruments of delicate temperament rarely played, they become untuned and discordant. I had arrested Geo only once in my career, for drunk and disorderly, when his grandson had gotten married six months ago.

They disappeared over the next hill, and I walked back toward the truck with Dog. I could hear the sound of a diesel motor coming from the front gate and echoing off the hills like a skipping stone as I hiked back toward the main entrance. A top-of-the-line, deep green Chevrolet that proclaimed RED-HILLS RANCHO ARROYO on the doors was pulling a gleaming dump trailer pinstriped the same color up to the gate. I looked around for Duane, then walked over.

Ozzie Dobbs Jr. was undersized and overly cheery, smiling with small, square teeth that looked like Italian tile. He was wearing a large cattleman's style hat, and a green-checkered cowboy scarf was tied at his throat with a square knot and not the usual buckaroo one the cowboys in these parts preferred. The window whirred, and I noticed he let it down enough to be heard but not enough to let the cold or stink in. "Uh-oh. What's the problem, Officer?"

I patted my leg again for Dog to follow and carefully picked my way to the side of the shiny truck. "Oh, an unidentified individual may have dropped down on the evolutionary scale." I leaned on the window, tipped my hat back, and smiled at Ozzie's mother, who was in the passenger seat. "Hello, Mrs. Dobbs."

Betty Dobbs was approaching eighty but was still a looker with a fine bone structure that had held up to the years and sad eyes, which made you want to tell her anything she wanted to hear. She had been my ninth-grade English/civics teacher, and at the time I'd considered her a harpy. Now retired, she was known to volunteer for every civic organization imaginable, from the county animal shelter to the friends of the library and the hospital auxiliary.

"Hello, Sheriff. It's a lovely evening, isn't it?"

Evidently, the smell and the cold hadn't invaded the cab yet. "Yes, ma'am." I looked around again for the younger Stewart, but only the dogs were in the office. "Got your water bill, Ozzie?"

He grudgingly pulled the yellow slip from the seat but held on to it. "Yeah, I've got the damned thing but I gotta tell you, Sheriff, I got about three more loads, and I was hoping you fellas would cut me some slack."

I glanced back at his covered trailer. "Well, I understand you've already dumped one load today. What've you got back here?"

He stared at me for a second, probably wondering where I'd gotten my information. "Mostly brush I clear-cut from down by Wallows Creek."

"All right." I glanced back toward dump central, where I'd last seen Santiago and the solid waste facility engineer. "I'm not sure where Duane is or where Geo's going to want you to put it, but you better back up and run it through the scale."

He sighed. "I will, but then the commissar is gonna want

to charge me. I don't want to say anything against anybody, but you give some people a little power and it goes straight to their head." He gave an apologetic glance to his mother and then started in again. "I have yet to come up here and not have that old bastard go through every load I bring into this place. You'd think I was trying to drop off nuclear waste." I held up a hand, but it had little effect. "Now, he knows I've lobbied the county to shut this place down and move it a little farther out—and that's a fight I'm going to win, but as to that private junkyard of his . . ."

"Ozzie."

His face reddened, but he continued. "The amount of ground seepage, antifreeze, transmission fluid, gasoline, and oil that comes off this hill and down into Rancho Arroyo would be a disgrace to any government agency, and I can tell you that I'm not above making a few phone calls and turning this into a Superfund site."

I spoke with a little more authority this time. *"Ozzie."*

He stopped and glanced at his mother again, finally resting his eyes on his vehicle's dash. Mrs. Dobbs moved a little past the profile of her son and looked at me imploringly. "I apologize, Sheriff. Ozzie Junior's had a trying day, and I'm afraid his nerves are on end."

I allowed a commensurate amount of silence to pass. "That's fine, Mrs. Dobbs." I studied the side of her son's face, but I think he was embarrassed to look up. I stepped back, calling for Dog to accompany me. "I'll say something to Geo, Ozzie."

His mother, unwilling to leave things unsettled and impolite, leaned across and called out to me. "How is your daughter, Sheriff?"

I smiled and raised my voice to be heard over the diesel. "Cady's fine, ma'am."

"Still with the law firm in Philadelphia?"

"Yes, Mrs. Dobbs."

"Betty, please. Are we going to see you at the Redhills Rancho Arroyo Survival Invitational this weekend?"

As a reputable and highly visible member of the community, I received an invitation to the goofy golf tournament every year, but since I wasn't even a fair-weather golfer, I always ignored it. The Redhills Rancho Arroyo Survival Invitational was one of those midwinter golf tournaments where they played in parkas with optical orange golf balls, white not being a winter color for golf. "I'd love to attend, but I don't golf, Betty."

"Yes, but that lovely friend of yours does." She smiled. "The Native American fellow?"

"Henry Standing Bear, he's Cheyenne." Even women in their eighties smiled at the thought of Henry; it was, as always, annoying. "He's at my jail right now."

Her forehead furrowed. "Oh, no."

"Nothing professional; the pipes in both his house and where he works froze, so he needed a place to stay."

"Doesn't he golf?"

"Yes ma'am, he's a scratch player." I shrugged. "He's good at everything."

"He broke your nose, as I recall."

"Eighth grade, at the water fountain."

"Didn't he go on to college?"

"Yes, ma'am—Berkeley."

She nodded in remembrance. "I don't suppose you could convince him to play? The benefits from this year's tournament are going to the American Indian College Fund, and it would be wonderful if we could have a Native American participate."

I waved, trying to indicate that the conversation was ending. "Well, when I get back to the office I'll mention it to him."

She continued to smile, but Ozzie pressed the button for the window. Mrs. Dobbs sat back as he put the truck in reverse, and I saw that Saizarbitoria and Geo were walking side-by-side down the inner road, the Basquo still holding the cooler under his arm, his hat now functioning as a makeshift mask.

About fifty yards away, Geo said something to my deputy, and they parted company—Sancho toward me, and the dump man, still holding the rifle, toward the scales.

I leaned against the grille guard on my truck and watched the young man approach with a slight hitch in his step and a general attitude of dissatisfaction. He reminded me of me.

He pulled up about two steps away and lodged the web of his thumb over the butt of the seventeen-shot Beretta at his hip. "All right, I set a preliminary grid with the twine, but I gotta tell you that in my learned opinion the thumb arrived in the cooler and we have nothing to gain by digging up the surrounding area."

I crossed my arms and nodded. "You don't think we're going to find the rest of him out there, huh?"

"No, and Mr. Stewart says there hasn't been anything disturbed in that area for a couple of weeks now and given the fragile nature of the container . . ." He squeezed the cooler till it squeaked. "I'd say it's a new arrival." He studied me. "Is digging up the entire dump in the freezing cold for the next two weeks going to be my punishment for leaving?"

I ignored him and asked another question. "You gonna check the permits for the weekend?"

"Yeah. The place is closed on Sundays, so it had to arrive either late Friday or Saturday."

"Well, get the paperwork from Geo, and we'll . . ."

I was interrupted by a series of shouts coming from the direction of the scales. I turned in time to see the scarecrow figure of Geo Stewart with the .22 rifle held at port arms standing on the scales in front of Ozzie Jr.'s truck. The developer gunned the engine on the vehicle to impress his intentions upon the dump man, even going so far as to lurch the one-ton forward so that the chrome grille guard was almost touching him. Butch and Sundance were leaping in the air in an attempt to gain enough purchase to burst through the office Plexiglas.

I held up a finger to the Basquo. "Just a second—I'll be back in a minute." I hustled across the broken ground, raised a hand, and shouted. "Hold on, hold on!"

I guess they couldn't hear me—or maybe it was that they just didn't want to—but Geo didn't retreat, and I could see his mouth moving in response to what looked like Ozzie's spitting tirade. I was about thirty yards away when the truck lurched again, and the junkman was thrown backward.

Geo hit the railroad-tie ramp with a liquid thump, and his head cracked against the hard surface of the creosote-soaked wood, the rifle falling to the side with the *ch-kow* sound that indicated it had gone off. At its discharge, the truck stopped but, as near as I could tell, it was still in gear.

"Put that thing in park!"

I scrambled forward—Dog was beside me now and was barking. I could see where the round had glanced off the windshield, cracking the glass and shearing a deep groove through the trim and the front of the cab.

I placed a hand on the elevated sill of the driver's window, reached in through the narrow opening, turned off the motor, and snatched the keys from the ignition. "Are you two all right?"

Ozzie didn't move, but his mother, pale and breathless, replied, "We're fine, but what about George?"

I slipped from the door and moved to the front of the truck where Geo was stretching his neck to one side as he lay there on the ramp. He was feeling the back of his head. I kneeled down and supported him, and his hat fell back, exposing the waxy, pure white skin where the sun had never touched him. "Are you okay?"

He closed his eyes and then stretched them open, alternately flexing his jaw.

"Geo, are you all right?"

"Whoo-eeha." He moved his mouth, with the fog from his breath condensing in the frigid air, and then drew a hand up to swipe the saliva from the corner of his mouth before it froze. "I didn't shoot nobody, did I?"

I smiled down at him. "Just the truck, but I think it'll make it." We both chuckled. Dog was standing by the scales and barking at the wolf mutts that were now taking turns jumping against the window. I did a little barking of my own. "Enough!" He quieted down, and my eyes drifted past to Saizarbitoria, who stood with the cooler and evidence kit at his feet where he'd dropped them.

His sidearm was drawn and, even from this distance, I could see his hands shaking. I watched him until he became aware of me; he half-turned, lowering the Beretta.

Betty Dobbs was out of the truck and now crouched beside the shaken junkman, who looked up at her and smiled brilliantly from beneath the dirt and whiskers. "Are you all right? I didn't shoot you, did I?"

She laughed and shook her head at him.

I cleared my throat and started to stand. "Betty, could you keep an eye on him for just a second?" She smoothed his hair back, and I figured George was in better hands. "I'll be right back."

As I stood, I became aware that Ozzie Dobbs Jr. had tried to open his truck door, but that the railing on the scale had him penned. "Did you see that? That crazy son of a bitch tried to shoot us!" He was still spitting, and his Chiclet teeth showed in a thin-lipped grimace.

Remembering Dobbs's keys were still in my palm, I stuffed them into my pocket and held a hand out to silence him. "Stay where you are."

He looked around, unable to see Betty or Geo at the front of the truck. "Where's my mother?!"

"She's taking care of the man you just tried to run over."

I turned my back to him and approached my deputy, all the while attempting to get a handle on the surge of adrenaline that continued to bottle-rocket through my veins. The Basquo hadn't moved and was still turned a quarter away from me with the pistol at the side of his leg, his upper lip trapped between his teeth.

"You all right?"

He didn't say anything.

"Are you all right?"

He strained to speak. "Yeah."

I looked back to make sure I was the only one who had witnessed him drawing his weapon. I turned to Sancho and gestured gently toward the semiautomatic. "You wanna holster that thing?"

"Yeah . . . yeah."

As he secured the Beretta, I turned and saw the strangest thing I'd seen all day, and I'd seen a lot of strangeness up to this point. George Stewart and my ninth-grade English / civics teacher were entwined in a passionate kiss.

3

"Other than his long johns, how is he?"

Isaac blinked behind his thick glasses. "He bruised a few ribs and cracked the back of his head; personal hygiene notwithstanding, he's in remarkable shape for a man his age."

"He's had a rough day."

"It says a lot for hard work in the fresh air."

"I'm not so sure that would strictly define the environs of the dump."

"Municipal Solid Waste Facility." Evidently Geo had educated the Doc, too. "To each man, his own paradise."

I rolled my eyes. "Well, since we're on a subject literati—have you seen the moving finger writes and having writ?"

"I have."

The Basquo was talking to Janine at the end of the hallway, so Isaac leaned in closer and, speaking sotto voce, looked up at me. "Walter, you know as well as I do that that thumb is probably the result of some local cowboy having dallied up a little too quick at one of this weekend's team ropings."

"In February?"

He adjusted his glasses. "Have you forgotten how many indoor arenas we have in the surrounding area?"

I studied my boots and went to one of my recorded responses. "Well, we're checking all the leads."

He made an exasperated sound in the back of his mouth. "It was in a cooler with crushed beer cans and melted ice from the IGA."

"Maybe it hitchhiked there." I got a smile out of him with that one. "I don't think we're being overly zealous in treating this as a possible missing person—or part of a missing person."

"Walter, this was some roper squeezing his finger off, putting it in the cooler for safekeeping, and then getting so drunk that he either passed out or simply forgot about it. He's probably woken up this morning and realized he's missing a digit."

"Thumb."

The intensity in his deep-set eyes increased. "And will probably be in here later to consolidate the damage." He paused and took a breath. "Now, do you want to tell me what sort of criminal conspiracy this is in which you are attempting to involve me?"

I glanced back toward the front desk, pushed off the wall, and draped an arm around Doc Bloomfield's narrow shoulders to steer him toward a little more privacy. "You've been working with the Basquo on his recovery since the knifing?"

He nodded. "Yes."

"How's he doing?"

The Doc paused. "In what spirit is this question asked?"

"How about physical."

We'd walked to the end of the hall and were now confronted with the set of double-swinging doors that led to the ICU. I stopped and retrieved the majority of my arm but left a hand on the Doc's shoulder.

"The initial damage was the penetrating wound six inches to the right of the midline with an extending incision and hemorrhagic effect that included the left perinephric fat and the kidney itself. The organ suffered a ninety-five percent loss in its filtering abilities and was removed, but the other kidney will most likely continue to operate at peak efficiency especially because the young man is in inordinately fine physical condition."

"Yep, but how's he doing?"

Isaac propped an elbow on his arm and cupped his chin in his hand. "Well, there was some additional infection that seems to have affected the left oblique muscles, but other than that, he's fine." I nodded but didn't say anything. "But that's not really the part of him you're worried about, is it?"

"Not really."

"He's exhibiting some psychological neurosis?"

"I don't know if I'd call it neurosis."

A smile softened his face. "What would you call it then?"

"Back in the day, Lucian used to refer to it as bullet fever."

He exhaled a gentle laugh at the thought of my old boss, who had been the previous sheriff of Absaroka County. "And what, exactly, are the symptoms of bullet fever?"

"Numerous—the first being a strong urge to find something else to do for a living, preferably in an occupation where people aren't trying to slice you, dice you, and julienne fry you."

"Sounds sensible."

"Nobody ever said it was a sane line of work, Doc." I sighed. "He's a good kid, tough and brave as a summer day— I just think this is the first time he's ever gotten a good look into the abyss, and he's maybe brought a little of it back with him."

"It sounds as if this condition might be familiar to you."

I nodded and smiled. "Yep, I had a little dose or two."

The Doc shook his head, mildly scolding. "All right, what is it you're planning to do?"

"Well, whether he stays or goes I want to make sure he knows he's all right. In the long run it's best for him to learn that he's not bulletproof. I just want to remind him that he might be just a little bullet-resistant."

"And how are you intending to do that?"

I took a deep breath and tipped my hat back. "Haven't a clue, but I figure that if I keep him occupied with the thumb it'll at least hold his interest until I come up with something."

"Walter, I don't need to remind you that you are not a professional in dealing with these types of things and that there are people who . . ."

"I know that."

"Your friend, Dr. Morton, at the VA over in Sheridan?"

"Yep, but that would make it official, and I'm not sure Santiago would be willing to go for that."

The Doc pulled at his nose, readjusted his glasses with a middle finger, and studied me for a long moment. "What do you want me to do?"

I shrugged. "Nothing illegal, but if you could feign a little ignorance about the nature of the evidence and possibly keep it quiet if anybody comes in with a telling injury . . ."

He pulled the all-knowing clipboard from his chest, flipped a page over, and read. "Mr. Felix Polk of Route 16, Rural Delivery Box 12, appeared here yesterday at approximately 11:22 a.m., wanting to know if anybody had shown up with the end of his thumb because he, and I quote, 'Wanted to get it back and have it made into a key chain,' unquote."

I took a breath. "Well, this might end up being a little harder than I thought, but I'll think of something." I started to go but then remembered that I wanted to ask him about Mrs. Dobbs. "Hey, Doc, do you remember Betty Dobbs?"

He thought for only a second. "School nurse and teacher. Retired, isn't she? Married well, as I recall, but he died two and a half years ago, I think." He didn't hesitate in adding, "Salt of the earth. Why?"

"Just curious."

Ozzie Dobbs apparently wanted to press charges, but I thought that Geo didn't, so I took the trail of least resistance and went to visit the junkman first. I knocked on the door of his room, but there was no response. I could hear the television, so I waited a second and then swung the door back. Geo was walking around in a hi-here's-my-ass gown, barefoot, and looking for his clothes. He was still wearing his disreputable hat with the flaps sticking straight out at the sides, so it looked like Geo was clear for takeoff.

"Whatta ya think them nurses did with ma pants?"

Burned them, I thought, but I wasn't going to be the one to tell him. "I think you're supposed to be in bed, Geo. They have to give you one more going-over before they'll let you go; probably something to do with the insurance."

The response was predictable.

"Gaddam insurance." He stood there in the middle of the room with his fists on his hips. His tan, still holding through the winter, started just above his eyebrows and paused in a deep V at his throat along which there was a substantial scar that appeared to run from ear to ear. The tan then recommenced at his wrists and ventured to his fingertips. I guess they had cleaned him up, with or without his permission, because the rest of him looked like boiled chicken. "Somebody gotta feed Butch and Sundance."

"What about Duane or Gina?"

His answer was accompanied with a vague gesture. "Went off to Sheridan to go to the show and visit friends."

"How about Morris?"

"Drinks."

I thought about how I was supposed to have met Vic an hour ago, and how my current popularity was plummeting along with the mercury. "Well then, I can take care of that."

He studied me from the corner of his eye. "Got a bird."

I walked over and lowered the volume on the television.

"I can probably take care of that for you, too." It was Natalie Wood and some guy I can't remember singing in *West Side Story*. I thought it an odd choice for the junkman but pretty good programming since we were coming up on Valentine's Day.

"Got nary a feather."

I turned back to look at him. "I beg your pardon?"

"Lindy. Got nary a feather."

"The bird?"

He nodded. "Plucks 'em all off in spite."

"In spite of what?"

"Daughter-in-law run off; only one that could stand the bird."

I thought about it. "Geo, didn't your daughter-in-law leave a while back?"

"Ten year ago, June 12th." He evidently felt the need to add. "Parrot can live a long time; could be the spite."

I crossed to the visitor chair and sat in hopes that he'd settle on the bed so we could discuss recent developments. "Geo, I need to talk to you."

To my relief he came over and predictably beat me to the punch of my visit. "Not making a charge."

I smiled at him. "I'm glad to hear that."

He sniffed, probably unused to smelling anything but himself. "Perfect right to."

"Yes you do, but then Ozzie Junior'll probably bring up the fact that your gun went off."

"Accidental."

I nodded. "I agree, but I just wanted to nip any problem

we might have in the bud." I stretched my leg. "Geo, I'd like to ask what that was all about. Do you and Ozzie have something going on I should know about?"

His attention focused on his feet, which were aligned with the legs of his chair. "Nope."

"Nothing?"

He pushed his welding cap back, revealing the stunning whiteness of his forehead and a perfect widow's peak.

"Nope."

I waited a moment and then stood. "All right then."

"When are you gonna feed Butch and Sundance and the bird?"

It seemed like an urgent request. "Tonight?"

He nodded. "Dog food's in the garbage can in the mud-room, birdfeed in the urn on the shelf by the cage. They's cat food on the back porch for the raccoons."

"Raccoons."

He nodded. "Make sure they got water in the heated bowl and stay out of the basement, there's snakes."

I took a deep breath. It was turning out to be a long day. "You want me to feed them, too?"

"Nope."

"Snakes, Geo?"

"Yep."

"In February." I stood there looking down at him, not-ing again that he was composed of thin, drawn muscle that displayed every strand and sinew. "Are those wolves of yours going to try and eat me alive when I go back there?"

The smile faltered a little on his lips, and not for the

first time I noticed there was an odd elegance to the man. "Nope."

I wasn't sure if I believed him.

The effects of the drops were gone, and I no longer needed a personal chauffeur, so Dog and I drove the eight miles to the dump in the dark alone.

I cut the motor on my truck but left the headlights to shine on the snack bar/municipal solid waste facility office. I cracked the Bullet's door open, and Dog looked at me expectantly. I looked at the office and could see them waiting, dark eyes flaring in the window. I grabbed my Maglite from the seat, reached in, and clicked off the headlights. "No, I think you better stay in here." He didn't look happy, but I closed the door behind me and slowly made my way toward the patched-together shack.

I shined the beam of the big flashlight onto the Plexiglas and into the two sets of glowing eyes. I placed a hand on the aluminum knob but then thought it best to introduce myself from the safety between us, so I put my other hand against the thick, clear plastic and spoke softly. "Okay, if I open this damn door and either one of you makes the slightest sign of aggression, I'm leaving the two of you to starve. You got me?"

I tried to think of the last time I'd been bitten by a dog and could only come up with a nasty little shih tzu that had nipped my elbow in the Busy Bee Café during rodeo weekend two years back. One of the big, lean heads stretched forward. I'm not sure if it was Butch or Sundance, but he licked the clear plastic against my hand. "All right, here we go."

I pulled the door open, and they continued to sit there, looking at me like hundred-and-twenty-pound bookends.

"Okay. Good dogs, good boys."

I reached a closed fist toward the one that had licked the Plexiglas and watched as the black-and-white muzzle moved forward for a sniff and then a lick. I rolled my hand over and let the wet tongue lap across my palm. His fanlike tail swept back and forth, and I thought so far so good, which caused me to make a mistake and reach for the other wolf mutt, who up to this point hadn't made any movement or sound.

The rumble in his chest sounded like the internal combustion of a high-compression motor and just as urgent.

I looked at him. "Hey."

He backed away just a little and pulled up one side of his muzzle to show me the business end of a canine tooth as he continued to growl.

"Hey."

He backed away until his butt bumped against the far wall, which really wasn't far enough. His lip dropped a little, but he stayed there watching me as I ran a hand over the head of the friendlier of the two in hope that if he saw the other dog respond well he might loosen up a bit. I turned my focus marginally to the dog I was petting. "Good dog . . . If historical reference is any good in judging personality, I'm betting you're Butch."

He looked up, and I was relatively assured. The other dog was no longer growling and dipped its head as I kept petting the friendlier one. "C'mon, Sundance . . . C'mon, Butch."

I took the path from the office that led to Geo's house and headed off at a slow walk past my truck. Butch kept pace at my left as we followed the frozen, hard-pack road—Sundance tagged along behind. I glanced at the truck and could see that my backup was watching and committing every movement to memory. We walked past the chain-link fence; the sign on the other side read STEWART JUNKYARD—NO TRESSPASSING, spelling notwithstanding.

The gate was held in place by a rubber bungee cord but still moved a couple of inches squealing in counterpoint with the wind that was picking up from the mountains. I stopped and held the metal-framed gate in one hand, thankful I was wearing gloves so that my flesh didn't stick, and ushered the first dog through; the other one stood and looked at me. "C'mon."

He waited a short moment and then followed, keeping his distance as I looked down the path at the gables of the big house.

Douglas Moomey had built the place in the late 1890s, but after the death of his brother in the Boer War, he was called back to England from a life of drunken remittance to a life of drunken privilege. The only thing he'd left behind were illegitimate children who spoke with a vague British accent and the house. A local cattle rancher bought it and the surrounding property, and it remained in his family until the late forties, at which point Shirley Vandermier, one of the local call girls, acquired it as a result of an heir chasing aces and eights.

There was supposedly an old tunnel that had run from the whorehouse to a livery almost an eighth of a mile away, which allowed the local ranchers and cowboys ingress and, more important, egress in times of emergency—such as when the sheriff might be looking for patrons of the establishment.

As I stood among the random, rusted automobile carcasses that were stacked around it, it was hard to imagine the place in its original glory. The gigantic house squatted on a native moss-rock foundation like the place had grown there. The night clouds raced over the roof like fleeting spirits, and the tendrils of a long dead cottonwood's split trunk ran its bony fingers through the clouds. Only the insistent bite of the northwestern wind and subzero temperatures reminded me that it was Valentine's Day and not Halloween.

There was no paint to peel, so the structure had slowly gone monochromatic from its balustrades and verandas to its shriveled and checked shingles. More than a few of those shingles lay at my feet, most likely victim to Geo's latest stint as chimney sweep. There was a plume of smoke coming from the blackened bricks, and it looked like there was a light on somewhere in the back of the house; I figured that Gina and Duane must have come back from the movies early.

The dogs had stopped at the base of the stairs to turn and look at me. I gave the entire house one more quick glance. "I'm coming."

Automobile parts, scrap metal, and large, derelict appliances were scattered on the porch as well as the patchy iced yard. I picked my way around a Ford nine-inch differential, a

'50 Willys Jeepster grille, and the seat from a mid-sixties Impala. The steps were warped and cupped but held as I climbed onto the porch.

"Sheriff's department."

I waited but there was no response, so I opened the front door and followed the wolves inside. There was a set of stairs in the entry hall with a stained oriental runner complete with tarnished brass rails on each rise. The carpet had been tracked black, and the worn spots at the center of each tread showed the oak board underneath, the distressed wool threads drifting in the air of the opened door as if the stairwell had been disemboweled.

The green wainscoting had crinkled its stain and pulled away from the surface of the wood like a skinned alligator, and brocaded wallpaper hung in strips from the plaster-and-lath walls. In the partial moonlight of the parlor windows, the human hair that had been mixed with the plaster curlicued from the wall—mixing hair with plaster was a common practice of the period, but it was still a little unsettling.

There was a door under the stairs that must've led to the basement. Snakes.

Junk was everywhere—stacks of moldy books, newspapers and magazines, a portable air compressor, a broken ladder, and a floor fan with no blades were just a few of the items within reach. Amazingly, though, the air felt humid.

The dogs were waiting for me in the archway of the back hall that led to what had to be the kitchen, but I detoured to my right and stared at the bluish-gray trapezoids of moonlight revealing boot prints that disturbed the dust on the floor.

There were two large, overstuffed reading chairs facing the fireplace and, as the chimney had indicated, the smoldering remains of a fire.

A small, round, battered Chippendale table with a Coleman lantern planted on top sat between the two chairs. None of the furniture looked to be in particularly good condition, but one chair had a sheet carefully draped over it with a large book spread open on it, binding up. Overtaken with curiosity, I took the five steps and leaned in to read the gilt writing on the tattered cover, THE COMPLETE WORKS OF WILLIAM SHAKESPEARE.

I stuck a finger between the pages, lifted up the volume, and flipped it over. Act 2, scene 6, *Romeo and Juliet*, not the most memorable excerpt from the play—a few lines close to the bottom of the page had been underlined with a dull pencil which, upon closer examination, was also on the seat of the chair. I picked it up and placed it in the center of the open book and read.

> They are but beggars that can count their worth;
> But my true love is grown to such excess
> I cannot sum up sum of half my wealth.

My estimation of Geo Stewart was rising as I closed the pencil in the collected works, eraser out, and returned it to the seat of the chair. I glanced back into the entryway, but the dogs were not there—probably waiting for me in the kitchen. I stepped to the fireplace and unhooked a well-used fire iron, crouched, and started stoking the remnants that remained between the glowing amber eyes of the owl-shaped andirons.

There were a few sparks and the ends rolled to the center, re-igniting the fire and giving the place a bit more cheer and, needless to say, warmth.

There was a noise from the kitchen, and I figured I'd better get to feeding the wild bunch before they decided to take it upon themselves. I stood and started for the main hall, looked through the glass partition toward the pantry, and thought I saw someone.

I froze and stood there without moving, blinking my eyes steadily, thinking it must've been the residual effect of this afternoon's drops, but the image of a woman dressed completely in nineteenth-century clothes passed through the hallway behind the beveled glass.

With the light reflecting through the hinged doors of the kitchen and the stained-glass side panels, I could see she was wearing a deep red ball gown, complete with high collar and a bustle. I thought I should investigate and had just started toward the swinging doors, when they both opened.

"Oh, my lord . . ." She placed her hands at her chest and looked at me, wide-eyed. The doors flapped closed behind her. "Oh, my lord."

"Mrs. Dobbs?"

I finished off my slice of apple pie and took a sip of my coffee, the communal silence weighing heavily on the two of us.

We sat at a small table by the kitchen window; the kitchen, as opposed to the rest of the house, was spotless. There was a gigantic, six-burner porcelain stove with four ovens, a massive refrigerator, and cabinets that had been scrubbed within an inch of their grain. The floor and the walls up to the chair rail were those tiny, octagonal tiles set in a pattern that, even in the dim lights of the antique fixtures, glistened around the room like a jeweler's showcase. The only thing disturbing the décor were the two lumps of wolf-dogs that lay snoring in the corner by the back door.

"Good pie. Good coffee, too." I set the thick china cup down.

She nodded and continued to sip from the mug she held in both hands. Her pupils were a soft blue, but the edges looked hard and dark, reminiscent of the blue-willow china that was carefully displayed in the highboy by the stove. Her hair was long, and the way she looked it was hard to remember that she was probably a member of AARP and that she'd been the one who had introduced me to big Bill Shakespeare in the ninth grade.

"Nice dress."

She laughed, and I figured I was getting somewhere. She put her coffee cup down and folded her hands in her lap. "You must find all this a little strange."

I shrugged. "A little."

She pointed at my plate. "It started with an apple."

"It always does."

She laughed some more, a melodious sound that made me want to be funny. "I was stealing them from George." She half-turned in her seat and gestured outside. "There's a lovely little stand of apple trees off the path and up near the old cellar. I was there last fall and was picking apples for apple butter—that or looking for a tree tall enough from which I could hang myself."

I said nothing.

After a moment of not looking at me, she continued. "He wasn't angry—as a matter of fact I think he was surprised and pleased to see somebody. We talked, and he offered to get some paper grocery bags and help me carry the apples back home. The next week I brought him some apple butter." She laughed again, without any prompting from me. "You know why I like George so much? Because he doesn't apologize for anything; he just does what he pleases and doesn't concern himself with what other people think." She leaned forward and propped her chin up with the palm of her hand. "It seems like I've spent most of my life apologizing for things, and it seems to me that if I hadn't been selected to absorb some of George's sly yet beneficent spell, my life might now be quite different."

She stopped talking, started to say something but then changed her mind. We sat there in the silence till I gave her an out. "Could I have some more coffee?"

"Why yes, of course." She stood, smoothed the elaborate dress, and crossed to the stove where she plucked the white-speckled coffeepot from a burner she had turned to low. She refilled my cup, placed the pot on a knitted holder at the center of the table, and watched me drink. "I guess I should explain that hanging remark, hmm?"

"You don't have to."

"It's been a rough couple of years with Ozzie Senior dying."

I fiddled with the handle of my cup. "I'd imagine so."

"I mean, it wasn't a surprise; he'd had health problems for quite some time."

I smiled at her with all my heart or as much as was in my throat. "Mrs. Dobbs, you don't have to explain any of this to me." I sat back in my chair. "You see, I would file this under personal business. I learned a long time ago that matters of the heart are well outside my jurisdiction."

She smiled with a little down-curve before the kick at the corner of her lips. It was similar to the smile that Vic had used to a devastating effect. "Thank you for that, Walter." She looked down at the laced fingers in her lap. "Maybe I just needed someone to talk to about all this."

I took a deep breath and let it out slowly. "In that case, I'm all ears." I fingered the disfigured one. "Or ear and a half." I smiled. "Does anybody else know about this relationship?"

She hugged herself and looked out the window, where condensation from the heat of the stove was clouding the view. "Ozzie Junior may have some suspicions, but that's all." She continued to try and see through the glass and finally got to the subject she was looking for. "Your wife died a few years ago, didn't she?"

"Yes, six . . . about six years ago."

She took a deep breath of her own. "If you don't mind my asking, in what way did it affect you?"

I told her the truth, because I thought it was something she needed to hear. "I wanted to die, and I don't mean that figuratively. They take a big chunk of you when they go."

She nodded, but just barely. "Yes."

"There's a friend of mine, an Indian . . ."

She smiled. "Henry Standing Bear?"

I shook my head. "No, another Indian, half Cheyenne and half Crow, by the name of Brandon White Buffalo." I paused to remember the words the large man had used while I'd eaten his carefully prepared breakfast sandwich in Lame Deer at the Sinclair station that bore his name. "He said that it's like losing a part of yourself, but worse because we're left with who we are after, and sometimes we don't recognize that person."

She sighed a soft laugh. "So, we're lost to ourselves?"

"Pretty much."

She poured herself a little more from the enameled pot with the clear, gemlike percolator top. "Do you still think about your late wife?"

"I do."

"How often?"

I smiled weakly. "Used to be every minute, then once a day . . . I guess I've toughened myself so that I only think about her when I see something that reminds me of her." She gripped her mug, and I noticed that the thin band of skin at her ring finger was still pale. "That give you hope?"

"Not overly."

"Well, you might be tougher than I am—most people are."

She didn't smile this time, and it was as if the hard edges at the outside of her pupils had become sharper. "I don't think I believe that."

I shrugged. "Either way, I'd never be able to get away with a frock like that." That got a laugh.

"I was wondering how long it was going to take you to get around to asking again."

"It's a very nice dress."

"Thank you." She was self-conscious now, so I waited. "George likes it. He found it at the dump. It was in a bunch of boxes that the community theater had thrown out when they stopped doing their annual melodrama."

I didn't think I should follow that line any further and it was getting late, so I stood and pulled my pocket watch from my jeans as an indication: ten-thirty-seven. One of the dogs raised a red-rimmed eye to glance at me as I collected my hat from the adjacent chair. "I assume you've fed the naked bird and the raccoons?"

She looked out the window through her reflection. "I have."

"Then I should be going."

She looked up at me but didn't move. "I was hard on you, wasn't I? I mean in school, back when you were a student of mine. I was hard on you."

I lied. "I'm afraid I don't recall."

"I do. I was always harder on the students I didn't think were living up to their abilities."

I wasn't thirteen anymore, so I asked. "Their abilities or your expectations?"

She smoothed her hands over her dress. "I always had the greatest expectations for you, Walter."

"I'm not so sure if I want to hear how I turned out."

She patted the table in front of her. "Quite nicely, now that we've mentioned it." Whether she was thinking out loud or assigning me a final grade, I figured the least I could do was respond. "Thank you."

She continued to study me. "Do you feel old, Walter?"

I laughed and thought about my medical exam, only this afternoon. "I guess we're not trading compliments then."

"No." She stammered. "No . . . I'm sorry, that's not what I meant. I think you're a very handsome man, very attractive, and certainly younger than I am, but there is a certain melancholy about you."

I decided to answer half of the question, if for no other reason than to relieve her embarrassment. "It's relative. When I'm with my daughter, Cady, I feel aged. When I'm with my old boss, Lucian Connally, I feel like a spring chicken."

She waited so long to speak again that the big dog's eye slowly closed, and the large, lean head went back to the tile floor. "Is there anybody you love?"

"I beg your pardon?"

She smiled and quickly added, "You don't have to answer, but I wonder how you feel when you are with them."

I recognized the nine-year-old unit parked behind my truck. More important, I recognized the brunette sitting on my hood despite the frigid cold, her back against my windshield and her head tilted up to examine the silver underbellies of the clouds. The moon was hidden, but her light showed through the strips of cumulus that stretched to the horizon like the heavens had been harrowed.

Even in tech boots, jeans, and a nylon duty jacket, she looked good.

"So, are you here for the environs?"

"Yeah, reminds me of the water treatment plants in South Philly." The blue-black fur collar of her jacket framed her lupine features, and she reminded me of the wolves I'd just left. The tarnished-gold eyes dipped into me. "So, you find the rest of Jimmy Hoffa or what?"

I laughed. "So, you've heard about the case of the century."

"A Felix Polk called in to the office to check for his lost thumb."

"Damn." I hooked my own thumbs into my jeans and watched my breath trail off south and east along with my words. "Was Sancho there?"

"No, he'd already gone home to check on his wife and the Critter."

Vic had taken to calling Antonio the Critter. "Everything okay?"

"Yeah. Critter cries, she calls, he goes."

"You get a statement from Polk?"

"Yeah, but the finger is taking the fifth." She shook her head at me. "Walt, what are you doing? I mean you've done some crazy shit before, but hiding people's body parts?"

I studied my boots and rolled my sore foot, giving it a little flex; it responded by hurting like hell. "It's the end of a thumb, and it's not like he's going to glue the damn thing back on."

She pursed her lips and continued to shake her head at

me. "By the way, the thumb in question is resting comfortably, yet not so appetizingly, in the commissary refrigerator butter dish. Now, I'll ask again. What the hell are you up to?"

I placed an elbow by her boot. It was still piercingly cold, but evidently she didn't feel like being inside. "The Basquo quit today."

She folded her arms over her chest and looked back at the sky. "Hmm . . ."

I spoke to her lean throat. "You don't seem surprised."

"I guess I saw that one coming."

I tipped my hat back and gave myself the luxury of studying her some more; the hard curve of her jaw, the sassiness that her face carried even at rest. "You spend more time with him than I do. What's your prognosis?"

She made the next statement cheerily. "He's fucked in the head." She shrugged. "Look, this is not the first time you or I have ever seen this. Maybe it would be best for him to go back to corrections." She looked straight at me. "Hey, did I just miss something or is there some kind of connection between Felix Polk's thumb and Saizarbitoria's future career path?"

I gently tugged at the lace of her boot. "Maybe."

"Oh shit, is this another one of your salvage operations?" I didn't say anything, and she sighed with a sense of finality. "All right, I'll leave that one for now—but in case you forgot, you were supposed to go look at a house with me and buy me dinner. So, I repeat, what the fuck have you been doing?"

"I left you a message on your cell." I looked up at her. "You wouldn't believe me if I told you."

"Doc Bloomfield said you'd gone to feed those dire wolves

of Geo Stewart's, and I thought they must've gotten you instead, so I came out here."

"Somebody had already fed them."

She glanced in the direction of the peaked gables. "It wouldn't happen to have been Betty Dobbs, would it?"

I made a face. "How did you know that?"

"Her son, Tweedledum, called in a missing person's."

"Great."

She studied me and smiled, revealing the canine tooth that was just a shade longer than the others. "Is there more to this story?"

Vic loved dish, so I pulled my hat off and rested my forehead on her thigh—I was the picture of abject despair. "Betty Dobbs, my ninth-grade English/civics teacher, is having an affair with Geo Stewart."

Her leg jumped, my head bounced, and I looked up at her as she covered her mouth with a hand. "Get the fuck out of here; Daughter of the American Revolution, P.E.O., *Who's Who*, grand matron of Redhills Rancho Arroyo is *shtupping* the junkman?"

"I think Municipal Solid Waste Facility Engineer is the title he prefers."

"Ozzie Junior is going to prefer to put a bullet in his unwashed ass. Is he aware?"

I put my hat back on. "Who?"

"Tweedledum."

"No."

"Can I tell him?"

"No."

"Why?"

I sighed and turned my back to her. "Because if he has to hear about it, I'd just as soon he heard it from somebody other than us."

She nudged my shoulder with her boot. "So how long's the old schoolmarm been getting her holster polished?"

I looked back at her. "Since apple season."

"Fuck me." I watched as her eyes played across the desolate landscape of the dump, and she distilled the situation to one wicked phrase. "Love among the ruins."

4

"You do not golf."

"No, but you do." I wasn't making much headway with the Cheyenne Nation. "It's for a good cause—the American Indian College Fund. You've probably heard of it—you being an American Indian and all."

"Yes."

I sipped my coffee and took another tack. "I'll carry your golf bag."

I could see that my best friend was desperately trying to find an excuse as he stared into his own mug. "Is it a foursome?"

"A what?"

He sighed a long breath like he always did when I was trying his patience. "Generally, these tournaments are played in groups of four."

Damn. "That means we have to come up with two more people?"

He paused and, even with his apparent reluctance, I had a feeling he was weakening. "Golfers, two more golfers."

"Right, golfers . . ."

He set his mug down, and his hands covered his face. I studied him, his neck and shoulders so full of muscles that it was a wonder he didn't creak when he turned his head. He was looking a little tired, and I was beginning to wonder if the winter was getting to him, too.

The recent storm had swept across the Wyoming/Montana border, taken more than a dozen Powder River Energy poles with it and, in a fit of perversion, had left all the water pipes on the Rez and the contiguous area to freeze and bust.

The Bear's bar, the Red Pony, was one of the first to succumb, and his home had rapidly followed suit. Henry had been our guest for the last two days and, with the rush on qualified plumbers, it was looking as if he was ours for the next week.

He dropped his hands and stood, walking to the window and staring with his dark eyes mirroring the gray light.

"You all right?"

He didn't move, but the voice sounded in his chest. "Yes."

"You don't seem all right."

He nodded, just barely. "Which is better, being all right or seeming it?"

I let the rhetoric settle in the room like mist after a rain. I knew better than to try and read the weather in him. Like the rest of the high plains, if you did he'd just change.

"It is Lee."

Henry's on-again-off-again relationship with his half brother was something he rarely brought up. "Didn't you see him in Chicago on the way back from Philadelphia?"

"No. I called him and left a message, and then he called and left a message for me. I finally got him to commit to a meeting at a small bar on Halsted, but he did not show. I sat in this bar for forty minutes before the bartender asked if I was Henry Standing Bear." He turned and pulled back the black hair to reveal a set of features, all of them jockeying on his face to see which would be the most striking. "I was the only Indian in the bar."

"I'm glad I wasn't there."

"Hmm." He turned back to the window. "Lee had called and left a message that he was not going to be able to make it." This was not exactly a new occurrence in Henry's dealings with his brother, but I remained quiet. "I had a dream about him and called three weeks ago and left a message, then called again yesterday, but the number had been disconnected."

I nodded and crossed my ankle, giving it a little relief. "Did you try that, what's it called? The place where you've tracked him down before?"

"The Chicago Native American Center. They have not heard from him longer than I have."

"He'll show up." I felt weak saying it.

"Yes."

"He always has."

"Yes."

I listened to the tinking of the radiators and the sound of my own breathing. "You going to Chicago?"

"Not yet." The response had an ominous tone.

I nodded at my desk some more. "Well, let me know." I thought about the conversation Vic and I'd had about Cady's upcoming nuptials and changed the subject. "Cady . . ." I paused. "She, well . . ." I paused. "She wants you to marry them."

"Yes, I know. She also wants to have the ceremony at Crazy Head Springs at about the same time as the Chief's Powwow in July."

I sat up a little. "How do you know all of this?"

"She called me last night while you were at the junkyard." Once again, he did not turn but his tone of voice changed along with the subject. "Who else do we have for this foursome?"

"Nobody—you and I are the core." At least he had said *we*. "Cady called you last night?"

"Yes."

"She didn't call me."

"You are not marrying them." He came back and sat in the chair by the door. "Why is it I have a feeling that this golf tournament has something to do with a case?"

"It might, but it's more preemptive than a case."

"I see."

I wasn't sure that he did. "I've got a little situation developing with Rancho Arroyo and the junkyard."

"To the best of my knowledge and what I read in the papers that case has been an ongoing one for the last few years." Henry was fully aware of the historic antagonism between the two parties and familiar with the Stewart garage as he always got Lola, his vintage '59 Thunderbird, serviced there.

"I have a more than sinking feeling that it may be coming to a head."

"And how, if you do not mind my asking, is a golf tournament going to assist in this situation?"

I uncrossed my legs, hitching my foot under my desk for balance, and leaned back in my chair. "I want to keep an eye on what could be potential conflict and was thinking that a higher profile for the sheriff's department might calm things down a little."

The sarcasm in his reply was wader deep. "Yes, that has always worked before."

"C'mon, it's not like I'm asking you to take a bullet—I'm asking you to go golfing."

"Do you remember the last time we golfed?"

I paused. "California; we had a great time."

"We were arrested."

I looked down at the blotter on my desk. "That was almost forty years ago, and we're mature adults now."

"Hmm." This *hmm* sounded about as convincing as the last one. "Did she ask about me?"

"Who?"

"Mrs. Dobbs."

I figured I'd not feed his ego. "Why would she ask about you?"

His head tilted back, and I could tell he was summoning up visions of his ill-spent youth. "I always found her attractive and thought she might've felt the same way."

"Well, she's available." That got him to turn and look at me.

Vic appeared in my doorway with the delicate down-curve before the kicked-up corner of her lip; it could've been a smile, at least the way rattlesnakes smile. I glanced up at her. "You don't happen to know any golfers, do you?"

She flicked her eyes at Henry and then back to me. "Not in a February where the mercury hasn't risen above the big fat zero I don't." She shook her head. "Have you got two hare-brained schemes going at once?"

I took my hat off and set it on my desk, brim up so the luck wouldn't run out; lately, I needed all I could get. "Just a little community-oriented law enforcement." I tipped the brim with my finger and watched it spin. "You think Saizarbitoria golfs?"

She readjusted her shoulder on the doorjamb. "You can ask him when he gets back from checking the bar code on that crappy cooler with every friggin' retailer in town. He should be in a really good mood by then."

"Speaking of, what kind of a mood has he been in?"

"Shitty, when he's in any mood at all. Most of the time he spends gazing out windows or at his own belly button."

I spun my hat some more. "Seems like textbook stuff?"

"Pretty much, but you combine that with sleep deprivation because of the Critter . . ." She grew quiet, and we all three listened to the radiator.

The intercom on my phone buzzed, and I punched the button. "Yes?"

Ruby's voice rattled from the plastic speaker. I don't know why she bothered with the intercom; I could hear her down the hall. "We've got a 10-50 out on the bypass. I don't suppose anybody would like to work for a living?"

Vic yelled over her shoulder. "Got it!" She pushed off the doorway but still stood there, placing her fists on her hips. "This shit with the Basquo is complicated. Have you ever considered that you may not be able to keep him?"

I glanced at Henry and decided to lighten the environs. "What, are you afraid of the competition?"

There was that little bit of silence as you wait for a response, the one that tells you that you might've just said something wrong. Her eyes sharpened, she stepped over and palmed Henry's coffee mug from my desk as a rudimentary form of housekeeping, and started out. I was about to say something when she abruptly turned, leaned in the doorway of my office, and studied me with a great deal of intensity. "No, I just don't want you to do what you normally do in these situations and get your tender little feelings hurt." I started to stand, but she turned, walked down the hallway, and called back, "By the way, dumbass, did it ever occur to you that I golf?" She turned and disappeared.

Henry stood and looked at me. "As your trusted Indian scout, it is important for me to warn you that you are now on perilously thin ice."

I grabbed my hat, lifted my jacket from the back of my chair, came around the desk, and followed her. "Vic . . ."

Henry joined me in the hallway as she looked back, shaking her head. "I played in the Mike Schmidt Celebrity Tournament back in Philly."

"Vic."

"And won."

We followed her into the dispatch area, and I noticed my Indian scout was careful to stay behind me. Vic paused at the steps just long enough to turn back and gesture with her fist out, finger pointing down. "Can you hear this? No? Then let me turn it up for you." She rotated her hand, and it was only then that I could see which finger it was—the South Philadelphia Municipal Bird.

From beside the dispatcher's desk, I watched as she sashayed out—the bell at the front door jangled viciously and the compression of the shock absorber most certainly had kept the heavy glass from shattering onto the sidewalk.

Henry's voice sounded behind me. "I do not mean to be critical, but if that is your recruiting technique . . ."

I was about to answer when I glanced over and saw Ozzie Dobbs Jr. waiting on the bench, his eyes a little wide. "Hi, Ozzie."

He stood, looked down the steps, and then back to Ruby. "Your dispatcher said you were in a meeting."

I nodded. "I was."

"Oh."

I heard the motor in Vic's unit fire up, and the tires squeal. "Ozzie, have you met Henry Standing Bear?"

He immediately became all smiles and extended his hand nervously the way people do when the only Indians they've ever been around are sports mascots. "You've got the bar out near the reservation, the Red Horse?"

The Cheyenne Nation smiled, suffering fools easily—hell, they'd been doing it for more than two hundred years. "Pony, the Red Pony."

I asked Henry if he wanted to have lunch with us, but he said he had things to attend to, including lobbying the Tribal Council about my daughter's wedding. I thanked him and told him to keep me posted about his brother.

My best buddy drifted down the hall, light on his feet

like some great cat. He slipped back into my office and disappeared. I turned back to Ozzie. "Ready for lunch?"

He looked more than a little uncomfortable. "Sure, but if you're busy . . ."

I pulled my jacket on and continued to listen as somebody, probably Vic, tore a strip off Fetterman Street. "Actually that was my other lunch date that just blew through here earlier, so it would appear that I am completely free."

"Great. Well . . ." He put his hat on, a snappy Gus type that added a good six inches to his height, and started for the steps. "I've only got an hour, so we better get going."

I shrugged at Ruby and Dog, who had raised his head to watch the action, and then followed Ozzie down the steps and past the photographs of the five previous sheriffs. Ruby's voice trailed after me. "Isaac Bloomfield called and said your eye appointment with Andy Hall is at nine a.m. on Thursday."

"Yeah, yeah, yeah . . ."

Ozzie had already crossed behind the courthouse and was approaching the concrete steps that descended diagonally toward Main Street, and he moved quickly. My foot was still worrying me, so I called out to him. "Ozzie, hold up." He waited at the top of the shoveled steps. "I got a little torn up a couple of months ago, and I'm still not completely healed."

"Sorry about that." He smiled, but I noticed his hands jiggled the change and car keys in his pockets. I guess he felt as though he should make some sort of conversation as we walked.

"Boy, that deputy of yours is a real pip."

I nodded as we made our way down the steps. "Yes, she is."

"And she golfs?"

"Apparently."

He nodded as we passed the barbershop and the Owen Wister Hotel and approached the door of the Busy Bee Café alongside Clear Creek. The windows of the café were steamed with an inviting warmth and gave me a little hope that no matter how long the high plains winter might be, I'd have a place to go and eat.

I started to take my traditional spot at the counter, but Ozzie kept walking toward a table in the back along the windows and away from the few patrons already in the place. The chief cook and bottle washer, Dorothy Caldwell, turned from the grill to give me the high sign, her hazel eyes following us with interest.

Ozzie pulled out the chair in the corner, which left me with my back to the door and the room. I wasn't used to that seat, but maybe developers in the modern West were more in danger of being shot in the back than sheriffs.

I draped my jacket over my chair and sat just in time for the queen bee herself to appear with two glasses of ice water and a couple of menus. Why she brought me a menu I'll never know, but it was a ritual and I found comfort in it.

She looked around as if this portion of the restaurant was one in which she'd never been. "You guys hiding from the law?"

I took the menu she proffered but then laid it flat on the surface of the yellow-speckled Formica table. "Yep, and if you see a deceptively diminutive deputy pull up, you'll let us know?"

She crossed her arms along with the tiny pad and stubby pencil and looked at me through her mostly salt and not much pepper bangs. "What did you do now?"

"I didn't know she golfed."

The expression on Dorothy's face didn't change. "That's a new one."

"Yep."

Ozzie, figuring that the conversation was complete, handed his menu back to her. "I'll have the BLT, hold the mayo."

Dorothy nodded, took his menu, and plucked mine out of my hands. "The usual?"

"Yes, please."

Ozzie looked uncertain. "What's the usual?"

She looked at him. "I haven't decided yet."

He paused for only a second. "I'll stick with the BLT."

As Dorothy retreated behind the counter, Ozzie turned back to me and spoke in a low voice. "Before we get started, I just wanted to tell you I was going to drop those charges against George Stewart."

I was a little shocked, and my face probably showed it. "Well . . . I was hoping that would be the case."

He took a deep breath and exhaled through distended nostrils, continuing to make eye contact with only the table. "The man is dangerous, but I figure we ought to let bygones be bygones."

My plan was to just let him talk, but it appeared that he was done. "That's very big of you." I looked around to make sure I was sitting with the right guy. "Just so you know, he hasn't filed any charges against you even though he bruised a few of his ribs and cracked his head open." I tried looking out the windows but settled for watching the drops of condensation roll down at a low rate of speed. "I guess Geo's not the kind to take that sort of thing seriously."

"And I am?"

I took a sip of my water just to slow us down. "No, that's not what I said."

The small man leaned in, the brim of his hat only a few inches from mine. "He walks up and down that fence line with a rifle like he's in some kind of range war."

Probably waiting for your mother, I thought, but kept that to myself. "He shoots the rats that you've been complaining about." I thought, with the turn of events, it was possible that Ozzie knew more about the relationship between the junkman and his mother, so I tested the waters. "Have you discussed any of this with your mother?"

He looked genuinely surprised at that one. "What?"

"Your mother, have you talked to her?"

He shook his head as if to clear my words from it. "What does my mother have to do with any of this?"

"Well, she was there."

His mouth hung open. I wasn't sure how much he knew about the situation, but I was certain he didn't know how much I knew. "Look, Sheriff, just because my name is Junior doesn't mean I have to check everything I do with my mother." He was really steaming up now. "Did you check with your mother about our meeting today?"

I took a breath of my own and waited as Dorothy planted two iced teas on our table, glanced at us, and then made a silent retreat. When she was completely gone, I turned to look back at him.

He was a good-looking man, small but athletic. I could only imagine how difficult growing up with his father, a truly hard man, must've been. How strange it was to inherit somebody else's dream and be forced to deal with the realities of it day after day. He was in a difficult position in more ways than one, whether he was totally aware of it or not. Ozzie Jr. must have had suspicions. It could be that these suspicions were what were fueling the current crisis, but only by making the situation clear could I deflect them and that meant betraying a trust; I wasn't that desperate—at least not yet.

"My parents have been dead about twelve years, Ozzie, but there's hardly a day goes by that I don't wish they were here so I could ask them some damn thing about fixing potato salad, wiring my house, or how I'm doing raising their granddaughter." I smiled, just to let him know we didn't have to draw our flatware and go for each other's throats.

His eyes were the same sad ones his mother had, and he was quiet for a moment. "I'm sorry; there really wasn't any call for me to say that."

"It's okay."

"No, no it's not." He took a sip of his iced tea and stared at the table again, and I got the feeling he wanted to slow things down a little himself. "I've been under a lot of pressure lately, and I've been saying a lot of things." He looked up at me. "Now that you mention it, my mother and I had an argument when she came home last night, and I haven't seen her since."

I thought that I'd seen Betty Dobbs close to ten. "When did she get home?"

"I guess it was about midnight, but then she went out again and I've been worried sick." He played with his napkin. "She said she saw you last night. Was that at the hospital?"

It's at this point that a smart man would lie, and a stupid one would tell the truth—I hedged. "No, I didn't see her at the hospital." He was waiting for more on that, but I shifted gears and took us back in the direction I'd originally intended. "Ozzie, I'm really pleased that you've decided to take this course with things. I think it's going to save a bunch of heartache down the road."

He continued to study me, and I thought about the damage we all did in life simply by being ourselves and getting up in the morning.

"I made your eye appointment."

"I know. Ruby said." I had stopped in at Isaac Bloomfield's office after discovering that George Stewart's room was empty. "Did you release Geo?"

The Doc looked up through his thick glasses at the floating dust motes in his office. "No, he pulled a Longmire."

I leaned in the doorway and hooked my hat on the handle of my Colt. "What's that supposed to mean?"

Isaac closed the book in his hands and reshelved it on top of the fifth of the precarious stacks that were on his desk. "He checked himself out and disappeared into the night, not unlike another individual we periodically treat here at the hospital whose escapes have become so regular that we have now made his name a part of the lexicon."

I dipped my head along with my smile and studied my boots in contrition. "Any idea when he left?"

"The night nurse reported him missing at one o'clock rounds."

I thought about it. "How did he get home? He didn't have a car, and as far as I know Duane and Gina were in Sheridan."

Isaac adjusted his glasses. "What?"

"Doc, did anybody see Betty Dobbs around here last night?"

He looked surprised. "That's the second time you've asked about her in twenty-four hours. Is there anything I need to know?"

"You don't need to know, and trust me, you don't want to."

I thought about the time line. It had been around ten-thirty when I'd left Betty and after midnight when her son had confronted her, but she could've collected Geo before or after she'd gone home. I'm not sure why it was I was dwelling on the details of the previous night; maybe it was habit, maybe it was because I preferred those thoughts to the Saizarbitoria debacle, or maybe it was something else.

The Basquo had checked all the medical records and was waiting for me when I got to the reception desk. He was sitting in one of the waiting chairs and gazing out at the gray day.

"Is Marie here yet?"

He looked up at me with an indifferent look on his face. "She's here with the baby now."

I stared at him. "Everything all right?"

He didn't move. "Yeah."

I nodded and sat in the chair beside him. "Well, good." He nodded this time but still seemed distracted, so I changed the subject. "What's the word on the cooler?"

"Nothing much. The bar code is actually three years old, and the cooler was bought at a Pamida discount store. The nearest one is in Worland, which is seventy miles away, and there's one in Moorcroft and Douglas." He paused for a second and finally looked at me. "You're not going to make me drive to Worland, are you?"

"No."

"Or Moorcroft."

"No."

"Or Douglas?"

"No."

His eyes returned to the window. "Good."

"Anything from the hospitals?"

"A guy died on a three-wheeler in Story over the weekend, but it would appear both of his thumbs are accounted for."

"I thought they outlawed those things."

Sancho remained still, his eyes reflecting the dead of the afternoon. "They did, but more than a few still turn up." He sighed. "How's the Municipal Solid Waste Facility Engineer?"

"Released himself on his own recognizance."

"Really?"

"Yep, and it's possible that Betty Dobbs is missing in the short term."

He took a long breath. "I've been meaning to talk to you about that."

"About what?"

He leaned in a little and spoke in a low voice. "Boss, were Betty Dobbs and Geo Stewart kissing?"

I laughed a short laugh and sighed. "Vic is referring to the case as *Love Among the Ruins.*"

"Wodehouse?"

I shook my head. "Evelyn Waugh by way of Robert Browning."

"It have a happy ending?"

I shrugged. "As much of a happy ending as a hermaphrodite having disfiguring cosmetic surgery to have her beard removed and an orphaned government official returning to a life of pyromania can be."

The Basquo rolled his dark eyes. "Now, why would someone write that shit?"

It was risky, but I thought I might be able to transition the conversation. "I think he was making a satirical statement about the inherent failure of the pursuit of happiness and the ability of any state to provide for it."

He nodded as he stood. "I can get behind that, but where do the bearded hermaphrodites and government pyromaniacs come in?"

"It wasn't his strongest work; maybe you should try *Brideshead Revisited.*" I stood. "Where are you headed?"

He looked at his wristwatch, another chronographic monstrosity like Vic's, with at least thirteen dials. "Marie should be finished with Dr. Gill so I thought I'd give her and the baby a ride home and then head back to the office and see if the NCIC has anything on the thumb."

I nodded, aware that that was the third time he'd referred to his son as the baby; at least he wasn't calling Antonio a critter. "How 'bout you let me take Marie and Antonio home and you can go ahead to the office?"

"You're sure you wanna do that?"

"Oh, I don't mind."

"Okay." I put my hand on Sancho's shoulder and steered him toward the glass doors that whipped apart like magic when we stepped onto the rubberized mats. He smiled, and I was starting to feel like a baby seal in a Louisville Slugger factory.

I knew where Dr. Gill's office was and leaned against the wall by the closed door, near enough so that I could hear them talking but far enough away to not understand what was being said.

I thought about Martha and how unprepared we'd been for our daughter. As it turned out, we hadn't screwed up that bad, and the ongoing project was now a lawyer in Philadelphia and engaged to a fine young police officer, who was Vic's younger brother. I think Martha would've approved of all but Vic, and then I thought about how unprepared I was for Cady getting married.

The door opened, and Dr. Gill looked at me over his

bristle-brush mustache. "Well, we were expecting a uniform but not the big star himself."

I took his hand and shook it. "Hey, Trey. Sometimes I take the more difficult jobs."

He turned and looked back at the beautiful young woman now standing in the doorway, who glanced up at me with a frank and appraising look. She held Antonio swathed in a blanket in her arms. She wore gloves, fur-lined leather ones, a simple green dress, a heavy, shapeless coat, and sensible shoes—a wise choice, considering the conditions.

"I'm your ride." She gave a brief nod and carefully made her way past me. I glanced back at Trey and shrugged. He smiled, waved a little wave, and shut the door between us.

"So, how's the Critter doing?" Had I just said *critter*? I stumbled ahead. "Colicky?" She watched her feet as she walked, the dark hair forming an impenetrable hood with only a small upturn at the end of her nose evident.

Again, the slight nod.

I had a mild panic attack, my natural response to feminine silence. "Cady, my daughter, was like that; the first six months, we thought we were going to die."

Marie and I turned the corner at the end of the hallway, and I followed her through the automatic doors. It had gotten colder, and she hunched her shoulders up around her neck in an attempt to protect the bare skin at the nape and pulled the tiny bundled person a little closer.

I opened the passenger door of my truck, and Dog leaned forward to sniff at them. Sancho had put the baby's car seat in, and Marie installed him. I supported her hand, and she slipped onto her seat. I stood there for a second and then closed the door. I climbed in my side, fired the engine up, and turned to look at her as she attached the seat belt. I thought she might say something, but she didn't.

I slipped the Bullet in gear and drove.

The wind was picking up; it was that lifeless time of winter when the shroud of the high plains stretches the sky's rinsed cobalt with smears of thin, vaporous clouds.

I turned off Fetterman and took a right onto Poplar. Marie tucked the baby's blanket and folded her hands in her lap—if the little guy was colicky, he was showing no signs of it this afternoon. I didn't make a conscious effort to talk but found words in my mouth with nowhere else to go. "We didn't think we were ready."

I watched the numbers on the houses increase—they were smallish cottages that the mines had originally constructed for their employees but that subsequent owners had added on to until it appeared that one carport joined with another deck which joined with another porch. The hues of the little houses at this end of town were defiantly vibrant; whistle-stop colors in graveyards. Cars were parked in grassless yards, and dogs were tied to leafless trees by chains that led into the black openings of insulated doghouses.

I slowed the truck at 441 and pulled onto a cracked concrete drive with a faded tin shelter that sagged at the back. There was a Nissan Pathfinder with a bumper sticker I remembered from the first day I'd met the Basquo that read IF YOU DIE,

WE SPLIT YOUR GEAR. I wondered if he had had a chance to climb any mountains since he had moved to Durant.

I killed the motor, cracked the door, and gingerly walked around the truck. She already had her door open and had unlatched the baby, presenting him to me. I took him carefully, and she got out of the vehicle. Her purse dangled from her elbow, and the three of us eased our way up the two steps of the tiny porch where, to my surprise, she pulled a set of keys from her purse and unlocked the door.

I wasn't aware of anybody in our town who went so far as to lock their doors; most people didn't even close them until really cold weather. They even left the keys in their cars with the engines running while doing errands downtown. We lobbied against such activities and went so far as to move the citizens' cars around the block in an effort to make them aware that they could be easily stolen, but it had little effect other than smart-aleck phone calls to Ruby.

"Would you like a cup of tea?"

I glanced down at her. "I'd love a cup of tea."

She nodded, one brief jolt of her chin.

I followed her into the house. It was small, had probably been built in the twenties, with a set of narrow stairs that rose to my right, living room to my left, and a small dining alcove that must've turned the corner into the kitchen. She continued on, but I paused at a nifty little wood-burning stove nestled in a river stone fireplace. The house was spotless, and there were sweet touches everywhere; lace curtains in the windows, hardwood floors waxed within an inch of their grain, and a deep red border with a twin set of gold stripes that raced the perimeter of the room. The furniture was old but sturdy, and there were a number of framed pictures on the mantel.

I took the two steps to the fireplace with the baby still in my arms—I think he liked the heat from the stove as much as I did—and I studied the photographs on the thick slab of dark wood. There was a wedding photo with the handsome groom and beautiful bride smiling at the camera, yet clutching each other like they knew what was ahead. There were a few shots of some older folks, about my age, actually—parents, I assumed—and one to my far right, a black and white with three individuals standing in some frozen coulee. The two flanking men were very tall, but my focus was on the center one, a young man with glacier glasses that reflected the mountain sky and adorned with the trademark Vandyke. He was smiling like a banshee, his fists planted on his hips, and a Tyrolean hat kicked to the side of his head.

Musketeer Santiago Saizarbitoria, mountain climber.

"He's very proud of that one." She'd shed her coat. The baby was making a few mewing sounds. "Can you continue to hold him while I make the tea?"

"Sure." I readjusted him against my chest and slowly twisted back and forth.

She considered me for an instant and then disappeared around the corner.

I peeled the edge of the blanket back and looked into the almost black eyes of Antonio Bjerke Saizarbitoria, aka the Critter. Even at three months, the swaddling looked like he'd been popped out of a Santiago mold. The dark eyes were wide. I extended a pinkie and watched as his little fingers wrapped around my proffered digit. "Howdy, partner."

I heard the ding of a microwave, and Marie appeared with two cups of tea complete with saucers.

I gestured for her to put mine on the mantelpiece. "The other two men in this one look familiar. Are they brothers?"

"Jim and Lou Whittaker—Jim was the first American to climb Everest, but that's Mount Rainier in Washington. San spent a few summers guiding up there for them."

"They must've named it after the beer." She didn't laugh. "Is that what you call him, San?"

She sipped her tea. "I call him lots of things, but that one's for public consumption."

I gestured with the baby. "And what do you call this one?"

"The Critter." I turned red, she grinned, went up on tip-toes, and peered over my arm. "He's awake."

I tried to get a little of the color to drain from my face. "Yep."

She looked at me, a little surprised. "And he's not crying."

I reached over and took a sip of my tea, which was briny, dark, and good. Maybe that's what I needed in the late afternoon, a little caffeine pick-me-up. "So, I'm getting the feeling that Sancho is a world-class mountain climber."

"He is, or he was." It was cozy there by the fire, and she showed no interest in moving. "Nothing happened, he just stopped climbing. The whole reason we moved here was so he could be near the mountains."

"It's probably hard to be a world traveler on twenty-one thousand dollars a year."

She glanced up at me. "Twenty thousand and sixty before taxes."

"Oh." I'd said it for comic effect, but she still hadn't laughed. "Marie, trust me, there's no one more aware of the shortcomings of the county budget than me." I took another sip. "So, if I give him a raise, do you think he'll stay?"

Her Basque eyes were metallic and shone like hematite. "Why don't you ask him?"

"I will, if you think it'll do any good."

She said nothing, and I was afraid we were going back to the silence. She set her tea on the mantel next to mine and flexed her hands as if they were lonely. "You think it's me, right?"

I paused. "Think it's you what?"

"Who's holding him back or something—keeping him from climbing, doing his job, everything."

I returned my cup to its saucer. "I didn't say that."

"It's what you're thinking though." Her voice carried no edge. She seemed to relax, almost relieved to have the subject broached. She took a deep breath and added, "Isn't it?"

"It had crossed my mind."

We listened to the wind pushing against the pocket-sized house and beating against it like the tail ends of a rope. She looked at the fireplace, the agates resting on the river stone like deep water under a fall, and I thought about what my Indian scout had said earlier, and how once again I was venturing onto thin ice.

"Whether he's doing this for you and Antonio or not, he's going to regret it, and I've learned from experience that it's not the things we do in life that we regret so much as the things we didn't do." I smiled at her, trying not to sound like her father.

The silence suited her just then, and I could tell she was fond of the rhythm of the little house. She looked at the baby in my arms and then at me, and it was like I was cascading into that deep water at the base of the falls. "Sheriff, promise me you won't let him get hurt."

5

"What kind of a horse's ass promise was that to make?"

He had a point.

Henry was seated on the old sheriff's leather sofa, was petting Dog, and smiling. I studied the marred surface of the chessboard and the open squares where I could possibly hide my king long enough to forestall the inevitable. The wind was continuing to blow outside, but it felt close and warm in room 32 of the Durant Home for Assisted Living. "Well, what was I supposed to say?"

The old sheriff picked up the cut-glass tumbler of Pappy Van Winkle's Family Reserve and examined the twenty-three-year-old bourbon, finally placing it on the prosthetic knee that had replaced the original since the forties.

"I never made a horseshit promise like that to any wife of anybody that ever worked for me, I can tell you that much." His index finger shot out from the glass, sighting on me from across the chessboard. "You go around makin' bullshit promises like that, you're courtin' disaster."

I moved my king and glanced at Dog, asleep with his head

in Henry's lap and taking up two of the three cushions on Lucian's sofa; it seemed that Dog and the Cheyenne Nation were the only ones who ever sat on the thing.

"Check."

As I reset the board, Lucian refilled our glasses. He rattled the ice in his, the mahogany eyes scanning his room as the sound of the wind stiffened, and he looked out the sliding doors. He sat like that looking like a line drawing in a Louis L'Amour novel—page 208, Twentieth-Century Lawman, Lucian Connally. "Let's see, we only had five altercations worthy of mention when I was sheriff and four of 'em involved you."

"Yep."

He'd always had the darkest eyes I'd ever seen, even in comparison with the Basques, or the Crow or Cheyenne, for that matter. The old sheriff dug into his vest pocket for his pipe and beaded tobacco pouch, which had been a gift from the Northern Cheyenne tribal elders. He looked at Henry for confirmation. "Still, I'd say his tenure as sheriff has been a lot harder on him than mine was."

The Cheyenne Nation smiled but said nothing.

I thought about my impromptu physical examination earlier this morning as a gust blew the pines outside so that they looked like they were raising their skirts and then pushed on the glass with a groan. More snow later, for sure.

I thought about Hatch, New Mexico; about a little adobe house I'd constructed in my mind with chilies hanging in the window and the lilt of Spanish voices drifting through the warm breeze. A place where there were no electric outlets on the parking meters to plug the engine block heater of your vehicle into, and where Gore-Tex and fleece were foreign words.

Lucian stuffed the bowl of the pipe full of Medicine Tail Coulee Blend tobacco, returned the pouch to his vest, and produced his old Zippo lighter. "You gonna move to New Mexico?"

I looked up at him, a little surprised. "Why do you say that?"

He lit his pipe, took a few puffs, surveyed the board, my next move, and spoke to Henry. "'S what he threatens all of us with, every winter."

The Cheyenne Nation nodded. "Yes, it is true."

The thick, double-paned glass flexed with the wind again, and it felt good to be inside with their company.

"So, what's really on yer mind, other than the change in the seasons?"

I lifted my tumbler and took a sip of the caramel liquid, allowing the medicinal burn to heal as much of me as it could from the inside. I paused, giving a moment of trepidation to the naming of my anxieties. "Bullet fever."

He continued to study the board, then moved a rook of his own and nodded. "The Basquo?" I nodded back. "How bad?"

"Pretty bad."

He let out with a long, slow exhale sounding like a locomotive stopping at a station. "You gonna keep him working?"

"For another two weeks—he gave notice today."

Henry looked up.

Lucian glanced at the Cheyenne Nation and then back at me. "Well, hell. What's he wanting to do?"

I hooked a knight out to greet his rook. "Go back to Rawlins; corrections."

The old sheriff grunted, then set the pawn in sacrifice to my knight, his bishop reclining on the baseline.

Henry breathed a laugh. "You want to run off to New Mexico, and he wants to run off to prison. It seems to me you are getting the better deal."

I turned and studied Lucian. "Where'd you want to run off to when those Basque bootleggers shot you?"

"To the county hospital to see if the sons-a-bitches could save my leg—and you can see how that turned out."

We all took sips of our respective bourbons, but Henry was the first to speak. "Sometimes things happen and places get sounded for us; things get touched that perhaps should never be touched."

This time Lucian pointed the pipe stem at me, something he did so often that I sometimes wondered if his finger had a safety. "Now I'm a big one for thinking—but I think you can give a man too much time to think. The Basquo's a thinker, and if you give him enough time he'll think himself out of his job." He glanced at Henry. "Whatta you think, Ladies Wear?"

The Bear lifted Dog's head and stood, downing his bourbon in one swallow. "I think it is time to go to jail." He crossed to the kitchenette, and Dog padded after him.

I smiled across the board at Lucian and moved my own queen out into play. "So, you don't think it's such a bad thing to take Sancho on a little snipe hunt with this chase-a-thumb?"

He shrugged. "At least until you can find something else for him to occupy his mind with." He puffed on the stem of his pipe and changed the subject. "Hey, I heard Geo Stewart's family took him out sleddin' yesterday."

I pulled out my pocket watch and studied its face in the dim glow of the painted hide lampshades. I figured Henry was right, and we needed to get out of there soon or we'd be facing one of Lucian's signature bologna sandwiches with instant coffee sprinkled on it for seasoning as our dinner. As it was, we were looking at either a frozen burrito from the Kum & Go or a potpie from the holding-cell kitchenette.

"The Indian says we gotta go." I walked past Henry and Dog.

He shook his head. "You ain't gonna finish the game?"

I placed my empty tumbler in the sink and returned to collect my hat and coat. "I guess my mind's somewhere else."

Lucian set his glass back on the small table, and I could tell he'd just as soon we stayed. "You know those Stewarts got more lives than a tin bear at a shootin' gallery." He looked at all of us and chuckled. "You know why Geo Stewart always wears a scarf or keeps his collar buttoned up on his shirt?"

"Nope."

"Got a scar 'round his neck, runs from ear to ear."

I leaned against the door. "I noticed it."

"Back in April of '70 we had a bad snow, dropped about forty inches overnight, and Geo finds himself short on supplies—mostly Four Roses, or Red Noses as we used to refer to it, and jumps on his motor toboggan and heads into town hell-bent for leather."

Henry asked. "Motor toboggan?"

Lucian shrugged. "'At's what they used to call 'em; military surplus, made outta someplace in Wisconsin."

"What happened?"

Lucian leaned back in his chair with his palms on his thighs. "Mike Thomas . . ." He paused for a moment. "He still got that spread out near the Stewarts?"

"Yep."

"Well, the snow got so deep that it filled up the cattle guards, so Mike's father had him string a strand of barbed wire across the ranch road to keep the stock in."

"Oh, no."

"Geo hit it at about forty miles an hour." He chuckled. "Mike and another artist fella, Joel Ostlind, found him that afternoon, and they had to use a digging spade to get him loose from the road where his blood had froze. Doctors said that the cold was probably what saved him." I opened the door for Henry and Dog but, just before closing it behind us, he added, "Another good reason for you to not move to New Mexico—it's warm down there, and you can bleed to death."

On the way back from the old folks' home, as Lucian referred to it, I conferred with the Cheyenne Nation, and we decided to partake of the best of both worlds and pick up a burrito at the Kum & Go and take it home to the jail to warm it up.

We were both surprised to find the much-used Olds Toronado parked out front and discovered Gina Stewart parked behind the counter. The same dirty parka was draped over her shoulders, and she was munching on some peanut butter crackers while watching a thirteen-inch black-and-white television, which was up on the cigarette shelves. She didn't even glance at us as we walked past the height indicators that were taped to the doorjamb to help identify burglars. I had spent a lot of time in the gourmet portion of the store and knew that the frozen burritos were stacked like tiny bundles of firewood in the fast-food section at the back.

Henry studied me as I peered through the glass. "You are actually going to eat this stuff?"

There was the shredded beef and cheese, the bean and cheese, and my old standby, the chicken and cheese. There was always the cheese with cheese, but I never felt full without the little bit of protein from the supposed-to-be-meat filling. In all honesty, I tried not to read too closely when I partook of this type of fine dining. Armadillo and cheese would be more than I could stomach. "You don't know what you're missing."

"Yes, I do." He wandered down the aisle to look for something more suited to his epicurian tastes.

I pulled a chicken and cheese out for me and an extra shredded beef and cheese for Dog and called after him. "Snob."

I put the veritable cornucopia of freeze du jour on the counter along with a tall-boy can of Rainier, pulled out my wallet, and waited for the young woman to see me. After a moment, she looked up, annoyed that someone was interrupting her evening, but when she saw me she brightened a little. "Oh, hi, Sheriff."

I laid a twenty on the Plexiglas that protected the plastic counter and read the poster that informed me about the available career opportunities in the country's third-largest convenience store chain with, easily, the most sexually suggestive name. "Hi, Gina, what are you watching?" I thought I could make out Cary Grant's voice and possibly Deborah Kerr's.

She chewed on a strand of her blondish hair. "It's that movie where the man and the woman are supposed to meet at the Empire State Building, but she gets hit by a car."

Must be the season for it, I thought.

She rubbed some crumbs off her jeans and dropped the empty cracker wrapper in a trash can behind the counter. "I think it's supposed to be romantic—you know, for Valentine's Day. I'm not supposed to be watching the TV during business hours, but the manager put it up there, and we don't have television at the house."

She paused as she looked past me to where Henry was opening another of the coolers along the back wall. "I get bored, and it makes me feel better when I watch a movie, but not because of the movie, though." She thought about it, and I watched her profile as she looked past my shoulder and continued to study the Bear. "I think about all the other people around the state that are watching the same movie, and it's like we're watching it together. I mean they're lonely, they're bored, and we're all watching the same thing." Her eyes came back to mine, and her voice dropped. "You have to keep your eye on those Indians; they steal."

I raised an eyebrow but ignored the remark. "It's more than just the state."

"Huh?"

I leaned back and traced the cable coming out of the display stand above me that then disappeared into the broken corner of one of the acoustic ceiling tiles. "It's cable, Gina, which means you're watching the movie with the whole country."

She smiled. "That makes me feel even better."

I smiled back. "How's Geo?"

She thought for a moment. "I think Grampus' fine, but I don't know. Since I missed my shift on Monday they made me come in and cover tonight." She leaned a little forward and confided. "I don't like working nights; a lot of creepos come in here."

Henry joined us with a bag of mixed salad and an unsweetened iced tea. "Present company excluded?"

She stared at him blankly. "Huh?"

I looked at him. "Gina here says she has to keep an eye on you Indians because you steal."

He nodded. "We do, but only small stuff, unlike you whites."

I pointed to the items I'd hunted and gathered. "I'll treat to save you from petty theft." I turned to Gina. "How much?"

Her fingers tripped across the keyboard of the cash register—she seemed relieved to have escaped the conversation. "Nineteen dollars and thirty-seven cents."

I slid the twenty a little closer so that Gina would notice. I couldn't think of anybody in our little community that I'd identify specifically as a creepo. "Creepos like who?"

She took the money and handed me my change. "Ozzie Dobbs for one. He's always coming in here, standing around and looking at my butt, and hitting on me. It's totally gross."

That was surprising. "Really." I took the change and stuffed it in my pocket.

A Volkswagen Jetta rounded the corner at Main, and the driver took advantage of the ice to hit the gas and drift the vehicle outrageously sideways. I raised my arm and hit the remote on my truck to blip the lights and draw attention to my unit, whereupon the driver slowed and drove on with a little more circumspection.

Henry's voice rumbled. "Rachael Terry—she is a wild one."

"Yep." I nodded, making a mental note to call Mike and Susie. I looked back at Gina. "Ozzie Dobbs, really?"

"Yeah, he comes in here once a week at least. That's the only reason I don't mind covering other shifts—at least then he doesn't know when I'm working." She picked up the beer and the tea and stood them in a plastic sack. Her eyes strayed back to the television. "He always wants to buy me things, which is nice 'cause Duane is tight as the bark on a tree." She dumped the frozen burritos and the salad on top. "You know, most people warm these up in the microwave before they eat them."

I picked up the package. "Buy you things?"

She shrugged her narrow shoulders, and the parka fell off. She was wearing an oversized, gray sweatshirt that had UNIVERSITY OF TEXAS in orange stenciled across her chest. "Yeah, one time he offered to buy me anything in the store if I'd give him a kiss." She glanced around. "Like I'd fuckin' do *that* for anything in *here*."

The lights on Main Street were swinging in the wind and blinking yellow, the way they always did after midnight, and it was as if the whole town, like a pinball game, had gone tilt. It was odd and depressing, thinking of somebody like Ozzie Dobbs targeting Gina; sometimes it meant something, but most of the time it was just the flotsam and jetsam of the human tide. "I'm concerned about the younger generation."

Henry nodded. "Do you think she paid for those crackers she was eating when we came in?"

I was looking forward to my burrito and figured I could rummage a couple of extra blankets from the linen closet at the jail, since on seriously cold nights it sometimes got a little nippy in the all-concrete holding cells. I wondered if I was getting to be like those old cons who couldn't sleep unless there were bars on the doors and windows—now that was a really depressing thought.

When we got back to the office, the flakes were basting themselves against a familiar, forest-green Chevy parked in the visitor's spot. From the sculpted drifts, it had been there awhile.

Both Henry and I could see that Ozzie Jr. was in the driver's seat, just sitting there, staring; speak of the devil soon to arrive. I shut down the Bullet and climbed out with our plastic bag, ambled my way around the front with Dog at my heels, and joined the Bear as we stood there looking at Ozzie, whose eyes were open but who still hadn't moved. I could hear the radio and could see the condensation in the windows from his breath. Henry and I looked at each other, the vapor from our breath whipping into our faces.

I tapped on the hood of the one-ton Chevrolet, and Ozzie's eyes shifted to us. I stepped closer and could see that he was dressed in the same clothes he'd had on earlier today but that there were smears of something dark on the sleeves of his jacket and the front of his shirt.

I slipped by the Cheyenne Nation. My hand fumbled with the door handle of the truck before I flipped it open and stuck my head into the cab. The heat was on high, the interior of the truck was stifling, and Roy Orbison was singing "Only the Lonely." It was blood on his shirt and jacket with some on his jeans and even on the brim of his hat.

"Ozzie, are you all right?" His eyes shifted to mine in a dull and listless way. "Are you hurt?"

His voice was slurred, and I could smell the liquor. "Walt, I didn't mean to hurt him."

I put a hand on his shoulder and saw that there was an empty bottle of expensive tequila on the seat beside him along with a collection of cheap valentines spilling from a bag. "Hurt who, Ozzie?"

"He was with her, Walt." His eyes darted around and toward Henry. "Hello."

I grabbed his chin and swung his face back to me, aware that for legal purposes, he had to say it. "Who did you hurt, Ozzie?"

"He walked her back like it was some kind of date."

"Where, Ozzie, where did this happen?"

Tears streamed from his eyes, and he sobbed, his lower lip pulsing in and out with his breath. "I'm scared, Walt."

"Ozzie."

"I didn't mean to hit him that hard, I swear I didn't."

I took his arm. "Come with me." He didn't resist, and I

took his keys. Henry helped me get him up the steps. I opened the door, flipped on the lights, and we seated him on the bench by the dispatcher's desk. "Henry, could you watch him?"

I snatched Ruby's phone from the cradle and hit the second auto-dial. Vic answered on the third ring, her voice a little groggy but deep and sultry. "And what fresh hell is this?"

God she sounded good, half asleep and snarky. "I need you at the office, *now*."

She snapped the receiver down on the other end, and I hung up, quickly punching the Red Cross emblem on Ruby's color-coded phone. Henry was kneeling in front of Ozzie, holding him up with one hand. "Ozzie, where did all this happen?"

He paused, but I guess I'd asked enough times that he finally got it. "My house."

"Is Geo at your house?"

"Yes." He slumped against the back of the bench, but the Cheyenne Nation kept him steady.

"Ozzie? What's your address?"

"101 Eagle Ridge, the one on the hill."

"911." I recognized Chris Wyatt's voice, and I told him what I needed and where.

There was a pause. "Walt, where the hell is that?"

The development was relatively new and still mostly unoccupied so even the EMTs didn't recognize the street addresses. "It's in the Redhills Rancho Arroyo subdivision."

"Oh. Okay."

I hung up the phone and hustled over to the watercooler to get a paper cup full for Ozzie. He reached out with a shaking hand to pet Dog, who was sniffing the blood on his pants.

I sat on the edge of the bench, glanced at Henry, and handed Ozzie the water. "Was it Geo Stewart that you hurt?"

He looked at the cup of water but didn't make any attempt to drink it. "I don't have any friends."

"Ozzie?"

"I really don't." He listed a little toward me, and Henry righted him. The small man looked at the Bear in appreciation. "Thanks."

The Cheyenne Nation nodded. "No problem."

"I mean I know lots of people—acquaintances, you know?"

I was forceful with the next question. "Is he hurt?"

He paused. "Yes."

"How bad?"

He began crying again. "Walt, I didn't mean to hurt him."

I nudged the paper cup toward his mouth. "Take a drink of water and tell me what happened."

The cup hesitated there for a moment. "Walt, I think I'm going to be sick." He burped, and then he heaved. "I'mhh . . . I'm gonna be sick."

Henry hoisted him up, ushered him into the hallway bathroom, and flipped up the lid. Ozzie no sooner sat on the floor before he leaned forward and spewed forcefully into the toilet. He seemed capable of the action without hurting himself, so I draped a washcloth onto his shoulder and stepped back along with Henry, closing the door to give Ozzie a little privacy. "If you need anything, we're right out here."

I could leave Henry in charge, but it wasn't his job. I had to wait until Vic got here to babysit Ozzie, then I could take off. I leaned a hand against the doorjamb, tipped my hat back, and thought about how I hated these kinds of cases.

"Are your nights usually like this?"

I threw him a look. "Pretty much."

Dog stood in the hallway as well and looked at the two of us uncertainly. I crouched down and put a hand out, and he hurried over. I pulled him in with my arm, and we all squatted there until my foot wouldn't take it any longer and I slumped against the wall. I sat with Dog's head in my lap, and the three of us listened to Ozzie Dobbs puke his guts out.

"I can stay with him until Vic arrives."

I sighed deeply. "That's okay, she's usually quick."

He continued to study me. "Then I will go with you."

"No need in the both of us going."

I heard the front door jangle and the couple of thumps as Vic's Browning tactical boots struck the steps on her way up the stairs. She vaulted across the dispatch area and was standing in the hallway in front of us in her fur bomber hat, down jacket, PHILADELPHIA POLICE DEPARTMENT hoodie, pajama bottoms, and duty belt, complete with cuffs, extra mags, and Glock. "S'up?"

I struggled to my feet as Henry stood. "I did not know you slept in pajamas."

"Gun belt, too. I'm kinky that way." Another round of regurgitation erupted from behind the door, and she raised an eyebrow at me. "If you called me from a sound sleep for a DWI then I'm going to kick you till you're dead."

*　　*　　*

I left Dog with Henry, Henry with Vic, and Vic with Ozzie. The roads were still relatively dry, and with the lights and siren I was able to make good time to the red hills east of town, especially since there wasn't a single other vehicle on the roads this late. I blew through the blinking red lights and straightened out on Route 16, bellowing and bringing all ten cylinders up like a pack.

I took the turn toward Geo's place but then steered off at the entrance to Redhills Rancho Arroyo, which was announced by a monstrous gateway of hewn logs about the size of my truck. I eased off the throttle so that I could make it through and past the empty guard shack. There was a slight downslope that led along the creek to five rambling million-dollar structures. It was an educated guess, since I'd never been to the Dobbs household, but the lights were on at the one squatting on the precipice of the ridge.

It was, of course, the mansion with the best view of the mountains.

I slid the truck into the driveway, grabbed a wool muffler that was on the seat, unclipped my handheld radio from the dash, and quasi-leapt into the drifts of snow that had collected on the concrete. I made my way to the door beside the wooden and windowed garage doors that probably cost as much as my house.

It was locked, so I pulled my Maglite out and made my way around to the back on the sidewalk that circled through the landscaping surrounded by nonindigenous, Colorado red-rock walls. The large sliding glass door was opened to a deck with light cascading from inside the house that painted stripes across the snow-covered lawn; there was a blood trail to my right.

When I got to the top of the steps, I could see where a few drops of blood had splattered across the travertine tile. There was a golf club lying on the floor, and it had blood on it as well. I stepped in the doorway with my heart palpitating like a friction motor, but there was no Geo.

Somewhere in the house I could hear someone crying, but it was muffled and distant. It was cold inside with more than a little snow blown in on the tile—I closed the door against the slamming of the wind. There was no blood on the thick carpet that led upstairs and, all in all, there was more blood on Ozzie than in the house.

I slipped my flashlight back into my duty belt. "Mrs. Dobbs?" There was no response, but the crying continued. I mounted the suspended steps that overlooked an expansive living room to the left and continued to the second door on the right. I didn't really want to intrude on the woman, but I needed a more detailed description of what had happened.

I knocked. "Mrs. Dobbs?" I heard a shuffling, and then the sobbing stopped. "Mrs. Dobbs, it's Walt Longmire. Can I speak to you?"

I listened as she padded to the door and turned the knob. When she saw me, she started crying afresh. "Oh, Walter . . . Oh, my God."

I leaned down so that I could be on her eye level. "Mrs. Dobbs, where is George Stewart?"

She began really sobbing now, and her hands clutched for

the lapels on my coat. "Walter, it was horrible. Ozzie Junior started screaming and George was shouting back at him and then he pushed him . . ."

I tried to get her to look me in the eye. "Mrs. Dobbs, where is Geo?"

She continued to study my duty shirt as she reconstructed. "Ozzie Junior fell, grabbed the golf club, and I swear he only swung it to warn George, but George stepped toward him and . . . and I just ran from the room." I nudged her chin up with my hand and finally got her to look me in the face. "Walter, Ozzie killed him."

I thought about the blood trail that I'd followed on the deck steps. "Mrs. Dobbs, did the fight take place in your kitchen?"

She caught her breath and nodded. "Yes."

"And that's where you left the two of them?"

"Yes."

I nodded and tried to smile a little reassurance into her. "Well, your son is at my office, and there's nobody down in your kitchen. In my profession, dead people tend to stay where they drop, so I think that Geo came to, noticed that nobody was around, and went home."

"Oh, Walter, do you think so?"

"Yep, I do. Head wounds tend to bleed a lot, but there's really not enough blood down there to indicate a serious injury." I straightened. "But if he's out there wandering around in this cold and snow with any kind of head wound, I have to go find him. Now, the EMTs are going to be here anytime now, and I need you to tell them to sit pat till I call in to them on my radio, okay?"

She sniffed. "Okay."

"Why don't you go down in the living room and wait by the front door?" I looked at her seriously. "And don't go in the kitchen."

She wiped her eyes with her fists. "I won't."

The weather had stiffened, and it was worse on the ridge above the Redhills Rancho Arroyo's back nine, with beads of snow sandblasting horizontally and my muscles grinding together like ice floes in a wind-lashed sea.

I couldn't pick up enough of the blood trail but found a small piece of Geo's Carhartt flapping on the barbed wire fence where he'd climbed over. I straddled the old three-strand attached to posts so aged they looked as if they might've grown there, pulled the tail ends of the muffler up from where it was wrapped around my hat, and played the beam of the big flashlight across the drifts.

I could still see the boot tracks in the foot-deep snow—he hadn't continued straight but had tacked against the wind. I twisted my hat down harder, so that the aperture between it and my scarf was like the visor on a knight's helmet, and pressed my face against the inside of my upturned collar. My stomach growled, and I thought about the two burritos lying on Ruby's desk; Henry had probably fed them to Dog.

I climbed the ridge and looked down at the path that skirted the junkyard/dump and saw where it ended at the back of the Stewart compound. With the abandoned vehicles and trailer houses, it reminded me of Khe Sanh in Vietnam—just a hundred degrees colder.

My radio crackled. Static. "Unit 1, we're 10-23 at 441 Eagle Ridge."

I plucked the radio from my belt and hit the button. "That you, Chris?"

Static. "Yeah. Mrs. Dobbs said to contact you for information about the victim."

I ducked my head to avoid the wind. "Well, get over to George Stewart's place by the dump and wait for me there. I'm pretty sure that's where he's headed."

Static. "Roger that."

I replaced the radio back under my coat. The trenches that Geo's boots had made continued down the canyon edge and arced toward the house. I followed as quickly as I could, but the snow continued to scour slick under my boots and the grade became slippery. I slid a little to the side in an ungainly split and then continued my descent, second-guessing my choice of leaving Henry Standing Bear at the office.

I was about halfway down the grade when I came to a second fence and a copse of naked apple trees crouched by a smaller path that led down the edge of the ravine toward the junkyard. Buried in the hillside across from the frozen idyll was an old cellar door that must've been the exit from the clandestine tunnel.

The spot where it had all started with an apple and a kiss.

The drift was at least a foot and a half deep in front of the doors, and they lay there undisturbed like peeling gray gates to the underworld. I couldn't see the boot prints any longer, so I backed up, crouched down, and panned the beam of the flashlight across the surface of the snow. The only thing I could see were the craters where my boots had broken through the hard crust of the surface. I stood there in a continual riptide of flakes that traveled quickly across the polished snow.

It was as if he'd disappeared.

I peered at the cellar opening again. It was strange, but there was a relatively new clasp and massive padlock hanging against the door, one of those locks with the rubber covering to protect it. There was nothing, though, to give any indication that he'd stood there, unlocked and opened the ancient doors or even continued in that direction. I turned the beam back toward the main pathway and caught sight of one snow-filled print that wasn't mine. He must have turned and continued down toward the junkyard.

It was a narrow path, just wide enough for a man. There was a wooden gate about two-thirds of the way down, nothing that would keep anybody out if they were serious. The footing was worse than before, and I had to take my time but soon arrived at the level space of the old quarry in the oldest part of the lot. I could date Detroit design by the surrounding stacks of automobiles, massive, skirt-fender beasts from the bulbous forties and sleek, high-finned quarter-panels from the futuristic fifties.

In the junkyard's protected environs, the wind had lessened, and the snow was wetter so Geo's tracks were easier to follow. I wondered why, if he was trying to make it back home, he had detoured here.

I made my way down the aisles of stacked vehicles and had just turned the corner at a '52 Lincoln when I saw eyes looking at me from the gloom of dark and distance. I raised the Maglite into two pairs of bronze iridescence.

The mutt wolves had their teeth showing as they made their deliberate way toward me between the stacked automobiles. I had been the jolly fellow who had freed them from the depressing dump office and taken them home to be fed, but now I was an interloper that they'd found in their assigned territory.

I made my voice stern. "Easy. Easy Butch, easy Sundance . . ."

They showed no sign of stopping, and even though I despised the thought of shooting them, I couldn't run. I hoped that maybe a warning shot would scare them off and reached down, unsnapping the safety strap from my Colt and fixing my hand around the grip.

At that movement, they froze.

My hand stayed on my sidearm, and I spoke between the snowflakes. "Well, you guys are smarter than I thought." They didn't advance, but they didn't run, either. I stood there for a moment and then shone the flashlight back onto the prints that turned a corner ahead and continued off to the right.

I stepped forward, but they still didn't move. "All right, let's call this one a truce. You guys go your way, and I'll go mine." I resnapped the holster and made my way around the corner of the Lincoln. They continued to watch me.

I made a cursory cast of the beam back toward the two dogs, but they remained immobile. Then I noticed that there were two sets of prints in this aisle. The new set were different from the junkman's, larger and with a more outdoor tread, an over-boot of some sort—probably Sorels. For comparative purposes, I placed my rubber-covered foot alongside—smaller than mine, probably a ten or an eleven.

I stayed to one side and followed both sets of tracks to another left. The snow was heavy now, but the wind had died. I looked up at the flakes that made me feel as though I were falling down and saw that some snow had been swiped away from one of the doors of an old, slope-backed, mostly intact Mercury Coupe.

The door hung open, and I could see one of Geo's antiquated logger boots hanging from the sill, the extended length of untied cord laces drifting back and forth across the open window of the vehicle on which the Mercury rested.

I hustled through the odd lumps of snow-covered junk and parts, finally resting a hand on the door handle of a partially crushed '47 Chevy that was at ground level.

Geo was slouched forward with a shoulder firmly planted against the steering wheel where the Mercury's horn would've been if it had still had one. He wore the welder's cap with the upturned flaps, the double troughs having now filled up with snow. The condensation of his breath had frozen his beard into a solid mass and thinned the blood in it so that it seemed transparent and pink. Thin icicles stuck out from his down-turned face like porcupine spines.

I fed a fingertip into my teeth and pulled my glove off, wrapping my hand around the junkman's wrist—the flesh was blue, cold. He looked down at me with the remainders of a faint smile, but it appeared that the glimmer of life was gone from the rime ice at his pupils.

It was also about then that I felt Sundance clamp his jaws into my right butt cheek.

6

"How's your ass?"

I responded conversationally. "Fine, how's yours?"

"Unperforated."

David Nickerson, Isaac's new resident, was on EMT duty and had just finished stitching up my posterior when Vic had barged in. I could feel the substantial breeze from the open door of the van and asked her to close it. She did and sat on the wheel-well hump I'd occupied only two days earlier. Vic had gotten Geo Stewart's body loaded into Durant EMT van number one, and it would appear that we were maxing out the available emergency vehicles for the area on a frozen and very early Wednesday morning.

"You always provide us with the most pleasant environs for our work."

"I try."

"I guess I should congratulate you on finding an entirely new place on your body for scars."

Nickerson straightened behind me. He had applied a large gauze patch over my wound, or at least that's what it felt like under the dull ache of the local anesthetic with which he'd shot my right cheek. "That's it."

I pulled up my underwear and Carhartt overalls, the emergency pair I kept behind the seat of my truck. "You're sure I'm not going to need any cosmetic work; that is my best side."

He smiled, and I took a few seconds to study the future of practical medicine in my county. He was a handsome kid with enveloping brown eyes and a comfortable face, one that I was pretty sure I was going to see a lot of in the future. "You sure you're old enough to be doing this stuff?"

The smile held, and he nodded as he put away the tools of his trade. "Diploma and everything."

He departed, leaving the van to Vic and me.

I pulled the sleeves up and shrugged on the shoulders, then zipped the front of the insulated suit and straightened the collar. "Geo?"

"Still dead." She turned her boot sideways, and we both watched as the collected snow slowly slid off. "It looks like the rural Rasputin finally ran out of lives. From a cursory examination, they say massive coronary, but they'll know more once they get him back to the hospital."

I thought about it. "Do you think the heart attack was due to the beating?"

She unzipped her duty jacket and studied me. "Difficult to say in all honesty but, if the man had stayed on the floor of the Dobbses' kitchen or even made it to cover, he might not be dead."

She took off her hat, ran a hand into her dark hair, and

studied me. "Who the fuck knows why people do the things they do when they're in that condition?" She paused. "Actually, you would probably know."

I came around the gurney and started to sit but then thought better of it. "Well, there's the disorientation of having been beaten with a pitching wedge, but it doesn't look as though he was hurt that bad." I sighed. "With the wind, it was tough going out there."

"That and the man is seventy-two years old with a history of heart trouble in the family. Didn't you say the son died of a heart attack?"

"Yep, but Isaac said Geo's heart was strong and that he didn't have the hereditary condition. He did have diabetes, though." I thought about it some more. "Why did he veer off and go to the junkyard when he could've just gone home?"

She folded her arms. "You just said it. Maybe he got disoriented out there in the snow, or he was just looking for the nearest shelter."

"A '48 Mercury Coupe with no windows?"

It was quiet in the van. "I don't know, maybe he thought he was going to the fucking drive-in." Her head inclined as she continued to study me.

I was getting irritated and it wasn't her fault, but she was the only one around to swipe at. "What're you smiling about?"

"You."

"Why me?"

She laughed. "You really don't want to charge Ozzie Dobbs with aggravated assault, do you?"

"No, and I don't want to have to hit him with a manslaughter charge." I put my hat back on and looked at her. "Did you find any keys on Geo?"

"What?"

"I've got a hunch I want to follow up on, but I need his keys."

Her smile tempered a little. "A big ring of them. I took them because I thought we might need to lock things up."

"What about the other set of boot tracks out there?"

She didn't completely accept the change of subject but let it pass. "It was Duane. Says he was after the dogs, that they sometimes chase a rabbit and won't come back, so he walked out there looking for them."

I still couldn't feel anything behind me, so I snuck a hand around to make sure I wasn't half-assed. "Speaking of, did Duane let them out after me?"

"Yeah. He says he saw the flashlight and turned the dogs loose."

"Where is he?"

"Outside in my unit. I thought you'd want to talk to him."

"Boy howdy."

"I can't believe he's dead." People respond to the death of a loved one in different ways; Duane's was the stunned way. He sank quietly into the backseat, picked his stocking feet up, and then set them down. We had his boots, and the smell of his socks in the close space was enough to take the hair out of our noses. "You're sure he's dead?"

"I'm afraid so." I was having a hard time sitting on one

cheek because even with the local, a dull throb was setting in. I took my hat off and put it on the dash of Vic's vehicle. I held her clipboard up so that I could make out the notes from her previous interview. "Duane, when did you come out here looking for the dogs?"

He pointed at Vic, who was in the passenger seat. "I already told her."

"Tell me."

He sighed, and his voice sounded like a recording. "Close to midnight."

"You turn the dogs out that late?"

"Yunh-huh, it's the only place I can turn them loose that's fenced in, otherwise they run off. Check with Mike Thomas, they been over to his place a bunch of times."

I flipped to the next page but then let it fall back and looked at him. "Duane, I need to ask you something."

He continued to stare at the floor mats. "Yunh-huh."

"When I found your grandfather, your boot prints went right up to and then past where he died. Is it possible that you walked by him when you were looking for the dogs and just didn't see him?"

He began searching the inside of the vehicle for answers. "I don't know. I just . . ." He clutched his knuckles together.

"Duane, why don't you tell me what you were up to this evening? Maybe we can get a closer idea about the time if you tell me."

He thought about it. "Gina and me went to the movies again in Sheridan."

"You guys go to the movies a lot, don't you, Duane?"

"Yunh-huh." He scratched his nose. "When we got home, I drank a few beers and kinda passed out."

Vic and I looked at each other.

I turned back to him. "Passed out."

"Yunh-huh. Gina woke me up when she went to work, and then I let the dogs out."

"What time was that?"

He looked confused. "What?"

"When Gina went to work and you let the dogs out, what time was that?"

"She usually goes to work around eleven-thirty." He thought about it. "Yunh-huh, it was eleven-thirty, I remember looking at the clock."

"You're sure?"

His gaze came up but didn't make my face. "Is that important?"

"Maybe." I put the clipboard down on the seat. "Duane, I'm trying to understand something and maybe you can help me with this. If your grandfather was trying to get home, why did he go to the junkyard?"

His eyes finally leveled on mine, and he looked genuinely confused. "I don't know."

"Well, his tracks led me down off the ridge to where the path cuts off to the junkyard. Do you know that spot, where the apple trees are?"

"Yunh-huh."

I waited.

He looked uncomfortable and picked at a hole in the thigh of his coveralls. The quiet settled on all of us like a wool blanket, itches and all. "Is there anything else up there?"

"Nunh-uh."

It was a quick response, too quick, as the cliché goes. "Aren't those old tunnel doors up there? The ones that run out from the basement of the main house to where the cathouse stables used to be?"

He wasn't so quick with a response this time. "Yunh-huh . . . Yeah, I guess."

I glanced at Vic, who clinched an eyebrow back at me quicker than Duane would've ever noticed. "So, why wouldn't your grandfather have just gone in the tunnel doors and made his way to the house and out of the weather?"

"Oh, those doors don't work."

I nodded and scooted farther up on my good cheek. "Then why is there a brand-new padlock on them?"

It took him a few moments to come up with something for that one, and when he did, it sounded like he had been coached. "Gaddamned insurance—they said we had to lock it up so kids wouldn't fall in there and hurt themselves."

"Can you get in the tunnel?"

"Nunh-uh, it's collapsed."

"From the basement of the house?"

He picked at the growing tear on his pants. "Yeah, I mean . . . a little ways, but there's snakes."

Again, he sounded like the dead man. "Snakes."

"Yunh-huh."

I looked at Vic and then back at him. "In February."

He looked at Vic and then back to me. "Yunh-huh."

There was a growing glow of gold-tinged red with just a sliver of platinum in the sky as Vic and I stood, looking off to the eastern horizon. The snow had stopped, but it was still diabolically cold and windy. I blew a thick pillar of breath and watched as it quickly dissipated between us. "Sailor take warning."

She studied me. "Yunh-huh."

Maybe our conversations were piling up in Nebraska after all. "Gee, Vic, do you think Duane is lying?"

She smiled and stamped her feet a couple of times, shuffling her Browning tactical boots and turning her full back to the wind. "As fast as a dog can trot."

I groaned, figuring this was the first of many dog remarks to come. "Did you get a lot of photos?"

"Yes."

"Print castings?"

"No, I did not haul plaster out there; it would've just frozen. We have his boots and believe me, the tracks are his—the boots match the prints, the prints match the boots."

"Fresh?"

She nodded. "We can look at them a little closer in the photos, but I'd say the timing works out pretty close to what he said in his statement. That part didn't change between my interview and yours."

She looked up at me from under the black rabbit-fur flap of her bomber hat, which indicated that after two weeks of negative temperatures, she was now serious about keeping warm. She resembled Anna Karenina, the kind of woman that if you want to kill, you have to hit with a train. I loved the way she looked in that hat, but I'd never tell her because she'd stop wearing it.

"I wanna look in the basement. Do you wanna look in the basement?"

"Yep."

She glanced back at Duane, still seated in her unit and wondering what we were talking about. "He's not going to want us to look in the basement."

"No."

"We need a warrant."

I started toward her unit. "Not necessarily."

I closed the junkyard gate and locked it with Geo's keys. Vic drove us back toward the Stewart house and adjacent lodgings. "What'd you do with the dogs, Duane?"

"I put 'em in the big house." He paused for a second as he continued to stare at nothing. "I feel really bad about that, Sheriff. I didn't know that was you out there in the yard."

He looked genuinely sorry, and I felt even worse about having peppered him with questions about his dead grandfather, but there was something about that basement that he and the recently deceased weren't telling me. "Hey, Duane, do those dogs have their shots?"

"Oh, yeah. Tags and everything."

"Well, do you think it'd be all right if we swung by the house so I could read them? I really don't want to have to take those precautionary rabies shots if I don't have to."

His eyes didn't make contact with mine when he responded. "Yunh-huh, sure." We drove down the lane and made a right. "You're not gonna shoot Butch and Sundance, are you?"

Vic glanced at me, and I shifted in my seat. "No, Duane, if I was going to do that, I would've done it when they bit me and not six and a half hours after the fact." Vic and I got out of her vehicle, and Duane made a movement to follow us. "That's okay, Duane, I think we can handle it."

He flipped the passenger seat forward and kept a hand on the door. "No, I better come in with you. They mind Gina best, but they'll listen to me. I don't want them making any more mistakes with nobody."

I held the door but kept it blocked with my body. "You don't have any shoes."

He shot a look down at his stocking feet, more holes than sock. "That's all right, I can just run into the house."

I glanced at Vic and shrugged. "Okay."

Duane hopped along in front of us, displaying a great deal of agility as he avoided the snow-covered junk in the walkway. He jostled the doorknob and called into the house. "Dogs!" When he swung the door wide, the two of them were standing in the entryway like twin sentinels.

The place was just as dreary as it was the other night and still mildewed, which is truly a feat in Wyoming's high desert.

It was warm in there, and I remembered thinking that it'd felt clammy when I'd discovered Mrs. Dobbs in the kitchen. I suppose Redhills Arroyo would be my next stop; breaking the news to Betty that her boyfriend was dead and that we were likely to charge her son with some form of murder.

What fun.

Duane brought the wolf mutts closer, and they were their old selves, smiling and wagging. I raised a hand, and Butch stretched his neck out to lap at it while Sundance stood just a little to the side and studied Vic as she closed the door behind us. I glanced at the basement door underneath the stairwell to our left and gestured toward the nearest hound. "All right, are you the one that bit me, you villain?"

Duane interrupted. "No, Sundance always attacks from the front. If you were bit from behind, it must've been Butch."

"And here I thought we were pals." I reached under his muzzle and swung his collar around in order to examine the tags. They actually were updated only this year, and I decided that I could now continue with part B of my plan. "Duane, could I have a glass of water?"

"It tastes like ass."

I stared at him for a moment. "What?"

He stood in the entryway, framed by the stained-glass side panels that led to the dining room. "The water here in the big house comes from the original well, and it's only about sixty feet deep. It's coal water and tastes like ass."

Vic turned her back, and I knew she was trying to keep from laughing. "That's okay; I'd still like a glass of water."

He started toward the kitchen and the dogs followed, but he stopped when we didn't. "You wanna come into the kitchen?"

I looked down at the melting snow on my over-boots and the filthy, thread-bedraggled carpeting. "I don't want to track into the house any more than I have to."

He acted as if he'd never heard those words arranged in

that order before, shrugged, and then ducked into the kitchen with the dogs at his stocking heels.

I stepped to my left and turned the handle of the basement door—locked. I pulled out Geo's key ring and quickly flipped through the older ones, finally selecting the smallest of the skeleton type.

Vic whispered over my shoulder. "You dog. This is all very interesting for me. I've heard of things like illegal entry, breaking and entering, collusion, and inadmissible evidence, but rarely does one get to see all of it at one time in person."

"Just a little ole-time law and order. Stick around; it's going to get worse. When I take a drink of the water, turn your head the other way and mumble *help*."

She stared at me. "Is this the accessory part of ole-time law and order?"

"Just put some feeling into it." I slipped the key in the door and unlocked it, opened and closed it, and then redeposited the ring back in my Carhartts just as Duane returned from the kitchen.

He held the glass out to me, and I couldn't help but notice that it looked yellow and smelled like sulphur; the sacrifices I made for my constituency. "Thanks." I stopped just as I was about to drink and shifted my ear toward the basement door. "Hey, did you hear something?"

Duane looked at me as he petted the dogs. "Nunh-uh."

Vic shrugged.

I brought the glass back up to my lips and took a swig of what, indeed, tasted like ass. I swallowed and looked around, especially at the brunette. "I thought I heard something."

Duane shook his head. "Nunh-uh, maybe the wind?"

I looked at Vic. "It sounded like somebody crying for help."

The young man pushed his greasy ball cap farther back onto his head. "I didn't hear nothing."

Vic looked at Duane. "I didn't either."

I studied the rusty liquid in the glass and took a deep breath as I raised it to my lips. "Well, I damn well better." Duane continued to watch me, probably amazed that anyone would take a second drink of the water. I got smart this time and just held the glass to my lips and shot a glance at Vic, who covered her mouth for multiple reasons.

She turned her head. "Help!"

Duane turned to look at her. "What?"

I gratefully placed the glass back into Duane's hands and stepped forward, leaning an ear against the basement door. "I'm sure I heard it that time." I twisted the knob as Duane's voice called out from behind me. "That door's locked, there's nobody . . ."

The door swung open, revealing a stairwell that turned at a landing below and continued to the left. There was a light switch to the right, just inside the doorway, and I flipped it on. The full force of heat and humidity wafted up from the basement as I took the first step down. "Duane, it sounds like there's somebody in trouble down here, so I'm going to have a look, okay?"

He moved to the doorway behind me, edging a little in front of Vic. "Nunh-uh, there's nobody down there."

I raised a hand at his protests. "Vic, did you hear something?"

"Maybe . . ." She tromped down the stairs behind me and whispered, "What's my motivation?"

Duane called after us. "Hey, there's nobody down there, she just yelled that."

As I turned the corner at the landing, I looked back up at her. "What, were you going to make me drink the entire glass of water?"

She smiled the crocodile smile. "I just wanted to see if you could do it."

There was another light switch attached to one of the basement support poles and a new, reinforced BX cable that strung on into the darkness. I put my hand on the switch as Duane joined us—it appeared the dogs wouldn't come down the stairs.

"Hey, you can't go down there without a warrant thing."

I glanced back up at him. "Duane, I've got an emergency situation, and you wouldn't want me to ignore it if someone is down here and hurt, would you?"

"Well, nunh-uh, but . . ."

I flipped the switch and glanced around as I stepped onto the dirt floor. It was your usual old house basement with a low ceiling and rough-cut beams and antiquated wiring with porcelain insulators and cast iron pipes that arrived from above and disappeared below. There was an aged washer and dryer that sat in a corner, unplugged, along with an operating hot water heater and a massive, coal-driven furnace looking like a giant metal octopus with a large chute that led to an opening along the hand-stacked foundation. There was the usual junk piled against the walls along with an inordinate amount of gardening tools, supplies, and at least eight fifty-pound bags of fertilizer.

A large blue tarp was tacked to the sill above and screwed into a four-by-four resting on the floor with a number of heavy-gauge extension cords disappearing underneath. As we stood there, the air pressure from whatever was on the other side billowed the plastic back toward us.

Vic stuffed her hands in the pockets of her jacket and leaned against one of the support beams as Duane joined me, still holding the glass of putrid water.

"I don't see any snakes, Duane."

"They're in the tunnel."

I gestured with my chin toward the blue plastic. "That way?"

"Yunh-huh, but it's caved in real bad. That's why we've got the tarp over it."

I walked to the front of the opening and held my hand to the side where warm, moist air was escaping. I looked down and saw that two large eyelet bolts were screwed into the four-by-four and then up at two large hooks where the wood could be lifted and held in place. I stooped and, even with the pain in my rear, began lifting up the wood and consequently the tarp.

Duane was at my side immediately and placed a hand on my arm. "Look, you can't go in there, you gotta have a warrant to be . . ."

"Duane, I've explained the situation and if you attempt to interfere with me any more, I'm going to ask my deputy over there to restrain you—and trust me, it's something she really likes doing."

I threw a glance back at Vic, who lowered a boot to the floor and began moving toward us in a smooth but determined gait.

Duane threw himself aside and sat on the bags of fertilizer; he was still holding the glass. "Fine, fuck it. Just go ahead and get it over with."

I raised the board and hooked it up as Vic joined me at the jagged opening in the basement wall where many a bandit and whoremonger had escaped the local constabulary. There were a few small indicator lamps strung out like landing lights, but that was all. The warmth and humidity hit like a wave, and we both stood there. I couldn't see anything but thought that there must be a switch somewhere, so I raised a hand past Vic's face and felt along the wall. It was there, and I flicked the heavy-duty toggle and watched as fluorescent lights throbbed on full with a monotone thrum.

Vic, as usual, spoke first. "Well, fuck me."

We both leaned forward in absolute disbelief. Humidifiers and heaters ran the distance half the length of a football field with hydroponic lights cascading life-giving warmth and vitamin D onto four-foot-tall plants that grew as far as we could see. I turned my head and spoke out of the side of my mouth. "Is that what I think it is?"

She nodded and looked back to where Duane sat at the opening of what looked to be the largest subterranean marijuana crop in history.

7

When I got back to the office, Vic was stretched out on the reception bench asleep, wrapped in a couple of blankets with a pillow stuffed against the armrest. Dog lay beside the bench and wagged a greeting in four/four time as I sat with care next to Vic's stocking feet—the only part of her that showed from under the gray wool.

I reached down and petted Dog, who fell over on his side next to Vic's tactical boots and closed his eyes. It seemed like a really good idea, so I pulled my hat down over my face and leaned back against the wall.

Vic moved her feet up onto my lap, and her voice was thick with sleep. "Well, now we know why Duane told Geo that there were snakes in the tunnel."

"Yep." I rubbed the thick knitted socks and listened to her purr. "I locked up the cash crop, and Gina has taken command of the household. She says she didn't know anything about Duane's cottage industry."

"Is she the one who works over at the Kum and Go, drives

around with people tied to her bumper, and always smells like the chronic?"

"That'd be the one."

"And you believe her?"

"Let's just say I thought we had enough people in jail for one night, and I've got plenty more problems to go around. Where's Henry?"

She pulled the blanket down, and her nose and the tarnished gold eyes appeared. "Asleep in your office."

I exhaled and wasn't sure if I had the energy to fill my lungs back up again. "How is the mad golfer?"

"Resting comfortably in holding cell A."

"And the pot grower of America?"

"Holding cell B." She adjusted, and I could see she was reaching underneath herself. "You want some more fucked-up shit?"

"Not really."

She recovered some loose sheets of paper that she handed to me. "Too bad, 'cause it's the only news that's fit to print."

I examined the pages. "What's this?"

"The answer from NCIC on Sancho's request for a report on the partial thumb, which came back as a negative—not enough print to work with."

"It's Felix Polk's. We know that because he's been everywhere in the county asking for it back." I rubbed my face with one hand. "That's another little chore I've got to go do."

She wrapped the blanket tighter around the trunk of her

body, emphasizing some of her more curvaceous physical attributes. "Uh-huh . . ."

I looked at her. "Now, why do I not like the sound of that?"

"Because I was bored and punched in Felix Polk and discovered he has a bench warrant with the Travis County Sheriff's Department in Texas concerning a failure to appear on a breaking and entering charge stemming from an incident in 1963."

"Is that all?"

She snorted. "Isn't that enough?"

"I don't think a more-than-forty-year-old bench warrant is going to be enough to occupy the Euskadi Avenger, especially now that we've got a real death on our hands."

She laughed outright. "Yeah, well, imagine how Felix Polk is going to feel about having his past and minor transgressions revisited. And as to Geo Stewart's death, there's not much of a mystery to that one."

"Maybe. Did you happen to notice that one of his shoelaces was undone?"

The look she was giving me could've been defined as incredulous. "So?"

"Geo was pretty careful about that type of thing."

She sat up. "Wait a minute, are we discussing the sartorial splendor of the man whose hair grew through his long underwear?"

"Yep, but he's also the guy who wore both suspenders and a belt and fully laced his logging boots."

She covered her head back up with the blanket. "Right."

I sighed and thought about the long drive I was going to have to take up the mountain. "Is that address for Felix Polk current? I was thinking of paying him a little visit before Sancho gets to work. You want to tag along?"

She didn't move, her head still covered. "No."

I looked at Dog, who dropped his head back between his outstretched paws. So much for man's best friends. I sighed and glanced down the hallway toward the two cells in back. "I don't mean to disturb your rest, but you say Ozzie Junior is in cell A?"

"Sleeping like a lamb and snoring like a lion."

"Well, it's good that he's getting some rest."

She snuggled back down in her blankets, and I was starting to wish it were a wider bench. "Yeah, imagine how he's going to feel when he wakes up and finds out he's headed for the big house."

"Are you Felix Polk?" The bandage on the man's thumb, the registration of the Jeep Wagoneer in the drive, and the name on one of the mailboxes at the end of Caribou Creek Road were pretty good clues, but this was official business.

The wind raced over the canyon where we stood, and with the altitude I bet we were standing in negative ten degrees. Felix Polk was a tall man, almost as tall as I am and close to the same age, with a large belly but in good shape if you didn't count the missing appendage. He had on a pair of chainsaw chaps and a hard hat with the built-in noise compressors flipped up so that he could hear me. Behind the cabin, some kind of machinery was running.

"You haven't got my thumb with you, do you?"

I smiled at him. "Mr. Polk, that's actually what I'd like to talk to you about."

He nodded. "C'mon out back, and I'll shut the log splitter down."

I followed him around the cabin and noted the architecture. It was pretty indicative of the period when the Bighorn National Forest had had to concede a few spots of land to long-term, hundred-year leases. Some of them were coming up for renewal and were a cause of anxiety to the locals, and the ones that were built in the late forties and early fifties were recently changing hands for a reasonable amount of money because of the concerns over the state's proclivity to cancel the leases.

This one was a handsome structure, the logs weathered to a solid gray with the old Oregon cement in between recently patched. Green asphalt shingles and wooden cased windows framed the small porch at the front, which led down a shallow slope to a pump house next to Caribou Creek.

There were stacks of firewood under every eave of the cabin, and a lean-to behind it held another eight cords at least. Evidently Felix Polk was expecting the winter to last as long as I was.

As nice as the cabin was, it was the environs that were the strong point. The house was nestled into a small box canyon with massive rock walls thrusting above the lodgepole pines. The majority of the privately owned structures in the mountains were situated in clusters along service roads or by the reservoirs such as Dull Knife, but this one was isolated with the only way in or out a dirt road that ran a winding three-quarters of a mile back to Route 16. It was just the kind of place to which you hoped to someday retire, and Felix Polk had.

"Twenty-two years at Dynamic Tool and Die; company went belly-up, but I had enough scraped together to buy this place. A truck driver who delivered a bunch of salvage equipment to us down in Austin told me about it."

He set a cup of coffee in front of me, and I wondered if I dozed off and my nose landed in the mug, if I'd drown. There was a fire burning in the old brick fireplace, and the cabin was cozy and warm. The furnishings looked to be from the sixties, and there were built-in bookcases chocked with a lot of military history and mass-market paperbacks with titles like *Death Hunt*, *Dead Zero*, *Dead On*, and *Death Blow*; all in all, there was a lot of death on those shelves. The most disconcerting thing was the Nazi flag that hung over the fireplace. Felix Polk caught me looking at it. "My father's; Belgium, 1944."

"The Bulge?"

"Yeah. I think he hated the British almost as bad as the Germans. He used to love pointing out that nineteen thousand Americans died in that battle and the Brits only lost two hundred."

"More to the point, how many did the Germans lose?"

"'Bout a hundred thousand casualties."

I was tired but felt as if I should make a few stabs at small talk; besides, the other stab, the bite wound, was keeping me awake. "How long have you had the cabin?"

"About seven months now." He poured himself a cup and

sat across the kitchen table from me with a Dynamic Tool & Die mug. "It was in pretty bad shape, but I was able to work on it all through the summer. I already burned a lot of firewood living up here, so I got that industrial splitter."

I gestured toward his bandage. "That how you lost the end of your thumb?"

He laughed and nodded. "Hell, yes—pinched it right off. I got my glove caught in the damn thing and didn't even know I'd done it; felt a little funny so I pulled my glove off and damned if the end of my thumb didn't stay in it."

"Ow."

"Yeah, it got pretty bad. When I went into the hospital over in Sheridan, they stitched it up and give me some pills. I made the mistake of takin' a few of them with a couple of beers and couldn't get off the sofa in there."

"Why the hospital in Sheridan? The one in Durant is closer."

"Needed gas for the splitter, and it's cheaper over in Sheridan."

"Did they notice that part of it was missing?"

"Yeah, they asked me about that, and it was then that I remembered that I'd made a run to the dump. I was drinkin' beer while I was splitting and had that cooler out there, so when I fished the end of my thumb out of my glove I just put it in and forgot about it."

I glanced around at the general unkempt quality of the cabin and asked, "You have a family, Mr. Polk?"

He nodded. "Used to. Had a wife that died, and I got a daughter, but then she died and I don't hardly hear from the granddaughter anymore." He studied me and looked at the ring finger on my left hand. "You a widower, Sheriff?"

"Yep."

He sipped his coffee. "Kids?"

"Yep, a daughter."

He nodded. "Seems like we've got a lot in common."

I needed to get to the point of my visit. "Mr. Polk, are you aware that there's a bench warrant for your arrest in Austin?"

He stiffened. "What?"

I leaned back in my chair. "This is not an official call, Mr. Polk, it's just that one of my deputies ran your name through the database and came up with an outstanding charge of breaking and entering."

He was surprised, to say the least, and then outraged. "From back in the sixties?"

"1963, actually."

"Do you know what that's about?"

In all honesty, I was tired and just didn't care. "Mr. Polk . . ."

He stood with his back to me and then turned to lean against the refrigerator. "I stole my own truck." He picked up his coffee cup and poured himself some more as a little of the outrage left him. He motioned toward me with the pot, but I declined. "I had this International Scout that dropped an automatic transmission and this fella fixed it, but charged me double. I promised him I'd pay him, but he kept my truck and wouldn't give it back. Well, I had a job to go to so I broke into the mechanic shop and stole my truck; got picked up by a deputy three days later, spent a week and a half in stir."

"Did you ever pay the bill?"

He puffed up a bit and wouldn't make eye contact with me. "No, I figured that with the ten days I spent in jail we were even." He shook his head in disbelief and stared at the green swirl linoleum on the kitchen floor. "Over forty years ago, and you show up on my doorstep."

"I'm not here to arrest you, Mr. Polk."

His eyebrows crouched over his eyes. "What?"

"As a matter of fact, I'm here to ask a favor concerning your thumb."

With the holding cells filled to capacity, I was forced to take a nap in my office, which never works because everybody can find me.

"Ruby says to remind you that you have an eye doctor appointment tomorrow morning."

I tipped my hat up and looked at Vic holding a fistful of the Post-its that my dispatcher usually left on my doorjamb. "I'm sleeping." I lowered my hat.

"She also says Isaac Bloomfield says Bill McDermott discovered something and wants to talk to you about it."

I raised my hat again. "Discovered something where?"

She sipped her energy drink, and I thought about asking her for some—I could use a little energy. "Something about Geo Stewart. I called Bloomfield but he wouldn't tell me." She sorted through the square yellow pieces of paper that represented my personal agenda. "I get the feeling he doesn't like me."

"He likes you fine, he just doesn't like your language."

"Fuck him."

"Uh-huh." Figuring my nap was over, I put my hat on my desk and pulled my sheepskin jacket down from where I was using it as a blanket. "Anything else?"

"You were snoring."

"Sorry, it must be my wounds." I glanced up at the old Seth Thomas clock on my wall—it was still losing about five minutes a year; I should be so lucky. It was past lunch, I still hadn't had anything to eat—Dog had consumed both burritos—and I was famished. "I'm really hungry."

She stood and flipped the Post-its onto my desk. "Well, let's go and eat—as far as I know, Geo Stewart isn't going anywhere."

Even though the mercury had yet to break two degrees, we walked to the Busy Bee Café. "How did the meet with the nine-fingered man go?"

I pulled my gloves out and stuffed my fingers into them quickly, so as to keep all of my own. "He promised to not roam the county in search of his thumb."

"In trade for?"

"His thumb."

She shook her head. "Does he really want to make a key chain out of it?"

"He didn't say." A few of the assessor's office ladies shot out of the back door of the courthouse, and we waited as they passed. "I also figured I'd call up the Travis County Sheriff's Department and see if I could get them to drop the charges. The story he told me sounds legit, and I don't think they're going to want to pursue." We rounded the corner of the court-house. "Where is the Basquo, anyway?"

"At the hospital again."

"I guess Antonio's got colic."

"Yeah, well at least the Critter's got a house to live in."

She seemed distant, and I figured I had to do a little bridge mending. "Do you want me to go look at that house with you today?"

She walked along the sidewalk that crossed the court-house's south lawn with her hands stuffed into her coat pockets and her ball cap on her head; she'd obviously seen me admiring the fur hat. "No."

"I'll really do it this time."

"Someone put a higher bid in on it."

I stopped, but she kept walking. "Oh."

She turned at the top of the stairs that led down to the commercial portion of Main Street, all two blocks of it, and looked at me. "My life."

I joined her at the precipice. "Yep?"

"Sucks."

I stood close with my back blocking the wind and looked down at her. "How so?"

"I'm stuck in this one-horse town with this crappy job that doesn't pay shit and an on-again/off-again relationship with my boss."

I nodded. "Gee, you're right, your life does suck."

She hit me with an elbow. "It needed wiring, plumbing, and the foundation was going to have to be shored up, and some asshole paid more than the asking price."

"We'll find you another one."

"I wanted that one."

"I'm sorry."

She kept her head down, and I leaned in till the brim of her hat was against my chest. She took a while to respond, and the clouds of her breath billowed up past my face like a rapidly cooling steam bath. "Yeah."

We stood there like that for a while. "Pretty big step, buying a house."

I felt the bill of her hat nod. "I figure I'm of an age where I need to start making some decisions in my life."

"Am I one of those decisions?"

"Could be."

She was right; ours was an on-again/off-again relationship, where the off-again part was mostly my fault. We'd had a smoldering attraction that had bloomed into a stoked furnace ever since an incident in Philadelphia had presented itself, but I still couldn't reconcile the difference in our ages, that we worked together, and that only a few months ago her younger brother back in Philadelphia had proposed to my daughter.

"Look, I know that right now our ages don't make that much of a difference, but ten years from now . . ."

"Fuck ten years from now."

She looked up at me with those tarnished eyes, and I tried to think about what else I wanted to say. We continued to stare at each other and, as usual, I opted for the path of least resistance. "C'mon, it's cold, I'll buy you lunch."

"I want a house." She turned, and I followed her down the steps. "Hey, I know, maybe I could buy Sancho's house."

★　　★　　★

Henry was back at the office when we returned, and I made him accompany me to the hospital. Durant Memorial had a morgue, or a standard treatment room that served as a morgue—it was room 31, a piece of information that wasn't shared with the common populace.

"Wouldn't you say this was like finding a hole in a pincushion?"

"He was injecting himself three to four times a day to control his glucose levels, but there are two things abnormal about these three injection points. The location where most of his injections took place is in the normal areas of the body, the front and the outside of the thighs, the abdomen, except the area around the navel, the upper and outer areas of the arms, the area just above the waist on the back and the buttocks. You'll notice where these injections were made."

Bill McDermott held the junkman's leg up for my inspection; I could see that there were three larger holes, which punctured the area behind the knee. "How in the world did you find them?"

"Blood."

"What's number two?"

"The size of the needle that went in there three times is a lot larger than the one regularly used for insulin, hence the blood." I studied the young medical examiner on loan from the state of Montana. It's something our neighbors from the north did as a courtesy in the depths of the Wyoming winter when the hour-and-forty-five-minute trip from Billings compared favorably with the five and a half hours from Cheyenne. Bill McDermott had changed since the last time I'd seen him. He looked worldlier and more affluent, which is what three months in Europe with Lana Baroja could do for you.

"When are you going to make an honest woman out of Lana?"

"She doesn't want to be an honest woman." He took a sip of his ginger ale and glanced at Henry, who stood quietly against the wall with his arms folded. Bill turned back and smiled at me, his long, blondish hair hanging in front of his face. "I heard your daughter is getting married."

"I heard that, too." I gestured back toward Geo Stewart's body. "Was that the leg that had the untied boot?"

Both Isaac and the Montana ME nodded.

"Why inject him behind the knee, if indeed someone did?"

Isaac placed his hands in the pockets of his lab coat. "Closest point to the major artery in the leg, and it's possible that it would go unnoticed."

"So you're saying somebody murdered him."

McDermott was cautious. "We're saying it's possible that somebody murdered him."

"With what?"

"Air."

I walked over and leaned against the wall beside Henry. "I thought that only worked in made-for-TV movies."

Isaac decided to take up some of the slack for Bill. "Depends on the condition of the victim, body position, and most important, the amount of air introduced into the system. It's been reported in some medical journals that as little as twenty milliliters could do the trick, but that's still quite a bit of air."

The Cheyenne Nation's voice rumbled beside me. "You would need a bicycle pump."

"That, or a veterinary syringe with something along the size of equine dosage." Isaac looked down at the dead man. "Despite the uncertainties, air embolism has served as a reasonably dependable method of execution for quite a while. In my home country I was confined first for being a Jew and then for refusing to assist in the gassing of mental patients. Psychiatric institutions were ordered to continue so-called mercy killings by less conspicuous means. I was told there was a program described as 'wild euthanasia,' which began at the Meseritz-Obrawalde hospital in 1942. While most of the murders were carried out with overdoses of sedatives, some patients were injected with air, which usually killed them within minutes."

"Would you need any medical knowledge to do this?"

The Doc glanced up at me. "Helpful, but not necessary."

When I got back to the office, I saw that Saizarbitoria's vehicle was backed up to the service entrance; I had put him in charge of collecting and then unloading Duane's illegal 4-H project.

"Hey, Duane." He looked up from behind the bars of his holding cell as I limped in with the last few plants. Vic closed the heavy door, took the plants from my hands, and disappeared.

"You gotta watch 'em in the cold like that, it'll kill 'em."

"I'm sorry to say, but for our purposes it doesn't matter if the plants are dead or alive." I pulled a folding chair over and sat on my good cheek. "Duane, I hate to add to your miseries, but I need to ask you some questions. Depending on whether I'm satisfied with your answers, I can either charge you here in county, hand you over to DCI, or to the Feds, who are not likely to let you off with a stint picking up trash along the side of the roads in an orange jumpsuit."

He continued to study the concrete floor and then mumbled a response. "Yunh-huh."

Vic returned and leaned against the wall. I looked back at Duane. "Whose idea was the marijuana?"

"Mine."

I shot a glance at Vic, who rolled her eyes, and waited a moment. "You're sure?"

"Yunh-huh."

"Duane, do you know what the sentencing guidelines are for this kind of distribution activity?"

"I wasn't distributin' it."

I took my hat off and held it between my knees by the brim. "My deputy, Mr. Saizarbitoria, spoke with the Powder River Co-Op folks earlier this morning after we did a little trash pull out at your place, and they said your electric bill for the last six months has been over seven hundred and fifty dollars a month." I took a deep breath and tried to explain the hopelessness of his situation. "Duane, possession with intention to distribute is not a specific intent crime—the quantity alone proves intent to deliver. The state of Wyoming doesn't need to prove specific intent with this amount of marijuana; knowingly possessing this quantity is a prima facie case."

He looked at me blankly. "We use a lot of electricity, watching TV and stuff."

Vic suppressed a guffaw as I continued. "Duane, I'm afraid there isn't a court in the land that would believe that even two Olympic-grade hopheads such as you and Gina could possibly smoke that much dope."

"Gina don't smoke it, jus' me."

I dropped my hat for dramatic effect. "Duane, I like you,

and I want you to listen very carefully to what I say next—I don't want you to be guilty of all this stuff alone."

Vic stepped from the wall and trailed an arm onto the bars. "Let me tell you, shitbird, I have heard some really lame-ass alibis in my life, but saying that you personally rocked the ganja to the tune of this much gear per annum is the worst alibi I've ever heard."

"It's true."

"It fucking sucks."

He started looking like he might cry. "It's true."

"It." She repeated. "Fucking. Sucks."

I retrieved my hat and stood, smiling at the young man to give him a little reassurance. "I've got a couple of other things to attend to, Duane, but then I'm going to come back and you and I are going to have another conversation, a conversation where you're not so completely guilty. Okay?"

He gathered a little fortitude and smiled back. "Okay."

Vic joined me as I walked around the corner, past the two Polaroids of our guests that we used to remind the staff that we actually had somebody in the holding cells. She studied me. "Business is picking up."

"Yep."

We turned the corner and looked in on Ozzie Dobbs Jr., who was still in his bloody clothes and was standing by the bars with his face pressed between them. "How's it going, Ozzie?"

"I want to press charges."

I nodded. "You were pretty upset about killing Geo last night."

"Yeah, but now that he's okay, I want to press charges."

It appeared that last night's repentance was limited. "What leads you to believe that he's okay?"

Ozzie Dobbs was the perfect picture of someone who had just had the bottom dropped out from beneath him. "He's not?"

"He died last night, Ozzie. He tried to make it back home in the snow and had a heart attack. Now we're not sure if it was the beating, the exertion, or something else—but Geo Stewart is dead." I stepped over to our little kitchenette and pulled a mug from the stack and turned it over. "You want a cup of coffee, Ozzie?"

He blinked and then looked at the two of us. "You guys are kidding, right?"

I stood there for a moment, wondering if more coffee was really going to help. "Not about the coffee I'm not."

He swallowed and nodded his head quickly. "I would love a cup of coffee."

I turned over another for myself and looked at Vic, who shook her head. I poured myself a cup and then one for him; I was guessing, but he didn't stop me from adding cream and sugar. I handed it through the bars, and he took it like a serum. "Geo's dead?"

"Yep."

"Oh, God."

I leaned against the bars and couldn't help but reassure the man. "If it makes you feel any better, and I'm breaking a number of laws myself by saying this, the beating may have been an aggravating factor, but I don't think you killed him."

He crossed back to the bunk and sat without looking at me. "You're just saying that to make . . ."

"No, I'm not. Now, I don't know how current you are on the situation with the Stewart family and your own, but I'm going to need some answers from you about everything that you might know."

He stared at the floor and then slumped with resignation. "I'll tell you everything I know, but can I get a shower? I'm worried that all this blood might be giving me AIDS."

I stared at him. "You weren't all that concerned last night, when you took the time to finish off a fifth of tequila."

"I wasn't in my right mind then."

Vic's eyes narrowed, and the iridescence was like a solar flare. "No shit, little beaver."

"Put your mind at rest, Ozzie. If Geo was HIV-positive, Doc Bloomfield would've told us by now." He didn't say anything more, and I figured after all he'd been through that it was the least I could do for him. "But, I'll get you downstairs for a shower."

Vic pushed off the counter and started toward the hallway. "If you can get through there without a machete; the basement looks like the Jamaican Botanical Gardens."

"Sancho says it's British Columbia Bud."

"Whatever."

Ozzie's voice carried after us. "Hey, Walt, can you ask my mother to bring me some clean clothes?"

When I got to the hallway outside my office, Vic was waiting for me on the other side of my open doorway. "Mrs. Dobbs already came by with his things, but she doesn't want to see him."

"Great, we'll just round up all the idiots and send the whole damn bunch off to Rawlins." I sounded a little fed up, even to me, and then noticed the odd expression on Vic's face. "What?"

She nodded to the open doorway between us. "Um . . . She's here. In your office. Right now."

I tried to exude an aura of blustering professionalism as I entered, tossed my hat onto my desk, and pulled out my chair. "Hello, Mrs. Dobbs."

She'd made herself at home and taken off her coat, the shopping bag with her son's clothes sitting on the corner of my desk. "I suppose I'm one of the idiots you're wanting to send off to Rawlins."

I sat and looked at her. "Not specifically. I hear you don't want to see Ozzie, but I think he needs your support right now."

"Walter, this was a completely unprovoked attack, and a man I cared a great deal for is dead."

"This is your son we're talking about."

She sighed audibly through her nose. "All the more reason."

I thought about the emotional linchpin that the entire episode hung upon and figured that if I could get her to focus maybe we could avoid all of this. "Mrs. Dobbs, is this the first time that your son has found out about . . . I mean, known for sure that you . . . ?" I waited for her to provide the rest so that I wouldn't have to come across with a more palatable version of *shtupping* the junkman.

"That I what, Sheriff?"

I was going to have to come across with a more palatable version of *shtupping* the junkman. "Umm . . . Is this the first indication that your son might've had . . . umm . . . concerning the intimacy between the deceased and yourself?"

She stared at me. "I don't see what that has to do with the matter at hand."

If I'd still been holding my hat, I most certainly would've dropped it. "Well, I think it has everything to do with it." I took a deep breath and let it out slowly, the way I always did when I was afraid I was going to say something I might regret later. "Betty, can't you see how this might raise something of an emotional response in your son?"

"Not to the point of beating someone to death."

"Well, we're still not sure that's what killed Geo."

Her voice elevated, just a touch. "I'm surprised at you, Walter."

I leaned back in my chair and wedged my good foot under my desk, this time trying to take the weight not only off the not quite healed broken bone in my foot but the still sore bite in my right butt cheek. Her arms remained folded, and I felt like I was, once again, in the ninth grade. "If your son is charged, it'll be for murder."

"Yes."

I leaned forward, trying to convey the seriousness of the subject even though I doubted Ozzie would have to do more than pay some heavy court and lawyer fees, and do community service. It was also possible that he and Duane would be picking up trash on the sides of the county roads in matching orange jumpsuits. "Which means he'll go to Rawlins."

"Yes."

"Prison." I paused. "Probably for the rest of his life."

She didn't pause. "Yes." Her head nodded slightly, and it appeared as if she was agreeing with herself. "I understand, Walter, but I just don't see anything else for it."

My mouth closed for a moment in hopes that some sanity might creep into the conversation, and I could just feel the beginnings of another of my headaches coming on. I was saved by the red light that began blinking on my phone and snatched up the receiver. "Yes?"

"Scott Montgomery on line one."

I made a face, even though I was glad for the interruption. "Who?"

"The sheriff of Travis County, Texas?"

"Oh, right." I placed the receiver against my chest and looked at Betty Dobbs. "Will you please consider what I've said, Mrs. Dobbs?"

She stood and shrugged on her coat. She tapped the bag on my desk. "These are Ozzie's things."

"I'll see that he gets them."

She nodded once with her chin, turned, and started to leave. "Walter?"

"Yes, ma'am?"

She stood with her back to me. "Are you aware that your door does not have a doorknob?"

"Yes, ma'am." She stood there for a moment more and then continued out.

Hoping for a sane person, I raised the receiver to my ear and punched line one. "Hello?"

"Sheriff Longmire, Sheriff Montgomery here. I bet you don't remember me."

He was right. "Have we met?"

"Why yes, at the Doolittle Raiders Reunion in San Antonio a few years ago. You escorted Lucian Connally down here, and we were both on that flight where the crew of the B-25, *The Yellow Rose,* let him take the stick?"

I vaguely remembered a heavyset man who was wearing a very large palm leaf hat, who said that he was also a sheriff. I also remembered thinking we were all going to die that day. "Do you have a mustache?"

"I do! Hey, if you and Mr. Connally ever make it back down this way, we'll be sure to show you Yankees a good time." He paused to take a breath. "They were looking to do one of the reunions down here at Austin-Bergstrom International, but we got beat out by Dallas. Hey, do you have any say in the committee that selects the locations for the reunions?"

"No, I'm afraid that I—"

"That's too bad, 'cause we sure would like for somebody to put in the good word for us. Have you ever been to Austin?"

"Well, no."

"It's a great town, you'd love it. We'd put on a heck of a show for 'em down here; everything's bigger in Texas."

The man's enthusiasm was contagious, and I found myself nodding at the receiver. "Sheriff Montgomery, I was wondering if—"

"Scott, just call me Scott."

I nodded some more. "Scott, I was wondering if you'd had a chance to take a look at that bench warrant that you have out on Felix Polk?"

Vic came in and sat in the chair that Betty Dobbs had vacated. She leaned forward and poked through Ozzie Junior's clothes.

He rustled some paper. "I'm looking at this fax your dispatcher sent down. We had a flood in the basement about ten years ago, and this warrant is so old. . . . What is it you'd like to do about this, Sheriff?"

I cleared my throat, and Vic looked up at me. "Drop it."

The response was immediate. "Consider it done."

"Simple as that?"

He laughed. "Walt, I'll be honest with you, this is a B-and-E that's over forty years old." He breathed into the phone, and I wondered what the temperature was in Austin, Texas. He spoke again, and this time his tone was a little more serious. "This fella a good guy?"

"Seems like."

"How'd he come up on your radar?"

"We found his thumb out at the dump—seems he pinched it off in a log splitter. We ran the partial fingerprint through and got nothing, but his connection to you guys came up with his name."

"He get it put back on?"

"The thumb? No. But I think he wants to make a key chain out of it."

There was a pause. "Sounds like he's suffered enough." His voice sprang back to conversational like a leaf spring. "Hey, you say you'll pull for us down here in Austin to get one of those Doolittle Reunions?"

"I'll do my best."

"Well, that's all we can ask, isn't it?"

I thanked him and hung up the phone. "World War Two fan."

"What about Polk?"

"Dropped."

"Cool." She reached up and flipped some of the clothing in the bag. "You gonna escort Junior to the shower?"

"Unless you'd like the honor." She pushed the bag at me again, but this time with a little more emphasis.

Ozzie's head remained down, but I suppose he felt as if he had to make some sort of effort at a conversation. "This is a nice jail, Walt."

I followed him down the steps. "We like it."

"I used to come here when I was a teenager, when it was the old Carnegie Library. I don't think I've ever been down in this part."

"Probably not."

We made the landing and turned the corner into something that looked like Johnny Weissmuller in *Tarzan with Possession and Intent to Deliver*. Santiago had arranged a number of event tables in the hallway, the dayroom, locker room, and all six of the regular cells. The Basquo was standing in the day-room with a clipboard and looked up as we stepped down. "Four hundred and eighty-three plants in all."

"Holy frijoles."

I ushered Ozzie over to the bathroom adjacent to the small locker area. It was a regular facility that had been converted by moving the wall and adding a metal, one-piece shower stall. There was a single utility bulb, which was the only source of illumination other than a window near the ceiling. "I don't normally do this, but I'll close the door and give you a little privacy. Just get undressed and toss your old clothes out here, and I'll hand you the new stuff when you get through."

He nodded. "Did my mother bring toiletries and a bathrobe?"

I looked in the bag. "Actually, she did." I fished a very pricey, plushy, Navajo-patterned robe from the bag and handed it to him along with a leather valet case. "Here you go." He disappeared into the bathroom without another word, and I closed the door behind him.

Sancho came over with his clipboard.

"What've we got?"

"It's up to you, boss." He shrugged. "If it goes to the U.S. attorney or the DEA, it means we lose jurisdiction, and it goes to Casper or Cheyenne. You want to go spend a week in Casper or Cheyenne testifying?"

"Not particularly." I knocked on the door behind me. "Ozzie, you undressed yet?"

His voice came through the door. "Um, yeah."

"You want to hand me your dirty clothes?"

"Okay."

The knob dutifully turned, and he handed me the wad of stained, filthy clothing. "Shoes?" After a second, they followed.

"Can I have my other clothes? It's kind of cold in here."

"You've got your bathrobe. I'll give you the clean ones after your shower." The door hesitated and then closed.

I threw the dirty clothes on the floor of the locker room and listened as the water in the shower stall came on. I turned back to Sancho. "So, we go local?"

"I don't think the feds would go for that, and besides, it might be hard on the county financially."

I attempted to be entrepreneurial. "Well, we do have a cash crop."

He ignored me and slid the clipboard under his arm. "What's Mister Greenjeans saying?"

"That he grew it for personal use."

The Basquo looked around the room at the product, his dark eyes narrowing. "You're kidding?" He shook his head in disbelief. "This is a high-profit, elevated narcotic value crop— sinsemilla."

I had a hard-fought knowledge of drugs, but my education was full of holes. "How can you tell?"

"All female plants. I'd say Duane's been hiding his light under a bush, so to speak. The cultivator has to be able to tell the male plants early in development and remove them, then by controlling the light regimen you hyperstimulate the female plants into producing buds." He looked around at the jungle that surrounded us again. "Like these."

I was pleased that a little of the old light was back in Sancho's eyes. It was possible that I could shut down the make-believe case of the missing thumb. "So what you're saying is that Duane's not just a pot grower, but the Johnny Appleseed of pot growers."

"He's using advanced cloning techniques, root enhancement hormones, and a lot of other stuff I've never seen."

The water was still on in the shower. "Ozzie, are you all right in there?"

His voice sounded over the noise in the metal stall. "Yes."

"Well, hurry it up; we've only got so much hot water in the building." I turned back to the Basquo. "You don't think Duane's smart enough to do this on his own, do you?"

"I don't think he's smart enough to tip cows."

"How about Gina?"

He leaned on the other bathroom door facing. "Between the two of them, they might be able to tip cows. Boss, he was using high-intensity discharge lighting, industrial-grade humidifiers, ozone generators, and CO_2 flow valves; there's about a hundred and fifty thousand dollars' worth of equipment alone down in that tunnel."

"Couldn't he have used the profits from an earlier crop to purchase all this stuff?"

He plucked the clipboard from under his arm, took a manila envelope from it, and handed it to me. "Receipts for all the equipment from a botanical supply company in Miami— all bought at the same time, six months ago."

"Why in the world would he keep the receipts for the equipment?"

"They were hanging on the wall in the tunnel along with the warranties, all of them registered."

"You're joking."

"Nope, I guess he figured if something went wrong with the equipment . . ."

I pulled a few of the slips out and looked at the dates. "You think somebody fronted the entire operation?"

"It sure looks like it."

The water continued to run in the bathroom, and I knocked on the door. "Ozzie?"

It took a moment, but he responded. "Yes?"

"Hustle it up."

I worked my way through the receipts. "I had a nice visit with your wife and Antonio yesterday." I tried to make it as innocent a statement as I could, so I added, "We had tea."

He studied the concrete floor. "I should have warned you—she likes tea."

"Hmm." I stood there listening to Ozzie's shower.

"I don't think my son likes me."

Once again, he didn't use the boy's name, but it was an opening that I wasn't about to let pass. "Why is that?"

"He cries whenever I'm around."

I stuffed the receipts back in the envelope. "I wouldn't take it too seriously; babies are odd that way and pick up all kinds of anxiety from their parents. A lot of times a stranger can hold them, and they just stop crying. Maybe it's because it's someone different, and they can sense that there are no expectations; I don't know. I'm not sure sometimes if my daughter likes me, and she's in her late twenties."

He nodded but didn't say anything.

"I offered you a raise."

He looked up. "Through Marie?"

"Yep."

"How much?"

"Another two thousand a year."

He didn't seem all that impressed. "What'd she say?"

I allowed myself a smile. "She said she didn't do your thinking for you." He laughed at that, and it was nice to see the old Sancho. I extended an arm and knocked again. "Ozzie?"

No answer. The Basquo and I exchanged a look. "Ozzie?"

I turned the knob and swung the door wide to reveal an empty bathroom with the water still running in the shower and the tiny bathroom window open to the outside. "You've got to be kidding."

9

It was the first time I'd put out an APB on a hundred-and-twenty-five-pound barefoot man dressed in a bathrobe.

"You know, I leave you two alone for five fucking minutes . . ." Vic was giving us a tongue-lashing as we hustled through the reception area. She snatched our radios from the charging station beside Ruby's desk and handed them around.

Ruby turned in her chair and looked at us with her phone receiver in hand. "Mrs. Dobbs wants to know if those clothes were the ones that Ozzie wanted?"

I waved her off and continued down the steps with my two deputies flanking each side. "Tell her we'll get back to her."

We blew through the doors and into a black glass wall of snow. I looked at the time and temperature on the Durant Federal sign across the street and noticed we'd warmed up to three degrees and that it was 4:45. He couldn't have gone far barefoot.

We circled to the right and the open window. We hadn't

bothered with bars since it was so small and high up and because I was practically the only one who used the shower.

"How in the hell did he get through that?"

I shot a look at her. "Determination." There was a wallowed-out spot in the snow where Ozzie had landed and a clear set of footprints leading diagonally across the lawn toward the back door of the courthouse.

The assessor's office was immediately to the right with a recessed room for their maps, and there were two sets of stairs that led to the courtroom above, one to the right and one to the left. The county clerk's office was down the hall, and the treasurer's counter was opposite to the right with a set of glass doors leading out to Main Street.

I looked up the steps. "If I was running around town with no shoes, a bathrobe, and a constitution like a hummingbird, I might stay inside, but that's just me."

Saizarbitoria leapt up the staircase and in a second was gone. Vic disappeared into the maze of the assessor's rooms, and I continued down the hall to the long counter in front of the treasurer's office. There were lots of mimeographed slogans and pithy remarks taped to the wall—IF YOU DON'T LIKE THE SERVICE, LEAVE, or, PROCRASTINATION ON YOUR PART DOES NOT CONSTITUTE A PANIC ON OURS. The signs were exemplary of the Absaroka County Tax Mob's attitudes toward uncivil service.

The usually garrulous ladies were standing at their desks and chatting like birds on a wire. "Sorry to interrupt, but have you seen a man in a bathrobe run by here?"

Trudy Thorburn, a diminutive blonde, pointed. "He went thatta way, Walt."

"Thank you." I placed the ends of a thumb and middle finger in my mouth and whistled loud enough to rattle the lights that hung from the ceiling. "When my deputies get here, send them after me."

I plunged back into the cold and looked for prints, but the sidewalks had been cleared and salted so it was impossible to discern any.

I could hear someone coming up behind me and turned to see Saizarbitoria at the top of the steps. He wasn't even breathing hard. Vic arrived, and I spelled out the plan. "Sancho, head back up the hill; Vic and I will split Main. I don't think he's dangerous, but if you spot him, hit the radio."

We split up. Vic crossed the street to the Office Barbershop, Crazy Woman Bookstore, and Margo's Pottery, any of which would have been an esoteric choice for a man in a bathrobe. As I carefully picked my way along the icy sidewalk, I couldn't help but wonder what on earth Ozzie thought he was doing. Whatever the charges, it wasn't going to look good that he'd escaped from custody—no matter how ludicrous that escape was.

I bypassed the engineering firm and the Office as they had already closed for the day and ducked my head in the lobby of the Owen Wister Hotel. The dark-haired young woman who was seated at the table closest to the door was rolling silverware into napkins and looked up. "Hi, Walt."

"Hi, Rachael. Have you seen a guy in a bathrobe run by here?"

She made a face. "Ozzie Dobbs?"

"Where?"

She placed the roll of silverware on the table and considered me. "He came in the door a few minutes ago and asked if he could use the phone there at the reception stand."

"Long distance or local?"

She smirked at me. "And how would I know that?"

"How many numbers did he dial?"

She glanced sideways and thought. "Local."

"Anybody use it after Ozzie?"

"No."

I studied the plastic phone. "This thing got a redial on it?"

"Yes."

"Hit it and write down the number and hang up. When one of my deputies gets here, give it to them."

"Okay."

"Thanks." I started to go but stuck my head back in and pointed a finger at her. "And stop sliding sideways on my main street."

I continued on to the Busy Bee and paused on the sidewalk to look in the windows. There was an elderly couple sharing coffee at one of the tables, and Dorothy was holding a pot behind the counter, but other than that, the place was empty.

I waved and continued across the Clear Creek bridge, tried the door at the Euskadi Hotel, but it was locked. The Copper Front had closed, but the Sportstop was still open.

Dave looked up from the cash register, his owl-like eyes peering over his glasses. "I don't suppose you're looking for Ozzie Dobbs?"

I made it to the counter in three steps. "Where?"

"Bought a parka, a pair of hiking boots, and a Stoeger

20-gauge coach gun with a box of shells." He threw a thumb toward the rear of the store. "And lit out for the territories."

"You sold a barefoot man in a bathrobe a shotgun?"

His eyes focused as the humor of the situation died. "There's no law against that, is there?"

I dodged a few clothes racks and strode through the ski equipment in the direction of the back door. "What did he buy that stuff with?"

"The man's rich, so I figured his credit is good." He was yelling now. "Was I wrong about that?!"

We were playing a different game now. In whatever deranged state Ozzie was, he was armed now. I unsnapped my .45 Colt.

I came out the back of the sporting goods store into one of the few alleys we had in Durant, and I started having bad thoughts about the last time I'd been in an alley and about headless Philadelphia assistant district attorneys but quickly ushered those memories out of my mind.

There were a few abandoned garages just off Main Street and a boot repair place, but nowhere I thought Ozzie might hole up. I studied the tracks and could see where a new set of hiking boot prints crossed the street, went between two of the garages, and on toward the Little League field and the city park.

I plucked the radio from my belt and turned it on, something I'd forgotten to do when I'd taken the thing. It squawked. ". . . And if you don't tell us where you are right now, the first person I am going to shoot is you!"

I keyed the mic. "I'm behind the Sportstop, headed over to

the ball field. Tell Sancho to go get his unit, stop in at the Owen Wister, and pick up a phone number from Rachael Terry. You can both meet me at the corner near the grandstand or over in the park by the public pool. And in other news, he's now armed."

Static. "What?"

"He bought a 20-gauge coach gun and shells in his detour through the Sportstop."

Static. "Jesus. Only in Wyoming."

I punched the button. "Did you get that, Sancho? He's armed."

Static. "Got it. You want me to skip the Owen Wister?"

"No, he can't be that far ahead of me, and I refuse to believe he's dangerous to anybody but us."

Static. "That's a fucking comforting thought." I returned the radio to my belt as Vic's voice went silent, assured that my kindly and courteous backup was on the way.

He'd skirted the field and crossed the street into the park. I followed the chain-link fence that surrounded the Olympic-sized pool that had been drained for the winter, and then the tracks disappeared.

I plucked the radio from my belt and keyed the mic again. "Vic?"

Static. "I'm at the ball field, which way did you go?"

"I'm across past the pool on the Clear Creek trail. Have Sancho drive around to the other side of the park and check Fetterman and the Stage trail." Santiago's voice broke in.

Static. "I'm getting the number now, and then I'll head over. You want me to just keep circling?"

"Yep."

There was a drivable bridge to my right, but something led me straight ahead. The public bathrooms were also to my right, but there were no fresh tracks. It had started to snow more heavily now, which figured, and it was like I was in one of those globes. I walked past the horseshoe pits and tried to see if there was a spot where he might've veered off, but the only prints I saw leading into the trees were those of a few loose dogs.

I figured if Ozzie had called somebody to pick him up, they'd be on the other side of the park. Obviously, his mother wasn't a part of the escape. Hell, she wanted him in prison. Who else was there? And why the shotgun? If he hadn't called someone to give him a ride, who had he called and why?

The banks of the creek had intricate, serrated shelves where the center of the stream had opened up to the rushing water below and held dripping stalactites like those in caves. The openings were large enough for a man to fall into, but he'd have to try—I knew, because I had about a year ago. The closer you got to the water, the louder the water became, but other than that, the place was silent.

There was no one braving the absolute cold of the park and besides, within fifteen minutes, it would be completely dark. My hand automatically went to my belt, but I guess I'd left my Maglite on the seat of the truck. The old-fashioned streetlights helped brighten the falling snow but not much else. They were placed around a protected picnic area that led to a large footbridge, which angled between a playground and a day care center.

I picked up his prints in their light. It looked as if he hadn't hesitated and had crossed the bridge toward Klondike Drive and the portion of town that stretched along Highway 16 West and up the mountain.

I hurried and crossed the bridge, pulled the radio from my belt, and hit the button. "Vic?"

Static. "Yeah?"

"When you get across the bridge, head right and check out the area around the day care. I don't think he went that way, but I want to be sure."

Static. "Got it."

There was a five-inch layer of snow on the swings that silently shifted in the slight wind, and I tried to think of something more depressing than empty playgrounds in the middle of winter but couldn't come up with anything.

The tracks continued toward the Clear Creek walking path that wound its way west past the old Wyoming Railroad locomotive that used to chug out past my place between the world wars. An extension of Washington Park, the greenway was about twelve miles in length and not as cultivated as the part in town.

As I started to cross the street, I saw the Basquo roaring up the hill on Klondike.

I stopped at the side of the road and waited for Saizarbitoria's vehicle to slide to a stop in front of me. He rolled the window down and looked up. "I called the number in to Ruby, and she indexed it with Qwest. It's the public phone in the bar out at the bypass truck stop."

"That means it's probably somebody on the move." I nodded and glanced over the roof of the car. "I think Ozzie took to the walking path."

He peered through the passenger side window of his unit. "Why the hell would he go there? What's he think he's doing, going bird hunting?"

I studied the dark path. "Not with a coach gun."

Sancho started to unbuckle his seat belt, but it was with a certain amount of trepidation. "You want to trade off, and I'll follow him up the trail?"

"No." I rested a hand on the sill and extended my other one. "You got your flashlight? I think I left mine in the trunk."

"Yeah."

He pulled it from the lodged location in the crack of the bench seat and handed it to me—a two-cell. Hell, I even shortchanged the kid on his flashlight. "Thanks. You head up Klondike here and take a right on Clear Creek Road, it follows the trail and you can use your spotlight—just don't drive off the ridge and into the water."

He didn't smile. "I won't."

The Basquo sprayed a little ice as he departed and headed left, up the other hill. He slowed at the ridge, and I watched as he focused the spotlight into the trees ahead of me. It wasn't like I was going to sneak up on anyone.

There was a phalanx of signs listing the rules for walking the pathway, the most important being no horses or unleashed dogs—it didn't say anything about shotguns. I walked between the concrete posts that marked the beginning of the greenway and started up the trail less traveled. There was a mitten that someone had found stuck on a branch with its palm facing me like a traffic cop.

Stop, go no farther.

I clicked on the flashlight, scanned the surrounding area, and saw a set of hiking boot prints leading straight up the middle of the path. I kicked off on my sore foot and ignored the ache from my bite wound.

The path was marked by small red posts at every tenth of a mile and, as I got to the first one, my radio crackled; Vic's voice was so clear in the arctic-like air that it sounded as if she were standing beside me.

Static. "Walt?"

I held the radio up to my face as I walked, the clouds of my breath freezing in the air and blocking my view momentarily. "Yep."

Static. "I checked the building, but all but one of the kids were already gone. The lady in charge said that nobody in a bathrobe had come by and that with the amount of parents coming and going there was no way he could've gotten near the place without being seen."

I thumbed the button. "It was a long shot, but I just wanted to be sure."

Static. "Where are you?"

"I'm on the extended walking path beside the creek. Sancho's flanking on Clear Creek Road. I've got shallow boot prints in the snow, and I think it's him."

Static. "Wait for me; I'm on my way."

"That's okay. I'm already a tenth of a mile in, so I'll keep going. I'm moving slow, and you'll catch up."

Static. "Walt, I know he's been pretty harmless, well, other than trying to beat another man to death with a pitching wedge, but now he's armed."

"You worried about me?" I couldn't help but smile as I listened to the jostling of her radio as she ran.

Static. "Yes, asshole. I have this image of you walking up to Tweedledum and saying hi as he blows your guts around your spine."

"I'll be careful."

Static. "You suck."

I clipped the radio to my belt and continued following the tracks. Leafless trees bowered over the path, and it looked more and more like some fairy tale. There was no wind, and now the only sound besides the rushing of the creek was the distant motor of Sancho's unit and the soft clicking of his emergency lights as he made his way along the ridge above. He was a little ways ahead, and I could see the sweeping spotlight working its way back and forth from across the creek bed to where the pathway rose and then disappeared.

There was a bench at the top of the hill, and it looked like Ozzie had veered toward it and even stood beside it for a moment before he went on. The trail became open to the right, and with the glow of the dusk-till-dawn lights on Fetterman Street, I could see the old sports field.

His tracks led me south where the cottonwood trees loitered near the creek. The path remained on the ridge and would actually meander through foothills for another seven miles, past the old power plant, finally ending at Mosier Gulch. There was a picnic area there, and it was accessible from the main road, so he could be using that as a rendezvous; still, Turkey Lane was closer.

I pulled the radio from my belt again and keyed the mic. "Sancho?" I watched as the spotlight stopped moving up ahead.

Static. "Yeah."

"Have you seen anything yet?"

Static. "No."

"Turn around and head back over to Fort Street and get out to Turkey Lane. If he's meeting somebody, I think that's the place."

Static. "Where the hell is that?"

"Left at the trailer park."

Static. "What if he crosses the creek and climbs the hill?"

"He doesn't have a flashlight, so I don't think he's going to get off the trail; I can barely see where I'm going with one."

The snow was picking up again and, with the dry cold, it was like walking in an ocean of snowy dust bunnies, with little puffs of frozen humidity rising from the path every time my boots hit the ground. There were a few juniper bushes and stands of chokecherry under which was another bench; Ozzie's tracks led to it, but again he hadn't stopped—five inches deep and undisturbed.

Was Ozzie looking for someone on the trail, and why was he stopping at every bench? And why the shotgun?

"Do you know it's already ten degrees below fucking zero?" Vic had caught up. She was holding something in her hands.

"What are you holding?"

"The ladies at the day care like you and thought we might enjoy some coffee during our cold pursuit."

I cracked the plastic top on the to-go cup; it smelled really good, and the warmth was intoxicating. "Very thoughtful of them."

We walked on at an accelerated pace, pausing infrequently to sip our coffees. I wanted to find Ozzie as quickly as possible, but I also didn't want to walk past him in the dark. Vic's flashlight prowled the brush to our right as I played mine over the bank leading down to Clear Creek, but Ozzie's tracks didn't veer from the walking path.

"I'm going to kill that little fucker when we find him. I'm freezing my ass off out here."

"You should've worn your fur hat."

"Yeah. Well, I didn't think I was going to be hiking to the Donner Pass." She slowed and sipped from her cup. I did the same. "He bought a shotgun in his bathrobe?"

I reattached my lid as we continued on. "Along with a parka and a pair of hiking boots."

"What in the hell?"

"My thoughts, exactly. I can't wait to ask him." I studied her upturned face and saw she was looking at a brief split in the clouds that revealed a half-moon.

"Is it supposed to warm up soon, say, turn of the century?"

"Nope, this cold front is supposed to settle in, and today was the high from now through the weekend."

"Three?"

"Yep."

"I quit too, and I'm moving to a place where the temperature is in double digits."

Both our radios crackled at once.

Static. "Boss, you there?"

I pulled mine from my belt. "Yep."

Static. "There's nobody here."

"Tracks?"

Static. "Nope."

"Well, you're our stopgap. Shut your lights down and see if anybody shows up, either from the road or the trail."

Static. "Roger that."

Vic sipped her coffee as she walked; a Pyrrhic victory. "What kind of shotgun?"

"20-gauge, coach gun."

"Why in the hell would he buy something like that?"

"Only thing that would fit under his bathrobe?" I shrugged and tried drinking from my cup as we walked but only succeeded in dribbling it on my coat. "I'd say he's afraid of something."

"Afraid of what?"

I recapped my coffee. "I'm not sure, but my mind would rest a lot easier if I thought it was us."

She stopped. "Do you see that?"

I directed my flashlight beam along with hers. Someone was sitting on the bench ahead of us in a new North Face parka, with a bathrobe that hung down to where a naked pair of legs bloomed from a pair of hiking boots with no socks.

I slowed as I came up beside him with my hand on my

sidearm and the beam of the flashlight directly on his face. Vic held to the side with her hand on her Glock. From all outward appearances, the shotgun on his lap was loaded and the remainder of the shells lay spilled in his lap. "Ozzie, if you shoot me I am going to be very disappointed in you."

He didn't answer, and he didn't move.

I kept the light on his face and noticed that his eyes were open, his jaw was lax, and a strand of spittle dripped from his mouth and hung from his chin like frozen spun glass.

I stepped closer. His eyes were unfocused, and the liquid in them was already beginning to freeze. I continued around him and could see the burnt spot and the small amount of frozen blood where someone had pressed a medium-caliber handgun to his chest and shot him directly in the heart.

I sighed.

Vic's voice came from behind me. "Happy Valentine's Day."

10

"A .32." Vic sipped her coffee. "We had a contract hit in Philadelphia, where some poor bastard rode around on a SEPTA line train for eight hours before somebody figured out he was dead."

I nodded philosophically. "When in Rome."

Bill shrugged. "I'll know more when I get him to Billings. The size of the barrel is usually indicated by the corona of soot, but if they used a silencer, which I'm assuming they did, the diameter might be affected."

The conversation was bringing on another of my headaches. "Anything else?"

"The wound was pinkish in color due to carbon monoxide produced by the proximity of the weapon."

I sipped my own coffee—it was the morning for it. "So there really isn't any doubt that this was up close and personal."

The young man smiled the half-smile he used when he had to tell me things I didn't want to hear. "Not in my mind. What were the tracks like?"

"I'm bringing my expert in this morning. He was up on

the Rez checking on the progress of getting his pipes thawed and trying to get permission for Cady's wedding."

McDermott smiled with his whole mouth. "Well, if anybody can get it done . . ."

I nodded as Dorothy brought over the pot and refilled our mugs and picked up our dishes and the detritus and debris of our food. "You three going to want anything else?"

I smiled up at her, thankful that she allowed us the back corner table for my indelicate forensic evaluations. It was not lost on me that this was the table where Ozzie and I had sat before.

Vic answered for the group. "I think we're good."

Dorothy set the check down between us and glanced at Bill McDermott as I picked it up. "I'd be careful, bad things happen to people who eat with this guy."

He watched her carry the coffeepot, along with our primary and ancillary dishes, back behind the counter. "Is everybody in this county a smart-ass?"

My deputy sipped her coffee. "Pretty much."

He studied me for a few seconds more and switched back to the subject at hand. "Often in these situations there's a mark on the victim where the killer has held the individual while shooting them; I'll keep an eye out for anything, but I swear it looks like somebody just walked right up to him and shot him in the heart."

"A professional killer in northern Wyoming?"

"Doesn't make much sense, does it?" I studied the pat-

terns of ice frozen in the low spots of the steps as we continued up. "And why would a hired killer shoot somebody like
Ozzie Dobbs?"

She didn't say anything, probably attempting to keep as
much of the warm air from the Busy Bee in her lungs until
we got back to the office. She tucked her face down into the
upturned fur of her jacket.

We got to the office, and I stopped.

She paused on the steps and turned to look at me through
the V-shaped aperture between her collar and her ball cap.
"What, you're going for a walk? It's fucking ten degrees below
zero."

I looked across the street at the bank sign again, which
told me the exact temperature—seven degrees below zero—
and time—9:05 a.m. "I need some information."

My mother had purchased a United States Savings Bond
from Durant Federal for me when I was a child, and I still did
all my banking there. I had my late wife's trust instrument
for my daughter, a checking account, a savings account, and a
money market account that probably now had about as much
in it as the savings bond's face value.

"Uh-oh, have we been robbed?"

Since we'd started using direct deposit a few years back,
I'd hardly ever set foot in the bank itself and was a little surprised at how much it had changed. John Muecke was the
president; hell, I remembered when he'd been a teller at the
drive-through. He was a handsome fellow, tall and tanned,
with silver hair, an easy smile, and a ready disposition.

I stuck my hand in his. "Anything you can do about that

sign of yours outside? People are getting grouchy it's been so cold."

He smiled a smile with perfect teeth. "They should go to Belize."

"That where you been?"

"Yeah, Michele and I have been going down there this time of the year for about three years now." I noticed he didn't let go of my hand. "Walt, can I talk to you for a minute?"

"Sure."

He let go, and I followed him past the tellers to the back corner of the bank. His office was the one with the best view of the Bighorns and was nicely decorated with a few paintings by local artists. I sat as he shut the door behind us and came around, sitting at his desk. "Walt, I've been meaning to talk to you about your daughter's trust fund."

"Something wrong?"

"No, nothing like that; in fact, it's doing incredibly well, especially considering the economy. I just thought it might be time to do something else with the money. Martha's trust expires when Cady turns thirty, and I was just wondering, as one of the executors, if she might like to transfer some of the funds from that account to something different."

"You have a branch in Belize now?"

He laughed. "No, but it's not an insubstantial amount of money we're discussing, and I thought perhaps with her birthday coming up, it was something we should talk about."

"Well, you should speak to her. I don't have anything to do with the trust, and I'd prefer to keep it that way."

He nodded his head. "Are you aware of how much money is in the account?"

"No, and I don't care to know. That would be Cady's business."

He wrote something down on the legal pad on his blotter. We sat there in silence as his look suddenly saddened. "Hey, I heard Geo Stewart passed away."

There hadn't been any formal announcement, but I wasn't surprised that word had escaped in our little hamlet on the high plains. "Yep."

"I guess the old guy finally ran out of lives."

"Something like that."

John leaned back in his Aero chair—it didn't flip over like the one in my office. "Is that why you came in?"

I waited a moment, and his eyes stayed on me. "John, I need a favor."

"Anything."

I leaned forward. "It's somewhat illegal."

"Okay."

I was expecting more of an argument but was willing to take what I was getting. "It's going to be a matter of public record tomorrow, but for today I'd just as soon you keep it quiet. Ozzie Dobbs is also dead."

He took a deep breath, and neither of us said anything for a few moments. "Suicide?"

"No." I studied him. "Why would you say that?"

He stared at the blotter and waited a moment before responding. "Walter, I have to go and attend to a couple of things." He pulled a folder from a stack at the side of his desk, the one on top, and opened it. It was thick. He held it up between us so that I could read the label at the tab, which read DOBBS. He laid the folder on his desk and stood. "Would you mind waiting here until I get back? It'll take me about five minutes."

I was having pretty good luck with people leaving me in rooms with open folders; so far this year I was two for two. "Okay."

He started for the door but stopped. "Could you leave me Cady's phone number? I think I have it but want to make sure it's current."

"Yep."

He closed the door, and I leaned forward, turning the folder toward me.

"How do you get eighteen million dollars overdrawn? I go seven dollars over and the fuckers charge me thirty bucks."

I tossed my hat onto my desk blotter. "As near as I could figure, Ozzie was using Redhills Arroyo as an investment opportunity. He'd sold a number of the development properties to partners, but sales didn't come close to paying them back and they all brought a collective suit against him. I guess Ozzie was in the process of declaring bankruptcy."

She leaned against my doorway. "When somebody closed his proverbial account?"

"Yep."

She hooked a thumb into her gun belt. "Henry called and said he'd meet you over at the walking path when you got back from your eye appointment."

I slumped a little. "Damn."

"Forgot about that, did you?" She smiled. "Ruby said to tell you that if you don't go, she's quitting, too."

I drove over to Sheridan for my eye appointment and sat in Andy Hall's waiting room, where I read an aged issue of some outdoor magazine proclaiming our area as one of the top ten in the country for sportsmen. Yep, come on out; it's open season on entrepreneurial junkmen and failed developers.

Andy stuck his head out a door and looked across the room at me—he is one of those guys who would always look like a young man. I figured he was approaching fifty, but he looked like he was thirty. "Walt?"

I stood and tossed the magazine on the side table. "Coming."

"You're limping."

"Yep, but I don't think it has anything to do with my eye." I followed Andy into the examination room, took off my hat and my coat, and sat on a chair not unlike one in a barbershop, but this one had electric power. "How's Jeannie?"

"She's good, but I'm never letting her on a four-wheeler again." Andy's wife had met with an unscheduled dismount a few months back. "How's the greatest legal mind of our time?"

"Engaged."

His eyes stayed on me. "You like him?"

"Yep."

He wasn't convinced. "What's he do?"

"He's a cop."

He glanced at the star on my chest. "Well, I can see how you wouldn't like that."

I nodded and thought about telling him about my reticence in having my daughter involved in another relationship so soon after the trouble in Philadelphia; instead, I fell back on some paternal boorishness. "You've got daughters; it just seems like you never stop worrying."

"No, you don't." It was quiet in the room, and then the eye doctor became all business by pulling some drops from a tray on the counter. "You seem kind of tired."

I thought about it. "It's a case I'm working on. I was up just about all night, and it just took a turn for the worse."

"I'm sorry." He tilted my head back and applied the drops. "Isaac says you're having headaches?"

"He seems to think it might have something to do with my eye."

"Frequency and degree?"

"About once a week, but they're not incapacitating or anything." Like a good professional, he withheld comment. "I'm probably sitting too close to the television."

"You don't have a television, Walt."

"I have an old one—it just doesn't get any stations anymore."

"But you still watch it?"

I nodded. "It's soothing."

"Sitting close to the TV doesn't do anything to your eyes."

"What about reading in bad light?"

"Nope."

I gave him the horse eye. "Next thing you'll be telling me is that carrots aren't good for 'em, either."

"Actually they are, but you can get vitamin A from milk, cheese, and a number of other foods, too." He smiled and took my head in his one hand while adjusting the examination light with the long fingers of the other. "Any vision loss?"

"No more than would be normal at my age."

He continued to study my troublesome eye. "Any double vision?"

"Sometimes when I look up." I figured I better come clean if I was going to get anything out of the visit. "I get some flashes sometimes."

"When?"

"When I turn my head too fast; just at the corner of my eye."

He folded his arms and looked at me. "Let's take a look at it and see what we're dealing with, shall we?" He placed what looked like a miner's light on his head and picked up a lenslike device and regrasped my head, tilting it back again. "You do have a lot of scar tissue around the orbit. Did you ever get an X-ray series done after the accident?"

"Which one?"

He shook his head at me, and the light from his forehead played back and forth across my face as he lifted my eyelid. "Which injury was it that you had when you started having these symptoms?"

"Probably the tough-man contest back in October."

"Tough-man contest."

"Yep, or it could've been from being rolled on by a horse, leg-whipped by a Vietnamese guy, pounded by a seven-foot Indian, falling off the back of a car in Philadelphia, the fight with a meth addict, or when I got frostbitten up on the mountain." He continued to examine me with a concerned look on his face. "It's been a busy year or so, or so Isaac Bloomfield keeps reminding me."

He sighed and kept tilting my head at differing angles. He stopped. "Hmm . . ."

"What?"

"Well, there it is."

"What?"

"A horseshoe tear of the retina." He let go of my eyelid and switched off the light on his head. "The viscous liquid from the eye has already infiltrated the rip so we'll have to use a gas bubble to lift the retina and laser it."

I didn't care for the sound of that. "Now?"

He took the light off and placed it on the counter behind him. "No, but we need to schedule it for tomorrow."

"Nope."

He looked surprised. I guess most people didn't argue with doctors, but I did it all the time. "What do you mean, nope?"

"I'm in the middle of a homicide investigation."

He sighed. "You know it could be misconstrued as malpractice to allow you to postpone the procedure for an entire week."

I was firm. "My choice."

"All right, next week; Billings or Rapid City, take your pick."

."Next week?"

"Yes, Walt. Next week." He smiled and continued to shake his head at me. "Let's be clear about this—you've had a tear in your retina for who knows how long. Generally headaches and double vision aren't associated with retinal tears, but those symptoms could be a result of an upglaze from an old orbital fracture and the flashes could be from a vitreous traction. Triad of symptoms for a retinal tear with subretinal fluid would generally be floaters, flashes, and curtain or veil starting to obscure the area in visual space that corresponds to the pathology."

I understood most of that. "Yep, but what's the worst that could happen?"

His voice took on a more somber tone. "You could go blind."

I thought about it. "In one eye."

"Well, that's an optimistic way of looking at it."

I thought back to a time when I was sure nothing like this would ever happen to me. "My father had eye surgery and had to stay in his bed with sandbags around his head for a week."

"It's much easier now and faster—same day." He repeated my options. "Billings or Rapid City?"

"Which one is warmer, do you think?"

"It's an indoor procedure." He was laughing.

Ruby was going to call Betty Dobbs to tell her that her son was dead, but I'd felt that a more personal approach might be needed, so I swung up to Redhills Arroyo on the way back to town, but nobody answered the doorbell and I couldn't see any lights.

I circled the house and followed my breath back to the kitchen doorway that led in from the deck. I looked in and saw Betty ferociously scrubbing the floor on her knees where Geo's blood had been spilled.

Notifying the next of kin had to be at the top of my list as one of the jobs I hated the most. It wasn't anything I thought I was particularly adept at, either, but I also didn't feel good about passing the chore on to anybody else.

I tapped on the glass, but she didn't hear me. I tapped louder, and she looked around, finally settling on me. She smiled and got up, dropping her sponge into a small mop bucket. She unlocked the sliding glass door and pulled it aside. "Hello, Sheriff."

"Hi, Betty. Can I come in?"

"Please." She moved toward the kitchen proper as I slid the door closed behind me. "Would you like some coffee?"

I didn't, but I would. "Sure."

"Have a seat."

She had a bandanna tying her hair back, an oversized sweatshirt on, sneakers, and a pair of pants that used to be called culottes. She looked like a magazine version of those housewives from the fifties, an image only reinforced by the singer/standard playing from an under-the-counter radio, Peggy Lee's "Is That All There Is?"

Great.

"Betty, would you mind turning off the music?"

She paused and turned to look at me as she poured us both a cup. "Don't like Peggy Lee?"

"No, she's fine; it's just that I need to talk to you."

She switched off the radio. "Black?"

"Um, if you would." I rested my hat on the table with the brim up, still attempting to catch all the luck I could.

She brought the mugs over and sat in the chair next to me. "I love those old songs; sometimes turn the satellite radio onto that channel and just cry for the fun of it." She smiled, and I thought about what she'd looked like when she'd taught Henry and me back in ninth grade. No wonder the Bear still had a little crush on her. "You look tired, Walter."

My eyes came up to hers, my pupils still moderately dilated. "I had a long night."

She played with her cup, making no move to drink from it. "I'd imagine Ozzie is very upset with me right now."

"Betty . . ."

"I suppose it was just the heat of the moment, but I don't have any tolerance for that kind of activity. And when he took it upon himself to go after poor George with a golf club . . . I still can't believe he's dead."

I leaned in and placed a hand on hers. "Betty, I need you to listen to me, because I've got something important I need to tell you." Her expression became one of concern, but she was silent. "I've got some very bad news. Ozzie is dead, too."

I watched that chill that encloses people when you tell them this kind of news, an emotional front that arrives with the reminiscences of a lifetime. She shuddered and slowly crouched back into her chair. Betty Dobbs would remember everything about this moment, the look on my tired, stubbled face, the smell of the disinfectant bucket at our feet, and the sound of the wind as it pressed on the otherwise empty house. Who knows how long it would take for her to recover, but what I did know was that if I mishandled this she would be haunted for a long time, the moment indelibly printed into her long-term memory.

I brought my other hand up, capturing both of hers in mine. "He escaped from the jail last night and died."

"He escaped?"

"Yes."

She looked at our hands. "How did he die?"

"It appears to be a gunshot wound."

"Did you shoot him?"

"No, we did not."

Another shudder ran through her. "Did he shoot himself?"

"No."

Her lips moved, but it was like a foreign film with the sound dubbed incorrectly. The words finally caught up. "He was murdered?"

"It's looking that way." I ducked my head in an attempt to get within her line of sight.

"Who . . ." She cleared her throat. "I don't understand. Why would someone want to kill my Ozzie?"

"Betty, nobody wants to know the answer to that question more than me right now, but I think we should concentrate on what's happened. Are there some phone calls I can help you make? People we need to contact?"

"No."

"Betty, you're very upset right now, and I just want you to know that . . ."

A ferocity leapt to her eyes, and it was as if somebody had pulled a switch. "What? That you know how I feel?"

"Well." I composed the next words very carefully. "It's different for everybody, but I had Martha and a close call with my daughter last year." She didn't say anything. "Is there somebody who can come over and . . ."

She looked away and took one of her hands back. "I'm sorry, but I'd like you to go now."

"Betty . . ."

"Please." She took the other hand away from me and turned in her chair. Her voice was soft but clear. "I'd like you to leave."

I took a breath, collected my hat from the table, and stood. "Mrs. Dobbs . . ."

"Please go."

I felt an involuntary tug at my neck muscles and nodded. "Yes, ma'am."

I sat in my truck and watched the wind sculpt the drifts in the driveway.

It was always like this when you were the messenger of death; the reaper himself didn't deign to deliver his own majestic messages but left that chore to us lesser beings, and the resonance of it stayed with you.

My radio crackled to life, and it wasn't Peggy Lee.

Static. "Unit one, this is base. Come in?"

I plucked the mic off the dash and keyed the button. "Hey, Ruby."

Static. "Saizarbitoria just called in and said your tribal reinforcement has arrived at the walking path."

I keyed the mic again. "Tell him I'll be over there soon."

Static. "Roger that." There was a pause. "Are you all right?"

"I am a clamorous harbinger of blood and death."

Static. "Did you go see Betty Dobbs?"

"Yep."

I stared at the Motorola but released the button on the mic. I sat there like that for a while, then was jarred by my own voice. "I like this channel, but I wish there was more music and less talk."

Static.

11

He crouched down, just outside the tape, and stared at the surface of the snow as though it were speaking to him. He inclined his head, and I could see the dark eyes underneath the long strands of black, broken only by a few intermittent threads of silver. When I saw him like this, I felt like a tourist on my own planet; I was here, but he was a part of it all in a way I'd never be.

I leaned against the grille guard on my truck and sipped coffee with Lucian, who had shown up at the office and trailed after us. I was surprised to see the old nickel-plated .357 in a hip holster at his side. "How's things goin' with the Basquo's bullet fever?"

I turned back to watch the Cheyenne Nation as he studied the tracks around the bench. "I don't know. Sometimes it seems like he's coming back and then other times . . ." I let my prognosis trail off.

The old sheriff allowed a respectable amount of time to pass as he rested his coffee on the hood of my truck, pulled out his pipe and the beaded tobacco pouch, and filled the bowl. He carefully lit it and smoked. "Had a deputy, Pat Cook—was before your time."

"I've seen pictures of him." My closest friend in the world, the man I'd grown up with, fought a war with, and lived the majority of my life in close contact with, grunted from beside the bench. "Something?"

The Bear considered without looking up at me. "I guess we are off for the golf tournament?"

"I believe so."

Lucian continued puffing, attempting to keep his pipe lit. "Winter of '70, I think. We got a call from out in the eastern part of the county 'bout this Poulson girl that was bein' abused by her daddy. So he loads up and heads down Route 192 to the place, little trailer house on the other side of the tracks. When he gets there, there's this twelve-year-old girl tied to the tire rack on a truck with nothin' but her underwear on."

He puffed on his pipe again; this time the embers glowed in the burl wood bowl as it overcame the cold and lit. "Pat cuts this shivering girl loose and tells her to go stay in his cruiser with the heater and heads up the steps of the trailer, but about that time this fella by the name of Fred Poulson comes out the front with a .410 pump."

The old sheriff shook his head and tucked his neck farther down in the collar of his Cacties coat. "Like he needed it; tall son-of-a-bitch with one of those big handlebar mustaches. Pat wasn't a very sizable individual, but he steps up and yanks the pump outta Poulson's hands and then knocks the coon dog shit outta him—whips his ass all the way around that trailer. Well, they make the first lap around the single-wide and around turn four Pat puts this Poulson on the ground. About that time he hears somebody rack a round into that .410 and looks up and damned if that girl didn't go pick up her daddy's shotgun."

Henry seemed to be focusing on the prints where Ozzie had been sitting in the brand-new Sorels. It wasn't where I would've started, but like I said, I wasn't connected.

"From a distance, she puts a round in Pat's face and chest, and then Poulson puts a round into Pat's back just for good measure. He and the girl jump in the family International, leaving Pat laying there on the ground." He tongued his lower lip between his teeth and held it there before it finally slipped loose with his words. "Lived—but his face was all boogered up."

"Whatever happened to him?"

"Ended up sellin' used cars off a lot up near Roundup." He watched Henry along with me as the Bear stood, repositioned himself, and studied the surface of the snow leading toward the creek. "I bought two of those little Broncos for the fleet off of him, and the next time I was up there I stopped in to say hey but he was gone." He sucked on the recalcitrant pipe. "Heard he was livin' up in British Columbia in a little town somewhere on Vancouver Island, but never heard from him again."

I let out my breath and watched as the fog hazed the air around us like a veil. "They ever catch the man or his daughter?"

"Nope."

Henry didn't move as I glanced at Lucian. "Vic seems to think I'm wasting my time."

"She might be right, but then she might be wrong, too."

The Bear's voice rumbled like a train. "He stood and then sat back down." His face with its strong features pivoted to the left and when he spoke, it was as if time were bending with his words.

I'd been up for an awfully long time, and maybe it was that or Lucian's story, but I looked at the sky and it suddenly turned dark with the night that was in Henry's words. I could see Ozzie Dobbs, and the snowflakes that had fallen now rose from the ground and suspended themselves in the air like tiny mobiles, reflecting blue, orange, yellow, and finally white.

"Dobbs had approached from the east, cautious, but motivated." Henry pointed. "You can see where the majority of his weight had been on the balls of his feet."

I could see Ozzie hurrying up the rise, the hood of his jacket pulled up to cover the features of his face, the shotgun held against his chest. The sky, reflected in the glow of the town, illuminated the bottoms of the speeding clouds.

"Then he stopped at the side of the bench." He pointed again, the powerful hand carrying the precision of a mitering tool. "There."

I watched Ozzie's specter as it stood by the bench and looked into the distance for someone.

"He then sat."

Almost as if ordered, the figure in the bathrobe, winter boots, and parka took a side step, pushed the snow from the bench, and sat with the shortened double-barrel on his knees. He was waiting.

"The assailant approached from the west; angling up from the creek. With the lack of visibility last night, Dobbs would not have seen this person until he was maybe twenty yards away."

Another figure could be seen in the gloom of my mind, with another hood raised, another face hidden. The Bear's hand circled the figure and swept to the left as if he were drawing in the air. The second individual came forward with their hands in their jacket pockets. Henry's other hand rose like a conjurer's, and Ozzie stood up again.

"Dobbs raised his weapon, his balance shifting with the movement—you can see it in the prints."

The two were facing each other now, but then the second person stepped away and turned toward the mountains. Ozzie sat, and the other person turned toward him. I watched as they spoke, but then the killer circled back toward the trail, probably to make sure that no one else was coming up or down the pathway. The conversation continued as the killer completed a circle and now stood in front of Ozzie like a clock striking twelve.

"You can see where the assailant stood."

I continued to watch as the killer's left hand came out from the coat pocket and rested on the small man's shoulder. They stayed like that for a moment, and then a gun appeared in the assailant's right hand.

"The hood blocked Dobbs's vision."

A semiautomatic pistol with the extension of a silencer rose in the flat light that was still reflected by the low-slung clouds, the barrel pressing against Ozzie's chest.

"Someone he knew, someone he trusted; someone who must have convinced him not to shoot his own weapon."

The Bear's hands came together, simulating the shot that had fired with a sharp crack.

Both Lucian and I jumped.

The Cheyenne Nation turned to look at us, his dark eyes swallowing the surroundings like twin drains. His head swiveled back to where the entire episode had played out. "You whites get too involved with these things."

Lucian caught a ride with Saizarbitoria, and I just hoped he didn't tell him the Pat Cook story. The Bear and I walked the two miles back down the trail. I wanted Henry to see all the tracks that had led from town. Our one piece of luck last night was that the snow had tapered off so that the prints were still visible.

As we walked, each of us on opposite sides of the trail, his breath billowed up from his face. "Cold."

"Yep." He stopped, looking at the ground between us, and I pulled up with him. "Something?"

He nodded. "Coyote."

"That's helpful."

We continued on. "Statewide, are there more murders in the winter?"

"No; there are more murders, rapes, robberies, aggravated assaults, and thefts in the summer, just like everywhere else. We get a spike at the holidays, but then it dies down."

"No pun intended?"

"Nope." He stopped again. "What?"

"Turkey; probably what the coyote was after." He talked as he walked. "This Ozzie Dobbs; he had a lot of enemies?"

I thought about it. "Well, I suppose so. You don't get something like Redhills Arroyo done without making a few adversaries."

He glanced over at me. "Like whom?"

"Well, the city council, the county planning commission, the three other guys who were thinking about doing the same thing . . ." He stopped again. "What?"

He pointed. "This would be where the coyote caught up with the turkey."

I cleared my throat. "Do you think we could try and stay on the case at hand?"

"Sorry." He continued on. "These would all be enemies of the father, yes?"

"Primarily."

"We need to discover someone who had something against the son."

"Or somebody who had something to gain by his death."

When we got to my truck, the radio was blaring something but cut off by the time I got the door open. The Cheyenne Nation climbed in the other side as I pulled the mic from the dash. "Come in base, this is unit one."

Static. "Where have you been?"

I keyed the mic. "Henry and I were having a lovely, early morning walk in the woods."

Static. "Mike Thomas called and said you might like to know that about five minutes ago, Gina Stewart pulled out of her driveway in the offending Oldsmobile with what looked like everything she owned stuffed to the headliner."

I looked at the Motorola. "Oh, hell."

Static. "Vic tore out of here in her unit but said she must've gotten on the interstate or taken old 87. I notified the highway patrol, but they haven't seen her either."

I keyed the mic again. "We will take the old road; it's the closest to us. Tell Vic to do a slow case around the streets in town."

Static. "Roger that."

Henry, used to my high-speed chases, made sure the safety belt was over his shoulder and firmly attached to the clasp. I started the truck and threw her in gear, spraying a fine trace of snow, grit, and shale dust in a rooster tail.

I'd just turned back to the roadway ahead of us on the way to 87 when the oxidized, copper-colored, laden '68 Olds Toronado flashed through the intersection. The car was doing a good sixty miles an hour when it went by, but the speed didn't deter the dirty blonde from attempting to light a cigarette as she negotiated the turn just past the Log Cabin Motel.

"Was that the aforementioned Gina Stewart?"

"Yes, I believe it was." I turned the three-quarter-ton's wheel and stomped on the accelerator, leaping the Dearborn steel onto the tail of the Olds, which was headed for the mountains.

"You might want to turn on your emergency lights and siren."

"Gimme a second, will you?" I reached down and flipped the switches.

I veered the truck around the corner and shot the distance past the Soldiers and Sailors Home, where the old guys usually sat and waved at traffic. There was nobody out there, testament to how cold it had gotten lately.

I could see the taillights of the Oldsmobile flare briefly as Gina slowed behind an eighteen-wheel truck; she passed him, forcing an oncoming pickup into the emergency lane.

I gave all ten cylinders their head, and Henry's hand crept up onto the dash as we blew past the semi and started gaining on her. With all the stuff piled in the backseat, it was difficult to see if she was aware of being followed, but she must have been, what with the siren and lights; to prove the point, she accelerated.

Whatever Duane and his uncle had done to the Olds to make it the Classic, it was evident in the twin six-foot black strips the front wheels of the Toronado left on the pavement when Gina punched it.

Henry glanced at me. "Wow."

I pulled the mic from my dash. "Base, this is unit one. I've got her on 16, headed west, up the mountain."

Static. "Roger that."

When my full attention went back to the road, I saw the brake lights come on the Toronado as it crow-hopped with all four wheels locked. I hit the brakes on my vehicle; the ABS served me well, and we stopped in a straight line well behind the Oldsmobile.

I'd already unsnapped my seat belt and was on my way out of my truck when I saw two gleaming black Dodge Chargers pointed in a nose-first phalanx that blockaded the highway in front of Gina.

The HPs in question looked like they'd stepped out of a recruiting poster. Rosey Wayman, whose sparkling blue eyes were giving her smile a run for its money, stood there in the middle of the road with her arms crossed, the short black gloves with the undone pearl snaps revealing the pale skin at her wrists—the only skin other than her face uncovered; and Jim Thomas, all six foot five of him, reminding me a little of me thirty years ago.

I could hear the Oldsmobile's radio thundering against the inside of the windows of the car. Gina hadn't moved. I waved at Rosey and Jim, who took a step back to show me that they were content to be providing backup.

As I approached the driver's side of the Olds, I could see Gina still puffing on her cigarette. The window rolled down with a dysphasic whine, and the full volume of the music, if you could call it that, assaulted my ears. She flipped some ashes onto the asphalt between us as she glanced at me from the corner of one eye.

"What?"

"A drive?"

"Yeah." She eyed my office and recrossed her legs. She had pulled a pen from the mug on my desk and was chewing on the cap. "I just needed to get out of that mausoleum. It's okay when Duane's around, but sometimes I just feel like . . . I don't know. The place is creepo."

I nodded and glanced at Henry, who was standing by the window. "A drive."

"Yeah." She was a little more defiant this time.

"With all your clothes in the car?"

She tossed it off with a nod of her head. "I didn't know how long I was gonna be gone. I thought maybe I'd go to the hot springs in Thermopolis."

"You had a chair in there."

She folded her arms into a classic defensive posture. "I thought I might need someplace to sit."

I looked down at the list on the piece of paper that rested on my desk. "And a box full of CDs and DVDs?"

She sniffed and pulled a lock of hair behind an ear. "Those were my favorites. I don't know what all this is about, but I have a right to go out in the car for a drive, don't I?" She let out a giant exhale of exasperation. "Look, can I have a glass of water or something? I'm not feeling too good."

I got up. "I'll get you some." I glanced at Henry, as his eyes returned to the girl.

There was a small crowd at Ruby's desk. Vic was, of course, the first to speak. "Well?"

I pulled a paper cup from the dispenser, pulled the toggle, and watched the water fill it up. "She wants a drink."

Vic propped an elbow onto Ruby's desk. "So? People in hell want ice water—I want to stick my boot up her ass."

I didn't say anything but walked back to my office and handed Gina her water.

"You know, you haven't read me my Miranda rights yet."

I sat on the edge of my desk and looked down at her. "I only have to do that if I'm going to arrest you. Do you want to be arrested?"

"No."

"Good, because I don't want to have to go feed the dogs, the raccoons, and the naked bird."

She sipped her water. "That bird is disgusting."

I tipped my hat back and studied her. I had to handle this one gently, or she'd just ask for a lawyer and clam up tight. "Gina, I know it's been hard lately . . ."

"You're damn right." Her foot bobbed in time with her indignation; her pink socks were rolled up over her acid-washed jeans, eighties-style. "And now I'm stuck in the Addams Family."

Henry shifted his weight and raised his head. My eyes returned to Gina. "And why is that?"

Her bobbing foot stopped bobbing. "I don't think that's any of your business."

"Okay, but there's something that's happened in the last twenty-four hours that's kind of changed the complexion of things."

Her eyebrows rose, followed by the eyes. "What now?"

"Your neighbor, Ozzie Dobbs, is dead." I watched her carefully, not so much because I considered her a strong suspect, but because she might've been carrying one of the pieces to this goofy jigsaw puzzle.

Her expression didn't change much. "Shit." Her hands came up and covered her face, and she crouched forward, the oversized sweatshirt deflating against her body and the remaining water in the paper cup splattering onto the floor. Her voice was muffled against her clenched hands. "Fuck . . ."

I put a hand forward. "Gina?"

When I touched her, though, she dropped her hands and looked at me as if I was asking about the weather. "I gotta go to the bathroom."

I sat there looking at her for a moment. "Okay."

I escorted her across the hall, and she closed the door. Henry stood, looking at me and the bathroom, where no sounds escaped. "You do not have a window in there, do you?"

The news of Ozzie Dobbs's death didn't seem to have affected Gina's appetite.

"So, what's this?"

I unrolled my silverware from my paper napkin. "We call it the usual."

She tucked the same piece of hair behind the same ear. "Looks like fried chicken."

It was fried chicken, and Dorothy served it with sweet coleslaw. She had picked up a couple of postcard recipes from the Brookville Kansas Hotel & Restaurant and had done a little tweaking. It was really good. Evidently Gina thought so as well—she had just finished a leg and was starting in on the breast as we talked.

I thought it best to try and steer the conversation back to her; in my experience, there wasn't much young women enjoyed talking about more than themselves. "Gina, how did you end up here?"

"I met Duane in Mexico about seven months ago."

"Mexico?"

"Yeah."

It was a little hard for me to imagine, and evidently it was the same for the Cheyenne Nation, whose eyes met mine. "Duane was in Mexico?"

"Yeah, Grampus sent him down to Cabo San Lucas for high school graduation."

I thought about it. "Duane stopped going to public school in the sixth grade."

"Yeah, but Grampus didn't see any reason why he should be penalized for dropping out. Duane's twenty-one and Grampus figured he'd have been out of high school by now no matter what. He thought a trip to Mexico might make Duane more worldly. It did—he speaks some Spanish and everything."

I tried to avoid looking at Henry. "So you met in Mexico?"

"Yeah. I saw him in this bar on the beach and just went right up to him and told him I was going to screw him blind—I think it really blew his mind." I glanced around the Busy Bee, just to make sure that the conversation was confined to our table. She smiled at Henry and then me. "And I did." We didn't know what to say to that, so her eyes dropped. "I guess Duane's in big trouble, huh?"

I risked a glance at Henry, but his expression remained neutral. "If I can keep the prosecution in-county, I'm hoping that I can keep Duane from doing much hard time. It's just I was thinking that you're in a position to help me figure some of this stuff out."

She straightened the fork on her plate. "Like what?"

"Well, why don't we start with Duane's little cottage industry?"

She studied the table, and her eyes started to well again. "I thought you'd want to talk about Ozzie . . ."

"Well, I do, but maybe we should start with the easy stuff first."

She sniffed. "Okay."

"What about the marijuana?"

The smile faded. "What about it?"

"Well, my deputy, Mr. Saizarbitoria . . ."

"He's cute."

"Yep." I took a breath; keeping up with Gina was wearing me out. "He said that the equipment and the procedures that Duane was using were pretty sophisticated and that he thought Duane might have a partner."

She dropped the chicken breast that she was eating on her plate and put her hands in her lap. "I don't know anything about that."

"I wasn't thinking of you but thought you might know who . . . well, you see, there was a lot of very expensive equipment that was bought in Denver, and I was thinking you might know . . ."

"It's just all so horrible."

"Yep, it is."

"It was Ozzie."

Henry and I looked at each other, and then both of us turned back to Gina. We had kind of figured that but needed confirmation. "Ozzie Dobbs."

She nodded her head. "Duane was talkin' to Ozzie up at the dump one time, and he said he knew a surefire way to make a lot of money. He said that if Duane knew a place where they could grow the stuff, he'd make all the arrangements and get all the supplies."

Considering Ozzie's financial situation, it made sense, and it wasn't the first time that money had made strange bed partners. "When was this?"

She wiped her nose with the sleeve of her sweatshirt. "About six months ago."

"Geo know about it?"

She shook her head and smiled through the tears. "Grampus? No. I think he knew something was going on, but he didn't really want to know, you know?"

I knew. "So, was there a crop before this one?"

"No, this was the first; I think they were thinking that they were going to get some kind of million dollars for the stuff."

"That's probably a pretty low estimate." Henry raised an eyebrow, but I remained focused on the young woman. "Now, don't get upset, Gina, but I'm going to move into the hard part of the conversation."

Her head bobbed like her foot had in the office. "Okay."

"I'm trying to figure out who would've had a motive in killing Ozzie, or Geo for that matter."

Her eyes met mine for the first time. "Wait, you think somebody killed Grampus?"

"It's possible." I waited, but she didn't say anything. "Would you?"

There was a pause. "Would I what?"

I said it slowly this time. "Know who might've killed Ozzie or Geo."

Her hands shoved deeper between her legs, and she shrank in the chair. "I don't think I should say."

"Gina, this is a homicide case, a capital crime, and anything you can tell me would be better for you in the long run."

She stared at her almost empty plate. "My momma once told me that when the police tell you it would be better if you did something, it meant it was better for them."

Henry bit his lip. I gave him a warning look.

I tried to think of a way to argue with that statement but came up with a dial tone. "Um . . . Well, what I'm hoping for is what's going to help us both."

She looked uncertain. "When you're trying to figure something like this out, you're probably gonna want to know who'd want to kill him, right?"

"Yep, if we can find somebody who had something to gain by Ozzie's death it makes my job a lot easier."

She said it quietly into the folded hands between her legs. "Duane, if he knew what was going on . . ."

"Gina, Duane was in jail when Ozzie was killed."

"I know."

"Well . . . Then he couldn't have been the one that killed Ozzie."

"Yeah. I know, but you were askin' who would have the most to gain if Ozzie got killed and that would have to be Duane, and Grampus, too."

I ran the previous week through my head, just to make sure I hadn't missed anything. "Gina, we'd already confiscated all the marijuana by the time Ozzie was killed, so there wasn't anything for Duane to gain by killing Ozzie."

She looked up at Henry. "Not for the money, no."

"What did you mean by 'If Duane knew what was going on'?"

She glanced down again. "The baby."

I whispered the next question in an attempt to be gentle. "You're pregnant?"

She nodded a quick nod and breathed the single word. "Yeah."

Henry ran a hand across his face and pulled the hair on one side over his shoulder. "You and Duane are having a baby?"

She darted a glance at him and then back to me. "Not exactly . . ."

12

"That's seriously fucked up."

"Yep."

"So while old lady Dobbs is *shtupping* the junkman, Ozzie is *shtupping* the granddaughter?"

I was trying to get a few more winks and had my hat over my face. "Allegedly."

"What's in the water over there, anyway?" She was sitting on the floor, was petting Dog, and annoying me. Considering the conversation, I was glad we weren't within earshot of Duane, still in the holding cells out back. "How does she know it's not Duane's?"

I continued to speak into the crown of my hat. "I don't know, but Ozzie was the only other guy she was supposedly *shtupping*."

She was quiet for a respectable five seconds. "Old lady Dobbs is going to be crazy for this."

"Yep."

I felt her shift her weight against the bench. "Does Duane know?"

"No, according to Gina." I lifted my hat. "Is this conversation going to go on much longer? Because I was thinking about trying to get a little more sleep."

She looked at her wristwatch, which was reminiscent of the one Sancho sported, a snappy little chronograph with more dials than Carter had liver pills. "So Ozzie was the financial backing and know-how for the doobage."

I rolled up to a sitting position. "Yes, according to Gina."

"Life according to Gina." She glanced up at me and paused in petting Dog. "Oh, I'm sorry. Are you through with your nap?"

"Yes."

"Good, then we can go over to the bar next to the truck stop and ask them about who Ozzie might've phoned yesterday from the Owen Wister."

The Bear was in my office making phone calls, which I assumed had to do with my daughter's wedding—which left Vic and me alone in the barhopping expedition.

"Henry seems preoccupied."

"Yep."

"Something up?"

"His brother Lee has gone MIA again."

She gave me her patented side-glance. "Doesn't that pretty much describe his brother's lifestyle?"

"Yep."

"Where?"

"Last word was Chicago."

She pursed her lips. "He headed out?"

"Not yet. He's still got Cady and Michael's wedding to plan." She was smiling now. "What?"

"I'm trying to imagine the Bear as a wedding planner."

The truck stop on the south end of the bypass was a place I infrequently visited, but my deputies were out there on a rotational basis, usually for drive-offs or for suspicious characters loitering around the truckers' lounge.

The phone call Saizarbitoria had traced had gone to the pay phone in the bar attached to the back side. Vic shook her head at a large neon sign that had a giant chick springing from an egg to do the two-step. The sign read THE CHICKEN COOP.

"I hate this place."

There were other signs hanging off the building advertising line-dancing lessons, mechanical bull rides, and Kuntry Karaoke on Saturdays. "I can't imagine why."

She opened the passenger door, got out, zipped her jacket up a little tighter, and straightened her gun belt. It was still blisteringly cold and, since the sun was setting, our hopes of getting above zero were plummeting. "It's like the Redneck Ride at Disneyland."

I got out on my side, smiling at Dog in the back. "They don't have one of those."

She met me at the front of the truck. "If they did, this is what it would look like."

We pushed our way through the old swinging doors and paused at the more substantial glass ones that were inside a shortened vestibule. There was a western boogie with accordion accompaniment scratching the paint off the inside of the place, and Vic paused to listen.

"What the hell is that?"

I tuned my ear and listened a little closer. "That'd be 'Three Way Boogie,' Spade Cooley."

She was wearing her fur hat again and a golden eye crept under it to look up at me. "Who?"

"Spade Cooley. He was the one who coined the phrase 'western swing' along with Bob Wills; got his start as a stand-in for a lot of the movie cowboys in California—murdered his wife in '61 because he thought she was having an affair with Roy Rogers."

My shapely undersheriff stared ahead in disbelief as she shoved open the inner glass door. "Happy fuckin' trails."

The place was as big as a barn and carried the same atmosphere. There was sawdust on the floor, along with a smattering of spent peanut shells. There was a bar to the left with rows of saddles mounted on swivel pedestals in place of stools. There was a much larger sunken area to the right that held a dance floor and, to the left, a fenced-in one with a mechanical bull and a pit full of mattresses on which the one-beer-too-many cowboys could land.

Smoking had been banned in most of the Wyoming bars, but a few still held their collective breath, and a thick haze of blue-tinted, elongated swirls hung in the air. There was a pretty good crowd in the place—a cluster at the far end of the bar and three couples out on the dance floor.

Vic took one look around and made a proclamation. "I'm going to the bathroom." She skirted the dancers as if denim might be contagious and entered an alcove where a pay phone hung, took a left, and disappeared.

I made my way to the bar and leaned into an open spot beside the brass railings of the wait station. The bartender was a young kid—handsome, tall, and heavyset. He leaned against the bar-back with his arms folded and talked to some patrons. An Elvis look-alike, he had sideburns that would've made a Civil War general envious, pointy-toed boots, ripped jeans, and a T-shirt decorated with, of all things, a bolo tie.

I waited.

He continued talking but glanced at me. I smiled, and his attention returned to the conversation he was having.

I waited some more.

He looked at me again and then said something to the group, who shared a few quick looks at one another. One man laughed but didn't make eye contact with me.

I waited some more, then reached across the bar and picked up an upside-down mug, flipped the Rainier tap on, and began filling my own glass. It was a bad thing to do on duty, but it was looking like if I waited till I was off, I'd be permanently on the wagon.

My actions got his attention, and he bulled toward me, slinging attitude as he came. "Hey, asshole! What do you think you're doin'!"

I pulled off the tap and retrieved my glass of beer before he could get there. "I just figured this was the only way I was going to get a beer."

He was in front of me now, puffed up and scrambling one

hand under the bar and reaching for my appropriated beverage with the other. "Gimme that!"

"No."

His hand came out with one of those short clubs that the truckers use to check tire pressure, and he rested it on the bar. "Give it to me now."

I took a sip and began unbuttoning my sheepskin coat.

"I said now, asshole!" He thumped the surface of the bar with the club.

I hitched a thumb into my coat and pulled it back so that he could see my .45 and a quarter of my star. I heard a few snickers from down the bar and watched as the majority broke up and moved away toward the tables on the other side of the dance floor like a miniature stampede.

I turned to look back at him. "Hi."

The billy club disappeared pretty quickly; I had to give him that. "Um, hi."

"You new around here?"

"No, I mean yeah."

I studied him and risked resting my mug on the bar. "Which is it?"

"I mean, yeah I'm new, now." He stood there for a few seconds more and then stuck out his hand. "Stroup, Justin Stroup. I'm from over in Sheridan, but I've been away."

"You lose your manners?"

"No. I, look . . ." He leaned in, his demeanor having changed rapidly. "I'm sorry, the boss says we're supposed to throw a lot of attitude. You know, to add some flavor to the place."

"You were about to flavor yourself into nine days." I smiled at him to let him know I was kidding and watched as Vic approached from the bathroom. She stopped at the jukebox. "Didn't you see me walk in with a fully uniformed deputy?"

He looked at her with more than a little interest. "Um, no."

This didn't give me a great deal of hope for his being able to tell me who'd received the phone call yesterday afternoon, but I asked.

"I have no idea."

The response was predictable but, with the attitudinal change, I was beginning to like him. I took another sip of my beer and nodded toward the alcove where the pay phone hung. "That the only phone in the place?"

"We got a land line in the office and one behind the bar here, but they're business phones."

"Big crowd last night?"

"Yeah. It was line-dancing night, so there was a crowd."

Vic took my beer and had a sip, in direct violation of Wyoming statutes; I could at least button my coat and be undercover. I gestured toward the bartender. "This is Justin Stroup."

"So." She flicked a look at him, and I could see traces of her lipstick on my mug as her eyes returned to mine.

I leaned against the bar; I refused to sit on the saddle stools. "When did you start work yesterday?"

"Six, like always."

"Well, this phone call would've been around five-fifteen. Were you here then?"

"No. Carla, the part-timer, comes in and gets me set for the evening. The afternoon crowd is really light—we don't even open till two."

I rested the mug on the bar and watched as Vic, completely unaware, swayed a little to the music as the jukebox shifted from Spade Cooley to a female singer I didn't know. "I don't suppose she's here?"

"No."

"Have you got a contact number?"

He took a few steps toward the cash register, slid a spiral-ring notebook out, and flipped it open. "Sure." He turned a page and slid it toward me. "Carla Lorme, the second one from the bottom."

"Mind if I use your phone?"

Vic had moved toward the dance floor and had lifted her arms. Her jacket was open, and her eyes were closed as her head tilted back, her movements in perfect synchronicity with the music that seemed a little rock-and-roll for the place. Her dancing was simple, but it always looked that way with people who came to it naturally; and boy howdy, she looked like a natural out there.

He pulled the phone from the bar-back and set it on the bar alongside the notebook without taking his eyes off Victoria Moretti.

I dialed the number, but there was no answer and no answering machine. As the phone rang, I read the address in the notebook. It wasn't far, just at the other end of the bypass, over the hill, and past the new high school.

I hung up the phone and shoved it and the notebook back toward him. "Thanks."

The other dancers had vacated the floor, and it was no wonder. Vic was getting warmed up, and her head shot from one side to the other, the dark hair snapping the smoky room like bullwhips. She pivoted and slunk, something that wasn't easy in the Browning tactical boots. I thought I recognized the melody from something my daughter had listened to. I inclined my head toward the young bartender. "Is that . . . ?"

"Lucinda Williams's cover of AC/DC's 'It's a Long Way to the Top If You Wanna Rock 'n' Roll.' I didn't even know it was on the jukebox; nobody's ever played it."

I continued to watch my undersheriff as she did a silent, self-involved Salome. "It's my new favorite song."

His voice carried from behind me and was a little wistful as we both watched. "Mine, too."

"I felt like dancing." She read the mailboxes as we topped the hill south of town; we were looking for 223. "We do that in the big city sometimes. Most of us don't particularly feel the need to take lessons and stand in a straight line to do it."

I widened my eyes and tried to forget the bit of pain I'd isolated behind the left one. "Or have a partner?"

"You could've joined me anytime; it could've been my Valentine's Day gift."

We almost missed the drive because of the piles of snow

banked against the roadside, but Vic saw it and pointed. I hit the brakes, turned, and fishtailed a little as we slowed and continued down a narrow lane that opened into an area that had been plowed so that a vehicle could turn around.

It was a small house, lodged against the hillside with a low fence leading around to one of those old-type garages, only large enough to accommodate models that didn't have names but had letters like A and T.

There was a light on in the back, and I pulled in behind a Toyota with local plates parked beside the gate. I looked at Vic. "You want to stay here?"

"No, I'm getting my second wind."

I nodded and killed the motor and we cracked open our doors, which sounded like twin glaciers splitting. "Suit yourself—I haven't found my first."

The small metal gate hung ajar, and I could see where someone had made an attempt to chip away the ice on the walkway but had given up. There was a concrete stoop and, beyond that, a front door that hung open. I could hear the forced-air heating system trying to keep up with the cold from the walkway.

Vic and I cast a glance at each other and placed our hands on our sidearms, Vic going so far as to unsnap hers. I was the first to reach the doorway and looked inside. It was tidy except that the braided rug was shoved to the baseboard and a picture next to the door hung awkwardly. There were scuff marks on the floor where it looked like there had been a struggle.

I pulled my .45 from the holster.

I cleared my throat and spoke in what my father used to

refer to as the field voice. "Ms. Lorme?" There wasn't any answer, the only sound being the valiant attempt of the heater to warm all of Absaroka County. "Carla Lorme, it's Sheriff Walt Longmire. Hello. Is there anybody here?!"

Vic looked at me. "Do you want me to get into character and say something?"

I gave her a look and stepped through the door into the small entryway. There was another door to my left, a stairwell going up, and what I took to be the living room to the right where a large flat-screen TV hung on the wall tuned to, of all things, *Cops*, with the sound muted. There was a desk with a computer that had a screen saver of some tropical island, and I tried to think about how long those things stayed on an inactive screen before hibernating.

There was a wooden chair, and a sectional sofa that half surrounded the room; a coffee table sat in the middle with a soft drink in an iced glass—another had been spilled onto the carpeted floor.

"Carla Lorme!"

I waited, but there was still no response.

I continued through the living room and another opening that looked like it led to the kitchen—I left the door to Vic. There was a coatrack lying on the floor with a bunch of women's coats still hooked to it.

I listened as Vic opened the door, and I continued toward the back of the house where it looked like a light was on. It was an overhead bulb, but the room was empty.

I heard Vic behind me, commenting on the television. "That's what I call irony."

I was in the kitchen now and noticed the Formica counters, the economy appliances, and old cabinets.

"You know how many cops it takes to screw in a lightbulb?" I glanced at her. "Ten; five to change the bulb, and five more to reenact it."

"Anything in the bedroom?"

"She didn't make her bed, and there was a cat."

I moved to the back and looked at another door that must've led to a cellar. "Anything upstairs?"

"Another unmade bed and a poster of Jessica Simpson. There's a bathroom up there, and two toothbrushes in the mug on the sink. The amount of hair product leads me to believe it's two women."

I glanced back at the computer in the living room. "You see the screen saver?"

"Yeah."

"How long before the screen on those things goes to black?"

She shook her head as she considered my absolute lack of knowledge concerning computers. "It's adjustable; you can set them so that it's on all the time."

"Oh." She continued to look at me as I glanced out the back door into the partial darkness. There were large drifts of snow and, like the Dobbs driveway, it looked like a frozen sea. I couldn't see any tracks in the reflected light. I turned my attention to the cellar door. "I'm trying to learn about the damn things."

"Yes, and we're all so very proud of you."

I turned the unlocked knob and swung the basement door

open, and it was at that point that someone shot a full load of pepper spray in my face.

"Yeah, he pulled the knob loose on the basement door and then slammed into the cabinets and knocked them off the wall. Then he broke through the back door into the yard; took the storm door with him."

I had my head in a tray with running water going into both eyes, so I was limited to what I could hear of the conversation. David Nickerson was working the night shift at Durant Memorial when Vic had brought me in. "So, you didn't apply the snow?"

"Hell no, the fucker's six foot five and weighs two hundred and fifty pounds so I just got out of the way. You should have heard the noises coming out of him; you know those old Frankenstein movies where the villagers chase after the creature with torches and set him on fire? It was like that."

The doctor straightened the bib on my chest and laughed but with a degree of professionalism. "He's lucky he got his eyes closed—that was some pretty potent stuff she got him with."

"It wasn't pepper spray?"

He laughed a little more. "Yes, but it's a dosage meant for bears."

"Jesus."

"Well, it's not going to do any good for that tear in his eyeball." I could see a blur as he leaned down to check the water flow. "That was smart thinking, getting out in the snow. Did he rub?"

"No. After the pinball effect in the kitchen, he hit the ground in the backyard and just kept throwing snow in his face. He was having a little trouble breathing and there was the topical irritation, but all in all it was pretty much textbook."

"How long did it take you to get him here?"

"Fifteen minutes, maybe twenty." I heard her move, and her voice came from another part of the room. "How's the girl?"

The young doctor turned off the taps, moved the device, and adjusted the table on which I was lying until it felt level. "I think she's fine. She banged her head and bruised her back when she fell. We're going to keep her overnight to make sure she's okay." I closed my eyes and kept them closed. "Now, did she fall down the basement steps immediately after she sprayed the sheriff?"

"Yeah, we were both trying to get away from him. There's a life-preservation thing that kicks in with us little animals when the big animals run amok."

He chuckled. "You seem unharmed."

"Hey, fuck you. It was like the running of the bulls at Pamplona." Her voice was light, and I could tell they were having a good time, regardless of my expense. "What was I supposed to do? Shoot him and put him out of his misery?"

I'd had about enough, raised a hand, and started to get up. The doc caught my shoulder and helped me. "How are you doing, Sheriff?"

I opened my eyes just a little and couldn't see much better than when they were closed. "Do you have anything for a headache?"

"Lots of things." His voice changed directions. "Can you keep him here till I get back? It'll just take a minute."

Vic's hands clasped my shoulder and steadied me as the curtain swished aside and the doctor's footsteps diminished across the tile of the emergency room. "How you doin', big guy?"

I cleared my throat and coughed. "What . . ." I coughed some more. "The hell . . ." I coughed again. "Was she thinking?"

Vic laughed, and I fought the urge to rub my eyes.

"Did I not call her sister's name enough times? Did I not say 'Walt Longmire, Absaroka County Sheriff's Department' enough times?"

I opened my eyes a little more and could just see Vic, who was standing very close to me. "She says that's the same thing the last guy who came into the house said."

I took a few breaths. I'd heard a little of the conversation in the truck but hadn't been in any condition to really listen. "Other guy."

"The one who took her sister about twenty minutes before we got there."

I took another breath. "Where is Claudia?"

"In the next room."

I stood, and Vic kept a hand on my arm. "The doctor said for you to not go anywhere."

"It's his hospital, he can probably find us." I opened my eyes fully and was just about blind out of my left. "In the land of the blind . . ."

With Vic's help, I made my way to another curtained room where a teenage girl was seated on one of the gurneys.

"Oh, my gawd, I am so sorry." Her voice was familiar as were the words. As near as I could tell, it was what she had repeated the entire trip here. "I am so sorry, oh my gawd."

Vic pulled a chair for me from the wall. "It's okay. I'm all right."

"You look horrible."

"It's okay, I normally look this way."

She began crying and as much as I could make out, she looked like she was about seventeen. "I am so sorry."

I cleared my throat. "Claudia, I need to ask you some questions about your sister."

She nodded vigorously. "Okay."

"She was abducted?"

"Yes. I mean, you guys don't think this is a joke or something? You think this is serious, right?"

I waited but didn't answer her question. "Could you tell me what happened?"

"Yeah. Um . . . We were watching television and saw the headlights of somebody coming up the driveway, so Carla gets up and goes to the door. I guess she must've opened it before whoever it was got there, and I heard her ask if she could help them, then they said something about the sheriff's department. Well, I got up when I heard that because it was my job this year to get the renewal stickers on the plates and I still hadn't done it." She looked at me. "Do you guys go from house to house about that?"

"No, we don't."

"Well, I started out front where they were, but he already had her."

I leaned in a little. "He?"

"Yeah. That would be important, huh? Yeah, he had hold of her and was dragging her outside."

"Could you see him, make an identification?"

She shook her head. "No, he was wearing one of those masks like a terrorist."

"A ski mask."

"Yeah." She thought about it. "Do you think it was Al Qaeda?"

"Probably not." I cleared my throat and concentrated once again on not rubbing my eyes or looking at Vic. "What did you do?"

"I ran back into the house and grabbed the bear spray that we keep in the kitchen cabinet, but then . . . I guess I got scared and hid in the basement."

"Did this person come back in the house?"

"No, I don't think so. I just was so scared that I stayed there next to the door with the pepper spray and waited." She started crying again. "Oh gawd, I am so sorry."

"Did your sister have any enemies, any new acquaintances or anything like that?"

"No."

"You're certain?"

"Yeah, I mean, neither of us have boyfriends. You know?"

I nodded along with her. "So, was he big?"

She nodded. "Yeah, almost as big as you."

"Heavyset or muscular?"

She took a deep breath and thought. "He had a lot of clothes on, so I couldn't say."

"What kind of clothes?"

"Dark, they were just dark. I don't know, just clothes; a coat."

"What kind of coat?"

She shrugged, embarrassed. "Lumpy?"

I continued to nod back at her, trying to keep her from getting frustrated and shutting down. "What was his voice like?"

"Rough, I think, but he wasn't saying a whole lot once he got hold of my sister; just a lot of grunting and stuff." She twisted her arms and legs together.

The interview was interrupted by the doctor, returning with a couple of pills in one of those paper cups and a root beer. Evidently, Isaac Bloomfield had told the young man about my habits. "Thanks."

I popped the tablets into my mouth and opened the root beer. "Was there anything else about his appearance that might've been distinctive? Anything at all?" I sipped the soda and felt the horse pills go down.

Claudia Lorme's face, or what I could see of it, looked sad. "No, I don't think so."

★   ★   ★

Very early the next morning, Dog watched as I staggered from the bench in the office reception area, stumbled over my blanket, and answered the phone. It was David Nickerson saying that during the morning rounds, when he'd checked on Claudia, she had come up with a distinctive aspect of the abductor's appearance.

I leaned on Ruby's desk and widened my eyes against the pain. A little flat light was shining through the windows to the east, and the thin fingers of the tree limbs looked as if they were intertwined in an attempt to hold on to whatever warmth there might've been out there. "What's that?"

There was a brief pause, and the young doc jostled the phone. "She says his thumb was bandaged."

13

Saizarbitoria had the misfortune of the first watch and had walked in with a fancy cup of coffee from the kiosk out by the new Wishy-Washy Laundromat at a little before seven. I couldn't see much, and my face still felt like it might fall off, so he drove my truck up the mountain.

"So, do you think Felix Polk kidnaps Carla Lorme because she sees him answering the phone at the bar?"

"Yep."

"Which means that Felix Polk is the one who received Ozzie Dobbs's phone call just before somebody shot him, which places Mr. Polk at the top of our to-do list?"

"Yep."

"Because he's the only guy we know of who is missing a thumb?"

"Yep."

He slowed as we made the steep grade alongside North Ridge and toward Grouse Mountain—the snow piled on the side of the road was almost at the top of the twelve-foot reflector poles. It was early, and there was no one else on the road. "So, how long have you known who the thumb belonged to?"

I fessed up. "Since day one. Felix Polk came in and asked for his thumb back."

"So why did you have me running all over the place trying to find out whose it was when you already knew?"

I opened my eyes and sort of looked at him. "I was trying to give you something to do until something else came along." He didn't look back at me but continued to stare out the windshield.

I could see his mouth moving as he thought, but he didn't say anything out loud. I looked through the side window. I was tired and my eyes hurt, but my mind was like a dynamo and refused to curl up and lie down. I took another breath and glanced at Saizarbitoria. You can't see things like what I'd seen and not have it change you, any more than the Basquo could have what happened to him and think it wouldn't change him.

When my eyes refocused, he was looking at me as if I'd said something.

"What?" His face remained immobile, and he turned back to the fog-blanketed road. "You said something. What'd you say?"

"Stay alive."

His eyes drifted halfway between the windshield and me. "What?"

"I said 'stay alive,' and I don't just mean physically. Don't let this one instance rob you of who you are and of everything you've got."

He leaned forward, peering through the gloom as if concentration would block my words. Neither of us said anything more, until I pointed out the barricaded roadway that led into the canyon where Felix Polk's cabin sat.

"The gate's locked." The air was cold but felt good on the scoured skin of my face.

"Looks like we walk in." I gestured back to Dog still seated in the backseat but poised to jump in the front if I opened the door. "Stay."

We tromped around the pipe blockade the Forest Service made the private property owners erect and started down the lane. The snow was piled high on either side where he must've used the front blade on the Jeep to keep the roadway passable. There were two tracks from Polk's Wagoneer running down the center, and the Basquo and I took a tread apiece to keep the slogging to a minimum.

The humidity in the air had frozen on all the surfaces of the trees, and it was like some forest prism. "The tracks look relatively fresh, if the snow's been steady."

Sancho nodded. "Yeah."

At least he was trying.

There was a larger opening farther down the road and a spot where you could turn around if you had to, then the darkened archway that led along Caribou Creek.

"How far to the place?"

"About a hundred yards, up on the right against the canyon wall."

He looked around. "Lots of trees."

"Yep."

"You want to split off and come up from the back, and I'll head straight in?"

I stopped for a moment and flipped the collar up on my jacket—the snow was filtering through the ground fog. The two of us stood there with our breath hovering in our faces. "Nope."

"How come?"

"Because my foot hurts, I'm tired, and my face still feels like I've been bobbing for French fries."

He shrugged. "You want me to hike in and go in the back?"

"Nope." I gave the Basquo what I thought was a gentle smile, but with the amount of feeling I had in my features, who knew what I looked like. "He's just a fellow who broke into a garage to steal his own truck thirty years ago and had the misfortune of pinching his thumb off in a log splitter. He might be the guy we're looking for and, then again, he might not."

Sancho nodded and pulled at the black hair on his chin. "Your call."

We both listened to the wind as it clawed its way over the top of the canyon. "We'll go straight in."

The trail led slightly uphill and turned a little so that we couldn't see the cabin. There were some logs along the road where Polk must've cut up some of the dead standing trees but had yet to haul them to the splitter.

Saizarbitoria was working with younger legs, but I had the inside curve, and we approached the Wagoneer at about the same time. The vehicle was parked in the center of the road with the bladed front pointed toward the cabin.

There was eight inches of snow on the hood, and I felt the surface where the heat had melted the snow to a skin of ice under the accumulation of powder. I looked up and took a reading on the flakes hanging in the air between us—ten, twelve hours at the least since the vehicle had been moved. That would've put it in the abduction ballpark.

"What are you thinking?"

I looked at the Basquo and glanced up at the shadow of the cabin, where you could see the overhang of the porch. "Could be he plowed this road last night so that he'd be able to get out this morning."

"Could also be that he was out kidnapping bartenders."

"Could be." I wiped the snow from a side window but couldn't see a ski mask lying there or Carla Lorme. "Could be not."

The wind was grazing the tops of the trees, causing them to undulate like hula dancers. The snow was sifting through the low-flying clouds, and it hung in the air like glitter.

"What the hell are you people doin' out there?!"

So much for sneaking up on the man.

"Mr. Polk, it's Walt Longmire."

"The sheriff?"

"Yes, sir. You mind if we come up?"

He laughed. "Well, you better, before you get so covered up with snow that you can't move."

I didn't look at Sancho but continued past the Wagoneer and toward the cabin. He trailed behind me and soon we were standing on the porch, which was covered with piles of snow curving over the gutters like hanging avalanches.

Felix Polk was dressed in what appeared to be his daily uniform—Carhartt overalls, thermals, and a flannel shirt/jacket. I noticed he was in his stocking feet. "You here to sell tickets to the sheriff's ball?"

I smiled at the old joke and gave the standard reply. "We don't have balls."

"That's too bad for you. Come on in."

We stepped into the living room of the cabin and the immediate warmth of the fireplace to our left. There were three doors adjacent to the main room, two bedrooms to the left, and a bathroom in the back and to our right; all the doors were open. "Mr. Polk, this is my deputy, Santiago Saizarbitoria."

The man did not, I noticed, stick his hand out to Sancho. "That's a mouthful. You Mexican?"

Sancho studied the Nazi flag over the fireplace, looked at me, and then pointedly at Felix Polk. "Basque."

The machinist looked unsure. "What's that?"

I answered. "High-altitude Mexican."

He still looked puzzled and gestured to the kitchen. "Coffee?"

"Oh, just more than life itself."

We followed him, and I thought I might have seen something stuffed at the small of his back. Polk poured us a few mugs and sat at his kitchen table as he had previously when I'd enlisted his help in my intrigues. "What's wrong with your face?"

I tipped my hat back and unbuttoned my coat. "I had a little adventure with some pepper spray."

He nodded but didn't look particularly concerned. "So, what brings you fellers up this high?"

"Mr. Polk, I've got a—"

Santiago interrupted. "You mind if I use your bathroom, Mr. Polk?"

He sipped his coffee, and I noticed that the bandage on his thumb was smaller but still evident. "Felix. I told your boss here, just Felix." He gestured toward the doorway. "Powder room's back there."

Sancho disappeared, and I figured he was casing the other rooms to see if Carla Lorme might be stashed in plain sight. I stretched my face and looked at Polk in the silence of the kitchen. "Lots of snow last night."

"That's for sure." He seemed uninterested in the conversation and smirked into his mug. "I was about to throw together a little breakfast; you fellers want anything?"

"No, thanks. I think we're fine."

He looked up and smiled in a personable way. "You're sure? I got eggs I picked up from a woman over in Tensleep, fresh as the day is old."

"That's okay." The Basquo reappeared, and I turned back to Polk. "Felix, we had a situation where a woman was kidnapped last night."

Once again, he didn't look overly concerned. "Really?"

Sancho stood, leaning against the refrigerator, and ignored the mug of coffee meant for him. "Yes, sir, and the only remarkable distinction that we have is that the man who participated in the abduction had a bandaged thumb."

Polk's eyes drifted to mine and then back to Saizarbitoria. "Uh-huh."

The Basquo unzipped his jacket and hitched his thumbs in his gun belt. "Well, you have a bandaged thumb, Mr. Polk."

The machinist made a comical face but kept his eyes on my deputy. "You've gotta be kidding."

Saizarbitoria was on a roll, so I let him continue talking to Polk. "Were you here last night?"

His eyes switched to me but had lingered on Santiago long enough to telegraph his displeasure at Sancho's line of questioning. "Where the hell else would I be in a blizzard?"

"Is there anybody who can corroborate that statement?" The Basquo's voice sounded a little strident, and I judged that some of it was general annoyance and some of it was aimed at Polk.

"Statement, huh?" He put his coffee down. "What? You here to arrest me?" I studied the man's face, and it was like there was something wild playing behind it, attempting to break through the skin.

I scooted my chair back and cleared my throat to get his attention. "Felix, we're not accusing you. We're just trying to get an accurate understanding of your whereabouts last night, say around nine o'clock?"

He looked me directly in the eye. "You go to hell."

We all sat there in the statement's afterlife. There are few enough things I do really well, but one of them is the ability to outwait someone in conversation. Polk looked sideways at his arm and then spoke. "I plowed my road out last night just before dark, and that's the only time I've stirred from this cabin." He looked back at Sancho. "And no, there aren't any goddamned witnesses."

Santiago shifted his weight against the refrigerator, and I thought for a moment he was going to try and slap his cuffs on the man. "You seem agitated, Mr. Polk."

"Damn right I'm agitated. I lose my thumb and suddenly become public enemy number one." He stood, carried his mug to the counter and refilled it, momentarily out of the Basquo's line of sight—and then he winked.

I sat there for a few seconds, making sure I'd seen what I thought I'd seen.

He moved back toward the table but stood there with his mug and stared at Saizarbitoria in defiance.

"Felix, did you just wink at me?"

He looked surprised and worried at the same time. "What?"

It was quiet in the kitchen.

"Did you just wink at me?"

"No."

It was a blatant lie, and I could see from the expression on his face that he knew I knew it. "Felix, you did. Just now, when you were pouring your coffee."

"What? No I didn't." He stood there glancing back and forth between my deputy and me. "What?" Suddenly, his shoulders sagged, and I became aware that he'd been tense enough to hold them in that fashion since we'd arrived. "God damn it . . ." His head dropped, and he stared at the floor.

"Mr. Polk?"

His voice bounced off the linoleum floor. "Well, how much of an outlaw do you want me to be?"

It was my turn to be a little dumbfounded. "Excuse me?"

He threw out his hands, and I saw Sancho reach for his sidearm. "For the kid, here? I'm supposed to be playin' like I'm some kind of criminal, right?"

It suddenly dawned on me that Felix Polk had been performing a role I'd partially assigned him in my last visit. I couldn't help myself and started laughing. Both he and Saizarbitoria looked at me as if I'd lost my marbles. "Felix . . ." I cleared my throat and carefully wiped my sore eyes. "Um, my deputy knows that the thumb we found was yours."

He looked at the Basquo. "He does?"

"Yep."

Polk shook his head in a dismissive manner and reached for something at his back and under his heavy shirt. "Well, damn it to hell." A snub-nosed .38 clattered onto the kitchen table.

Saizarbitoria had his semiautomatic out faster than a quick-draw artist could paint a line and had pinned the large man against the counter with a vicious reverse wrist-lock. "Don't move!"

I was up as quick as my high-mileage body would allow and rested a hand on Sancho's shoulder. "It's okay, he's—"

Polk pushed away from the counter, but Saizarbitoria planted him firmly, kicked his legs out, and held the Beretta at the man's head. "I said, don't move!"

"The damn thing's not loaded!"

I kept my hand on my deputy's shoulder. "Let him go."

He didn't look at me but eased the pressure. Polk turned, and the look on his face made it clear that he saw little humor in the situation. The Basquo released him completely, then stepped back, still holding his sidearm beside his leg. "Somebody want to tell me what's going on here?"

I put a hand out to keep Felix Polk where he stood, still leaning against the kitchen sink. "It's my fault. I think there's been a mistake, and Felix here thought that I wanted him to do more than I really did."

Sancho still held his Beretta at the ready. "What are you talking about?"

"I told you about how we found out whose thumb it was pretty quick, but I asked Mr. Polk to keep it quiet so that we could give you something to do." I sighed and glanced at Felix, whose face was almost as red as mine. "Understandably, he decided I was still plying that ruse and he needed to play along." I turned to Polk. "But I didn't mean that you should be playing with guns."

Polk folded his arms and looked at Saizarbitoria. "I thought I was going to get my damned head blown off."

The Basquo's eyes came up slowly as he holstered the sidearm. "I'm sorry, Mr. Polk. I had no idea." The dark pupils darted to me as he reached past me, picked up the Smith & Wesson revolver, and flipped open the cylinder. He checked to see if it was empty, then slapped it shut and rested it back on the kitchen table. "Can I speak to you for a moment?"

"Sure."

I followed him into the main room, and he fiddled with the doorknob. "I'm going to head back out to the truck."

"Look, Sancho . . ."

"I don't want to hear it." He turned the knob, stepped out into the cold, and closed the door behind him.

I stood there for a moment, feeling like a complete idiot, then turned and walked back into the kitchen. Polk was at the sink and was watching Saizarbitoria as he rounded the corner of the cabin and disappeared into the fog and snow. "Tough kid."

"Yep, he is."

One of his hands came up from the sink and covered his face as he turned toward me. His shoulders shook, and it took a few seconds before I realized that he was laughing. "You know, I haven't been handled like that in a long time, and I gotta tell ya, I thought I was gonna piss myself."

He continued to laugh, and I couldn't help but smile. "I'm really sorry about that."

"Ah, don't be silly. Nothing to it." He let out a deep sigh along with, I'm sure, the remainder of the tension his body held. "Looks like he might've taken it a little worse than me."

I looked out the kitchen windows but couldn't see much. "Yep. He's been having a rough time as of late."

Polk nodded. "I'll go out there and apologize to him if you think it'll do any good. I don't want him thinking that you had this all set up—I just thought this was what you wanted me to do."

"It's not your fault. I should've said something when we came in. I apologize again."

"My own damn fault. Hell, I'm the one that did it. I figured I was overplaying my hand with the revolver, but I didn't know how far you wanted to go."

I sighed. "Not that far."

"Yeah." We both stood there, and it was quiet except for the hum of the refrigerator. "They still looking for me down in Travis County?"

"No." I sat at the table. "The sheriff down there said that the statute of limitations had run out."

"That's pretty reasonable of 'em."

"I thought so, too." I took a deep breath and looked up at him. "So, you were here last night?"

He took a second to respond. "Oh. That part was real?"

"I'm afraid so."

"Well, yeah. I was." He sniffed. "I haven't gotten to the point in the winter where I have to go down and kidnap women yet."

"Yet, huh?"

He smiled and cocked his head. "Winter's long this high."

"This winter is long everywhere." I smiled back at him, but the sadness in my chest was dragging me down. "I better get out there and see what I can do to repair the damage I've done."

He stepped across the room and kicked the leg of the chair I'd occupied. "Have a seat and drink the rest of that cup of coffee. I don't think it'll do any of us any harm to take a little time and cool down."

We both sat, and he refilled our mugs.

Polk nodded into his. "Amazing what your mind can do to you, isn't it? When I got diagnosed with the cancer, I was living in a trailer about forty miles out of town and kept thinking that all my ol' buddies would come out and see me. You know, nothin' special, just show up with a six-pack and shoot the shit." He sipped his coffee. "I sat out there in a lawn chair, smoking cigarettes and starin' at my empty driveway for a couple of months. I'd go into town for my chemo and think I oughta call up so-and-so and see if they'd like to go bowl a couple frames, but I never did." He nudged the revolver on the table. "Went out and bought this thing and got to the point where I convinced myself that if any of the sons-a-bitches showed up out there, I was gonna shoot 'em myself." He studied the Model 36 on the table. "After a few more days, I figured there was really only one person that needed shooting."

He set the mug down and looked up at me. "Sold the place a week later, pulled up stakes, and got the hell out."

"Sounds like you made the right decision."

He thumped the table with the hand that was missing a thumb. "I've gotta go take a leak and rather than do it down my pant leg, I'm gonna use the head." He patted my shoulder. "I'll walk back out there with you and apologize to the young feller; it seemed like a dirty trick, and I'll make sure he knows it wasn't your fault."

I watched as he walked past me and took a right at the bookcases; after a few moments I could hear him relieving himself—he hadn't closed the door.

He was right—it was amazing the things you got used to, living alone.

I looked around the tiny kitchen and wondered if this was how I would end up, a rogue male pushed off from the rest of the herd, walking around in the same clothes for weeks, eating food out of cans, and forgetting to close the door when I went to the bathroom.

It wasn't an attractive thought.

I listened as the water in the sink came on. Maybe things weren't as bad as they appeared; at least Felix Polk still washed his hands.

It was more than possible that I was going to lose the Basquo, and that made me sad. I thought about what Vic had said about my harebrained schemes, acknowledging that this one had backfired and was probably going to cost me a damn fine deputy. All I could do was give him a good recommendation and, if he stayed within my realm of influence, keep an eye out to his future.

I thought I might've heard a noise on the porch, but before I could look up there was the startling impact of a firearm at close range.

I threw myself to the left and bounced off the refrigerator. I sat there looking at the shattered pane in the window and scrambled to get my .45 from my holster. When I drew my sidearm, I could see something move just to my right and aimed the Colt in that direction.

I brought my head around and could see the stocking feet of Felix Polk shudder, lie still, and then twitch.

When I looked up, Sancho was standing at the open door with his semiautomatic pointed at the large man who now lay on the floor. Santiago also shook, and he looked as white as I'd ever seen him. "He had a gun."

I stared at my deputy, then lurched up and crouched over Polk with a pair of fingers at his throat. There was no pulse, but his lips trembled and blood spilled from the corner of his mouth. His eyes stared at the ceiling. Center shot; the man had been dead before he hit the ground.

I looked at his hands and at the floor around him but could see nothing there. I looked back up at Saizarbitoria. "Sancho, there's no . . ."

He was on the verge of hysteria. "There was a gun!"

I stood and turned to make sure the .38 was still on the kitchen table. The Basquo watched me. "Not that one. Another one." His voice came from behind me. "It was lying on top of the hot water heater in a cabinet in the bathroom. That's why I circled back."

I searched the floor where Polk's blood was lining the tongue-and-groove planking like pinstripes. A postmortem gasp gurgled in the back of his throat as the pressure of his lungs sought to equalize with the air in the room.

I looked away and saw that just under the corner of the refrigerator was the wooden knob of the butt-end of the magazine—9mm Luger.

14

I watched him from the hospital reception desk.

The weather had followed us down the mountain and had settled over the town. It was still morning, but the snow had stifled Durant, and even the hospital seemed empty. If it hadn't been for the most recent of miseries, it would've been a lovely way for Sancho to end the week—to go home and sit by the fire with Marie and play with Antonio.

He was sitting in the waiting area, his profile sharpened by the snow that cemented itself to the outside of the glass with enough force to make the casings groan. I couldn't help but think that he was feeling like the window—thin, transparent, and liable to break.

"Yep." I kept my voice down as I spoke into the phone. "But we need that file after all. The situation's changed."

There was some noise in the background, and it sounded like Sheriff Montgomery was reconnoitering his thoughts. "He's been a bad boy?"

"Yep."

"You think he's a flight risk?"

I glanced up at the Basquo. "Not anymore."

He hadn't caught my tone. "Because we can arrange a warrant and have him brought back to Texas if you don't feel like dealing with this character."

"We'd have to ship him freight."

It was quiet in the Lone Star State. "Oh." He cleared his throat and sighed. "I'll head over to the records building today and supervise getting those files personally but no guarantees."

"I'd consider that a favor."

I handed the receiver back to Janine, and she stared up at me with that look you sometimes get from people, even people close to you, that reminds you of just how far the distance is between you and them. Our society, our culture, and our humanity depend on never crossing certain lines, and here we were, slipping back and forth as if they didn't even exist.

She fumbled with the phone, and I gave her a quick smile as I retreated across the carpeted area to Santiago. He was leaning back in the chair, slumped down with his legs stretched out and crossed at the ankles, his dark eyes focused on the hand that had shot Polk.

I thought about the connection between Ozzie Dobbs and Felix Polk and what it was that could've been worth both their lives. It had to do with the marijuana. If Ozzie was providing the bankroll, then perhaps Polk was providing the know-how. We'd have to check the ballistics on the bullet that killed Ozzie, but I was relatively sure that we had our man.

I needed to talk to sharecropper Duane.

When I glanced back up, the Basquo was looking at me. "How are you doing, boss?"

"Happy to be alive." He didn't answer but went back to studying his hand. "How about you?"

He took a deep breath and exhaled slowly, allowing only a fraction of the tension to leave his body. "Tired."

He looked it.

"Hey?" The eyes came back to me. "You killed a murderer, and you saved my life—that's a good thing."

"Yeah."

"Of course, I'm biased."

That got a smile. "I should go home."

"Yep, you should." We sat there in the smothering silence of the snow and our thoughts.

"I'm not sure if I have the energy."

"Well then, why don't you take a little more time." I stuck out a hand and gripped his. "You want me to call Marie and tell her everything's all right?"

"She doesn't know anything's wrong."

I nodded and thought about just how much drama had taken place in such a small amount of time. "Is there anything I can get you?"

His voice was brittle. "I could use a glass of water."

I patted his hand and then immediately felt like a fool for doing it. "I'll get it for you."

I filled the paper cup Janine gave me, and when I came out of the bathroom Isaac Bloomfield was waiting. "Changing of the guard?"

"I understand you were Maced last night?"

"Pepper spray."

He stood up on tiptoes to examine my face. "Your eye looks irritated."

"Pretty much all of me is irritated lately."

The Doc looked around the corner and down the hallway. "I'm assuming you want to know about the Lorme woman?"

"I do."

"She was beaten up pretty badly, and she's suffering from exposure. Where did you say she was?"

"In the pump house of his cabin, farther up the canyon and down by the stream."

The Doc shook his head. "She's going to be all right, but I was thinking of sedating her. I know you wanted to speak with her and thought this might be a good time." He rubbed his long nose. "Then there's the dead one."

"What about him?"

"I'm doing the preparatory phase of the postmortem to save that young man from Billings a little time, and I think you might want to have a look at the late Mr. Polk."

"Oh, now, why don't I like the sound of that?" How many times had I said that lately?

"When you're through with Ms. Lorme, I'm in room 31."

"The much vaunted room 31."

When I got back to the waiting room, Saizarbitoria was sleeping what looked like peacefully on the sofa. I put the water on a nearby table and fetched a pillow and blanket from the linen closet around the corner; I tried not to dwell on how intimate I was with the workings of Durant Memorial Hospital's emergency wing.

I didn't want to disturb the Basquo so I put the pillow beside him and covered him up with the blanket. I stood and looked out the windows; the visibility had dropped to the point where I was starting to question whether my eye was getting worse or whether it was that I just didn't want to see anymore.

"So, you'd never seen him before last night?"

"No."

"Never at the bar?"

She was shaking her head before I'd finished the question. "No."

"Did he say anything while you were with him? Anything that might help us figure this out? Anything at all?"

Carla bore more than a passing resemblance to her younger sister, and Claudia enhanced the kinship by sitting on the chair at her bedside. "He made a phone call while I was tied up in the car."

"With a cell phone?"

"No, it was at a pay phone."

I moved a little closer and sat on the foot of her bed. There was a large bruise running the distance from her jaw line to her temple, a terrific split at her lower lip, and the marks on her wrists where he'd used zip cords. "Where?"

She shook her head but stopped. It must have hurt. "I don't have any idea. I mean I was tied up with a pillowcase over my head and was on the floor. I couldn't see anything."

"How long did he drive after he put you in the car?"

She thought about it. "I don't know."

"Ten minutes?"

"No. More."

"Twenty?"

"Yeah, about twenty. Twenty minutes."

"He didn't go anywhere else, just straight up the mountain?"

She focused her eyes on me, sad that she couldn't help. "I don't know."

"It was a V6 Jeep. Was the motor straining to go up the mountain?" She nodded. "Then maybe it was the pay phone at the South Fork Lodge. Did you hear any other voices while he was stopped?"

"No."

"You're sure?"

"Yeah."

It was only a little better than nothing.

When I got back out to reception on my way to room 31, Saizarbitoria was still asleep, but Vic was waiting for me. She'd gotten the pillow under his head and held the Basquo's duty belt and Beretta.

I spoke in a whisper. "He wake up?"

She whispered back. "Yeah, but then went right back out."

"Give you any fight about surrendering his sidearm?"

"No."

It was state law that after a shooting, the officer had to hand in his/her weapon until a formal review had been completed. I sat beside her, and we both looked at him. "Just what he needs, to be on temporary leave right now."

She shrugged. "I figured I'd save you at least one shitty job."

"Thanks."

She unsnapped the safety strap on Sancho's semiautomatic. "At the risk of cheering you up?" I looked at her. "He came through."

"Yep." I smiled as I watched him sleep. "He did."

"How close was it?"

"Very close." I croaked a nervous laugh. "How stands the kingdom?"

"Amazingly quiet." She glanced out the window and into the maelstrom—it looked like heaven's comforter had ripped loose. "It's Saturday and snowing like a bitch, so the citizenry has shown a noteworthy amount of common sense in staying home."

"I love Saturday blizzards."

"Me too." She sighed. "We do have one visitor back at the office."

"Who?"

"Gina Stewart. She says she wants to talk to Duane, and she wants you there."

"Great. I get to hold her hand while she tells her husband that she's having somebody else's baby." I yawned. "I'm going to need you to call up South Fork Lodge and see if Wayne or Holli Jones spoke with Felix Polk or overheard the conversation he might have had there last night."

"Anything else?" She leaned toward me, bumping her shoulder against mine. "The ME is probably parked at the rest stop near Pryor Mountain, but his office says he's on his way as of about an hour ago and just think, we get to reintroduce Felix Polk to his thumb."

"It's the little things on the job that make it all worthwhile, isn't it?"

She smiled up at me with the wolflike tooth evident. "You know, I think I'm rubbing off on you."

About forty comments leapt to mind, but I let them all pass. "Could you call Ruby and ask her to make sure Gina stays in the reception area? After that, if you want to tag along, Isaac's doing a pre-examination on Polk."

"Oh, joy."

I stood. "I need to talk to Duane before Gina does."

She increased the wicked smile she reserved for special occasions and stood beside me. "Well, he's remarkably available."

One of the pre-mort procedures consisted of examining the body externally and getting the clothes cut off before rigor, if possible; consequently, Felix Polk now lay on the metal tray with no thumb and no clothes.

"What do you make of that?" The Doc folded his arms and stood by the small parts dissection table.

"He's hung like a fucking cocktail sausage."

The Doc and I looked at her as she shrugged Sancho's duty belt farther onto her shoulder. "Well, he is."

What Isaac Bloomfield was referring to was the amount of intricate tattooing that covered the majority of the man's body. "Prison tats?"

The Doc gripped his chin. "I'm no expert, but I would say yes."

I turned to Vic. "Go get the Basquo." She departed without further comment, and I turned back to Isaac. "Anything else abnormal that you can see?"

He shook his head. "Textbook center shot. I would imagine his death was relatively instantaneous. Why?"

I studied the tattoos on Felix Polk. "We didn't take photographs, and we transported the body. I just don't want there to be any abnormalities that might lead anyone to be asking questions about the action Sancho took."

He nodded. "You'll get a clean bill from me. You have the weapon Polk was holding when Saizarbitoria dispatched him?"

"I do. An antique Luger, locked and cocked, and if he hadn't done what he did it would be me lying here on the table, unsuited and unbooted."

The door opened, and Saizarbitoria followed Vic in. He was yawning but stopped when he saw the body of the man he'd killed.

"I wouldn't bring you in here, but with your time at Rawlins you're the closest thing to an expert that we've got."

He stood there for a moment more. It may very well be the case that confronting the body of someone you've killed is the hardest thing on earth to do. I watched him as he stood there, his foot on the gas but not moving. You convince yourself that what you did was the right thing, but there's that hard, cold fact that of all the things you can do as a human being—this is one you cannot undo.

He stepped closer, swallowed, and leaned over the corpse.

"Definitely state, possibly federal." He peered at the numerous shapes and designs. "Some of these are freehand, others are machine."

Isaac looked at him. "I didn't know that they have tattoo parlors in prison."

The Basquo shook his head. "They don't. The inmates make them out of a toy slot car motor, a hollowed-out ballpoint pen, a guitar string, and a nine-volt battery. It's a crono, 115." He looked up at us, aware that we had no idea what he was talking about.

Vic, of course, asked. "What the fuck does that mean?"

"A written infraction to give or get tattoos inside." His eyes returned to the body. "These things can tell you everything about the man if you read them correctly."

"Such as?"

"Who he is, where he's from, what he's done . . . Everything. I've seen guys stupid enough to put their DOC numbers on themselves."

There was a particularly extravagant heart with flames and three-leaved shamrocks, unfortunately near the bullet hole in the man's own heart. "Does the *AB* stand for what I think it does?"

He nodded. "Aryan Brotherhood, the white supremacist gang."

"What about the spiderwebs with the *FP*?"

"Those are his initials, and the webs represent doing time. The tombstones on his chest stand for the years he was inside."

I pointed at another one with a star and more tombstones. "That one?"

"Huntsville, Texas, the numbers mean from '78 to '83."

"*SWP?*"

"Supreme white power."

"*SB?*"

The Basquo shook his head. "I don't know, but we can cross-check the online systems." He indicated another batch of symbols. "The stone wall with railroad tracks here means San Quentin. Again, the numbers mean he was in from '85 to '97."

Vic chimed in. "Thank you, Johnny Cash."

I studied the dead man. "That's a long stretch."

The Basquo continued. "That's where and when the Aryan Brotherhood began, so I guess we have a founding member here." He shrugged. "They don't take to wannabes. If you bullshit your tats, they skin them off you with a razor-blade and a pair of pliers."

Vic seemed only mildly impressed. "Wow, the George Washington of Nazi fuckheads." She fingered the dead man's arm, where a pistol pointed out. "That means he's a shooter?"

"Yeah. It's odd that his tats end at his wrists and neck. This guy wears long-sleeved shirts, and you'd never see any of it."

I was getting an education. "That's not the norm?"

"No. They usually have stuff all over their hands, and sometimes on their faces." He took a deep breath and touched Felix Polk for the first time, then looked up at Isaac. "May I?"

"By all means." Isaac stepped forward and assisted him in turning the body.

The tattoos continued over both of the man's shoulders and ended with a woman's face. She was crying, and there were three teardrops. "Someone was waiting for him on the outside, and I'd say the drops are the number of kills."

"Three?"

"Yeah, one for the stretch in Quentin and another in Huntsville."

"The third?"

He shook his head. "Who knows? One where he didn't get caught, maybe."

Sancho and the Doc turned the corpse back over as I came around the other side to face Saizarbitoria. "This is the kind of guy who would kill someone if a multimillion-dollar weed operation went bad?"

The Basquo's voice echoed off the stainless steel. "In a heartbeat, and I'm willing to bet that not only was Polk providing the knowledge for the venture, but he was also in charge of the buyers. Blood in, blood out. These guys are heavy into drug trafficking, extortion, and pressure rackets. I bet he was producing for the entire AB. Usually you have to do a hit just to get in and then members are actively expected to score for the others in custody."

I sighed. "Isn't he a little old for this stuff?"

Santiago looked at him. "Not really. . . ."

I stuffed my hands into the pockets of my coat. "I've only got one question then."

The Basquo shrugged. "The partial thumbprint gave us nothing from the national records; Vic's verbal request on a name search must've popped up in Travis County but nowhere else."

"That wasn't my question." They were all looking at me as I continued to study one of the few portions of Felix Polk that held no information—his face. "How did Ozzie Dobbs meet somebody like this? And more importantly, how did he think he'd survive being in business with him?"

Nobody answered.

Especially not Polk.

The auxiliary baseboard heaters had kicked on in the jail to combat the extra-cold temperatures as Gina and I stood in the hallway.

She said she'd gone over and talked to Mrs. Dobbs. "You've been busy."

She put the cigarette I'd forbidden her to smoke back in the pack and stuffed it into the pocket of the pink parka. "Yeah, well . . . I just wanted to get it off my chest."

"All of a sudden?"

She shrugged. "Ozzie's dead, and I'm scared."

"Of what?"

Her brown eyes grew large in sarcasm. "Of being dead, too."

"Why would anyone want to kill you?"

"Because I'm carrying Ozzie's child?"

I sighed. "I don't think there's very much of a chance of anyone coming after you for that."

"Why?"

"We're pretty sure that the individual who killed Ozzie did it because he was involved with Duane's marijuana operation." The next part was only slightly misinformative. "And we've taken a man into custody."

"Who is it?"

"Fellow by the name of Felix Polk. Ever heard of him?"

The response was predictable. "No."

"You never heard Duane or Ozzie mention that name?"

"No."

"If I get you a picture of him, can you tell me if you've ever seen him?"

She sighed in exasperation, kind of like Cady did, but without quite the intelligence. "Why don't you just introduce him to me?"

I paused, wondering if I really wanted to add to the death count in Gina's head. "He's indisposed."

"What's that mean, he's in the bathroom?"

I figured the hell with it. "He's dead."

"Oh."

From her response, he might as well have been in the bathroom. Other people's deaths didn't seem to make much of an impression on Gina.

I needed to talk to Duane, but so did she. The problem is she wanted me to be a part of her conversation, and I wasn't too keen on the idea. On the flip side, I wanted her to be a party to my conversation, and she didn't seem interested in that. We were at an impasse, and the only answer was a very emotionally messy round robin.

"I am going to speak to Duane before you go in to talk to him."

"Why do you get to go first?"

"Because what you're going to say to him is going to be like an atomic bomb, and I'd just as soon get some answers before it goes off."

She folded her arms. "You think it's that big of a deal?"

I stared at her; I couldn't help myself. "That you're having another man's baby? Yep, I think that's going to put my questions on the back burner."

She shrugged again; the shrug really was Gina's art form.

"Duane, we know you had a partner in your little 4-H project and, since things have gotten more serious, I'm going to need you to tell me who that was."

He glanced at his young wife seated on a folding chair to my right and then back to me. "I didn't have a partner."

I sighed. "Do you remember that talk we had about this conversation?"

"Huh?"

I nodded in an attempt to get him to remember. "The one about coming back here and having another conversation where you weren't quite so guilty?" He was nodding along with me now. "That would be this conversation."

He stopped nodding. "Oh." He paused and looked at his wife again, and it was almost as if he had to try to remember. "Ozzie, Mr. Dobbs, had the money."

I pushed my hat back and scratched my head. "I figured that one out, but I also need to know who had the know-how."

"Ozzie did. He had these equipment books and all this other stuff that told you how to do it."

"What kind of stuff?"

"Notebooks."

I rested my elbows on my knees and leaned in. "I don't suppose you know where those notebooks are?"

"Nunh-uh."

I threw a glance toward Gina; the response was predictable—she shrugged.

I clasped my hands together and tried not to think about Sancho's remark that the two in front of me weren't likely to be clever enough, collectively, to overturn cows. "Did Ozzie ever mention a guy named Felix Polk?"

"Nunh-uh."

He really seemed pretty much incapable of lying. "So you've never heard that name before?"

"Nunh-uh."

Unfortunately, I believed him.

I cleared my throat. "Duane, I think Gina has something she wants to tell you."

15

"What do you mean it's not the gun that killed him?"

"It's not a match. I'm sending it off to DCI, but I did the prelims on the lead after McDermott dug it out of him and the markings are nowhere near the same as the one I tested—besides, Polk's gun was a 9-millimeter and the one that killed Ozzie was a .32."

I raised my hat and sat up, tossing the blanket that Ruby had used to cover me with a quick flip. My familiar and recurring headache blistered across my brain. "What'd you test it in?"

"A gallon of Jell-O and a box of sand."

I sat up, slumped against my desk, and draped a hand down to pet Dog. "Aren't we enterprising."

"Hey, don't be pissy with me for doing my job."

I held my temples for a moment. "I thought it was DCI's job."

"I was bored. I don't have a house and nobody bought me anything for Valentine's Day."

We both sat there for a moment, looking at Santiago

Saizarbitoria's duty belt, semiautomatic, and badge lying on my desk. I hadn't noticed it when I'd come into my office. "What's Saizarbitoria's badge doing here?"

"I guess he dropped it off when he turned in my unit. Ruby says he left it at her desk, and she didn't know what you wanted to do with it."

I sat there staring at the six-pointed star with the circle around it, the mountains with the tiny star over them, the open book, and the words that you could barely make out. *Vero est Justicia.*

Truth is justice. Indeed.

I stood and folded my blanket, laying it on the chair with the pillow. I picked up my hat and quickly walked around my desk, as though the Basquo's equipment might've been haunted. I glanced back at the badge. "Kind of has a note of finality about it, doesn't it?"

Vic looked up at me. "I'm sorry." She stood and held my hand as she pulled me into the hallway. "C'mon, I'll buy you lunch."

When we got into the reception area, Ruby peered at me from over her computer. "This means Felix Polk didn't kill Ozzie Dobbs?"

I yawned and then made a face, attempting to draw the pain from my head. "No, it means that Felix Polk didn't kill Ozzie Dobbs with the same gun with which he attempted to kill me. We haven't done a complete search of the neo-Nazi' cabin, but I'm sure we'll find other firearms there."

Vic stood beside me, petting Dog, who had followed. "And what if we don't find the .32 that killed Ozzie?"

"Then Polk disposed of it." My voice carried a little edge.
She studied me. "Or?"

"Or somebody else did it."

She didn't smile, but her eyes softened. "You're grumpy.
Get up on the wrong side of your chair?"

All three of them were looking at me now. "What it
means is that a deputy of mine with PTS just killed a kidnap-
per for pointing a gun at me and that there might be another
murderer running around out there somewhere."

"Then what would they, whoever they are, gain by killing
Geo and then Dobbs?"

I let out a deep sigh, and even I thought I sounded like a
tire going flat. "Somebody's circling the wagons."

Vic pushed me toward the stairs. "I'm hungry, so I'm betting you're starved."

"I am, so we'll grab something at the Dash Inn on the
way." I snagged my coat from the hooks on the wall beside
Ruby's desk and glanced back at my dispatcher. "Where's the
Bear?"

She looked up at us as Dog joined the group. "He hi-
jacked a plumber here in town and was last seen headed for
the Reservation."

My shoulders slumped. "If he calls in, tell him I need
him."

"Are we going somewhere?"

"We're going to head out to the Stewart place and look
for those notebooks that Duane was talking about or anything
else that might lead to a connection between Ozzie Dobbs and
Felix Polk."

Ruby looked past us and through the whiteout windows in the doors behind us. "If Henry is unavailable, who do you want me to call while you two are traipsing around the junkyard?"

"Get the Basquo back in here. Tell him it's an emergency."

"You know that's against the law."

"Whose?"

Ruby looked down and spoke the words neither Vic nor I would. "He quit, Walt. He's gone."

We'd only passed three other cars—well, trucks, actually—since leaving the office. Durant was like a frozen ghost town. The snow was another eight inches deep since I'd come off the mountain this morning, and the tires of my truck were completely silent as we slowly wheeled our way off Main Street and took a right onto Route 16.

Vic scrunched down in my passenger seat. "I guess we're getting all the snow for the winter at one time."

"Hmm."

She watched the side of my face and then spoke in a deeper voice. "How's the house hunting going lately, Vic?" The next voice was hers. "On hold." She once again spoke in a voice I was sure was supposed to be mine. "Well, we've been a little busy lately." She concluded the conversation with herself in her regular voice, but I'm sure it was directed at me. "Yeah. Well, you're an asshole."

She looked out the window, and now I drove in absolute silence, almost wishing for some tire noise.

We ordered three super-dashburgers—one for Vic, one for me, and one for Dog—with fries and two coffees. We sat there waiting at the drive-through window for our food, and I watched as another eighteen-wheeler slowly made its way off I-25 and parked alongside the road. WYDOT had informed us that they were closing the highway, and the trucks were piling up.

"So, how'd the Basquo take it when he found out the truth concerning the case of the missing thumb?"

I looked at her. "I'm sorry, is this a real conversation or another dramatic interpretation?" She stared at me for a long while, and I caved, incapable of withstanding the kind of silence she could put out. "He did the right thing."

She turned her head, and I watched her breath cloud the glass. "There are going to be questions."

"Yep."

"Especially since Polk's gun wasn't the one that broke Ozzie's heart." I looked at her. "Sorry."

My eyes returned to the road. "We'll find that gun."

"It doesn't look good with him quitting right afterward." Her voice was softer. "I'm just trying to look at it from the state attorney general Joe Meyer's point of view."

"I know."

She took her time before speaking again. "You should seriously consider whether you might've happened to have seen the reflection in the window of Felix Polk holding that gun to the back of your head."

I didn't say anything.

The food came along with a few biscuits for Dog.

"Thanks, Larry, you guys calling it a day? They've closed the highway."

He smiled and shouted as I handed Vic the bag of food and stuffed the biscuits in my pocket to give to Dog later. "Yeah, we're going home while we can still make it!"

I smiled back as he handed me our drinks and quickly slid his window closed. I hit the button to roll up mine, a spray of wayward flakes swirling in the open window as I watched Vic lodge her coffee into the passenger cup holder and mine into the center one. "A jug of wine, a loaf of bread and thou."

My dissertation was interrupted by Ruby. Static. "Unit one this is base, come in."

Vic looked at the radio and unwrapped her dashburger. "Your truck—your radio."

I sighed and pulled the mic from the holder. Ruby was still trying to win us over to a more businesslike attitude toward radio communication, and everybody had pretty much caved except for me. "What?"

Static. "I just got a weather report."

I keyed the mic. "How much are we supposed to get?"

There was a bit of jostling before the next communiqué and it became obvious where Ruby had found reinforcements. Static. "Ass deep to a nine-foot Indian."

I keyed the mic again. "Hello, Lucian."

Static. "What the hell are you doing out there?"

"Checking on the remainder of the Stewart clan."

Static. "They say we're gonna get eighteen inches by tomorrow morning."

"I won't tarry."

Static. "See that you don't; I brought my chessboard with me."

By the time we got to the dump/junkyard, Vic had fed Dog his burger and half of hers. I'd eaten mine in four bites and was just now finishing off my fries as we arrived at the Stewart driveway.

Mike Thomas was leaving as we got there, so we slowed and stopped. He pulled the '78 orange Ford alongside my truck and rolled his window down.

"What are you doing out in this weather, Mike? Neighborhood watch?"

He shrugged under his insulated coat and frowned, throwing a thumb back to the tarp-covered heap in the bed of his truck. "Was gonna drop a load off at the dump, but Gina said they were closed today and waved me off."

I looked up to emphasize the point. "Well, it is kind of inclement."

"I'm off to the Caribbean tomorrow, if it ever stops, and wanted to clear out my shop." He leveled an eye on me. "In sixteen years, I've never seen a workday when Geo Stewart closed. I guess it's all different now that he's gone."

"You heard?"

"Yep, and when I pulled up to the house to see what was going on, Gina was piling stuff into that piece-of-shit Toronado again like she was pretty intent on going somewhere else."

I glanced at Vic, then back to the sculptor. "You sure she

wasn't unloading? We caught her on 16 the last time you called and turned her back."

He thought about it. "Hell, she might've been unloading for all I know."

"Well, we'll go in and check on her."

He shook his head and began rolling up his window. "Good luck."

The Toronado was parked in the driveway close to the house, but the snow on it had been swiped off recently.

I stopped behind it and threw the truck into park. "Let's go."

Dog started his leap over the center console and into the front. "Not you. If those two beasts of theirs are in there, I don't need you starting anything."

He looked disappointed, but I left the windows down a little and shut the door after me. Vic was at the front of the truck when I got there. She glanced up at me. "I'm assuming you didn't mean me?"

We trudged through the snow to the driver's-side door of the Toronado. "Does that look like more crap than was in there before?"

My deputy peered through the frosted window. "Arf."

I studied the prints leading up to the house and onto the porch; three trips at least. It appeared that Gina was still intent on leaving, even with the weather and the warning.

The conversation with Duane hadn't been as bad as I'd assumed it would be, considering the nature of the subject matter. When she told him she was pregnant and that the father was not him, he seemed surprised but not particularly upset.

In the amount of time I'd been contemplating the Stewart social order, another quarter of an inch of snow had accumulated on the two of us. Without another word, we picked our way among the fresh prints to the house and met Gina coming out with a laundry basket full of clothes.

"Howdy."

She started with a short scream and almost dropped the basket. "Jesus Christ!"

"Sorry." Vic and I stepped onto the porch in an attempt to not accumulate even more snow. "What are you doing, Gina?"

She dropped the light blue plastic laundry basket after the question and took the smoldering cigarette from the corner of her mouth. "Leavin'."

"We told you to stick around."

"Yeah, well . . ." She glanced back into the open doorway of the house. "Grampus is dead, Duane's in jail, and I'm getting the fuck out of here. I don't give a shit what you told me to do."

Butch and Sundance appeared in the doorway, protective of Gina and obviously concerned that we were abusing their mistress. Butch, the one that had bitten me in the ass, was the nearest and was growling.

"In case you haven't noticed, the weather is pretty brutal, and the HPs have closed all the highways."

She took a strong puff on the cigarette, pregnancy be damned. "Fuckit. I'm still leavin', and you can't stop me."

I let that pass. "Something happen?"

"Morris came over, and I told him about the baby, and he went all ape shit."

"Geo's brother Morris?"

"Yeah, he's upstairs going through some of Grampus stuff."

"I don't know if I've ever heard him speak three words..." I could feel my headache coming back and wondered if they really had anything to do with my eye. "Would you like me to speak to him?"

"No. Fuckit, I'm leavin'."

"You're not going to get very far."

"I don't care." She started to bend over and pick up the basket. "I'm leavin'."

"I'm sorry, but you're not." The dogs caught my tone even if she hadn't, and were now both growling.

Vic unsnapped the safety strap on her Glock. "Call 'em off, or I'll throw a warning shot through both their fuckin' heads."

When you go to a dogfight, it's always good to bring the meanest bitch.

Gina casually glanced back and then screamed at them, "Shut up!"

The dogs went immediately silent. "Gina, if you leave here now you're not going to go anywhere except a ditch and then we're going to have to pull you out. Just stay put and let me talk to Morris, and then, if we have to, we'll give you an escort to a motel. Okay?"

She looked even more sullen than usual, turned with her load, and went back into the House of Usher, followed by the two Hounds of the Baskervilles.

There were more things piled by the doorway than

would've guessed would fit in the Classic, but who was I to judge. "Where is Morris?"

"Upstairs in Grampus' room. He said he was gonna get Grampus' gun and shoot me."

Vic and I looked at each other. "Really?"

She studied me as if I were a variety of moron she'd never met before. "Yeah, really."

"You stay here with Vic, and I'll go upstairs."

"Fine by me. I'm gonna get a pop in the kitchen."

"You guys wait for me in there." Vic nodded, and I took a step up the stairway. "Morris! It's Walt Longmire, are you up there?"

Nothing.

It was odd, and I found it hard to believe that Morris Stewart would've responded in the manner she'd described. "Morris! Sheriff's Department coming up the stairs!"

Nothing.

It was my first time in the inner sanctum of the house, and from the look of things on the landing, the upstairs wasn't any better than the downstairs. Junk cluttered the steps and continued down the hallway. There was a path down the middle, but car parts, stacks of papers, magazines, and cans of paint were stacked on either side. The place was an arsonist's dream. I thought about how they cleaned the chimney with a mop full of kerosene and shuddered.

"Morris, are you up here?"

There were six doorways in the hall; five of them had the doors closed with the sixth, the one at the end, slightly ajar. I picked my way through the debris and placed a hand on my sidearm. "Morris!"

I opened the nearest door—it was obviously Duane and Gina's. There were car posters on the walls and a huge canopy bed that looked like it might've been bought at a discount furniture place, the kind you see in tents alongside the road. The only light in the room was a digital clock that was an hour off. I stared at it for a few moments, thinking that there was something about it that was important.

Something about that clock and the time.

I decided I'd start at the other end of the hallway with the door that was slightly open and work my way back. The floor creaked under my boots, and I started feeling like Gina, trapped in the Addams Family mansion.

"Morris?" I nudged the door open—the gauzelike curtain on the other side of the room was flowing like the oversized sleeve of a ghost, to complete the analogy, and snow was piling up on the floor underneath the window. I moved to close it and go on to the next room when I saw something lying in a single bed to the left.

It was a tiny fold-out cot, really, but piled with sheets, blankets, and even a moldy buffalo hide. On closer inspection, the thing had horsehair tails hanging from the edges and intricate beading indicative of the late eighteenth century—probably worth a fortune but for the holes and the hair that was falling off of it.

Something moved under the pile of coverings, and I took the couple of steps to the bedside. "Morris?"

Whatever it was, it wasn't moving anymore, so I reached forward and peeled the blankets back. It was Morris, and there was a great deal of blood saturated in the dirty sheets. Th

blood had come from a bullet wound in his chest, almost iden-
tical to the wound that Ozzie Dobbs had sustained.

Then his eyes flew open.

"Jesus!"

His mouth began moving, but no words came out.

"Morris, stay still. I'll get you some help." I pulled my radio from my belt and hit the button. "Vic? Are you there?"

Nothing.

"Vic?" I released the button and yelled down the hallway
in a voice I was sure could be heard in the kitchen. "Vic!"

I placed a hand on the old man's shoulder. "I'm going to go
get help. I'll be right back. Hold on, Morris." I punched the button and yelled into the radio. "Base, this is unit one—come in!"

As I rushed down the hall and toward the stairs, Ruby's voice came through the speaker. "Unit one, this is base.
Over?"

As I passed Duane and Gina's room, it dawned on me why
it was important that the clock was an hour off—that Duane
had said Gina had left for work by the time he'd gotten up
from his nap, but in reality she'd reset the clock and gone out
to kill Geo. I jammed the radio to my mouth. "Ruby, get me
backup over at the Stewart place!"

Static. "Who?"

"Anybody. Everybody. Get me EMTs too. Morris Stewart
has been shot and is bleeding to death. Hurry."

I reached the landing and turned to find the front door once
again hanging open, but I cut left toward the kitchen. I stalled
at the swinging door I'd first seen Betty Dobbs walk through
and could see Vic lying on the floor, blood on her head.

I ran to her. I could feel the pressure of my own body exploding from the inside. I gently pushed my arm under her shoulder and pulled her toward me and up from the floor. froze as her head lolled to one side, and I could feel the air leap from my mouth. "No way, not like this. Not here."

She gasped a short breath, and it was then that I could see she was still breathing.

Her next words were quintessential. "Fuck me."

I held her head and spotted a frying pan big enough and old enough to have fed the whole Seventh Cavalry. I was lying on the floor by the refrigerator along with a large amount of spilled fried potatoes. There was a spot on it that was bloodied and held a tuft of brunette hair. I held her face up to mine.

She stirred again, and a hand came up, glancing off my arm and then dropping again. "What the fuck . . . ?" Her other hand came up and latched on to my sleeve.

"Are you all right?"

"My head . . . That bitch." Her eyes opened, and I could see where a blood vessel had burst in her left one. "What the hell did she hit me with?"

"Looks like a frying pan. I guess you should be happy she didn't have her gun." I propped her up a bit. "Are you okay?"

"No, my head . . . Yeah, I'm good." She started to sit up but her equilibrium was off and she wavered in my arms. "Shit."

I pulled her toward the kitchen cabinets and leaned her against them. "I've got backup coming with medical. Morri

Stewart's upstairs where she shot him in the chest—just like Ozzie Dobbs. Do you believe he's still alive?"

She stretched her jaw, and I could hear the popping noise. "When we're all dead, the only thing that'll still be alive will be cockroaches and a Stewart."

She was all right.

"Any idea where Gina and the dogs went?"

She tried to shake her head. "No idea. Did you check the car?"

"No, but we've got her blocked in, and I've got the keys."

She sighed, and I could tell it hurt. "I'll check . . ." Her hand slipped, and she jarred back onto her butt.

"Stay. When the troops show up, tell 'em Morris is upstairs in the last bedroom to the left." I stood.

She looked at me. "Where are you going?"

I pulled the .45 from my holster. "Hunting."

I could see from her prints in the fresh snow where she'd tried the car, but then that she had turned and gone back in, the dog tracks following hers. There was melted snow from her shoes and the dogs' paws that led down the stairs to the basement.

I turned the knob, but it was locked again. I reared back and planted a size thirteen into the wood by the knob plate and caught myself in the doorway as the wood exploded onto the stairs. I listened, but there was no noise from below, just the cold air from what I now knew was the cellar tunnel.

I flipped on the light switch and continued down the steps. She could've gotten her gun but wouldn't have taken the risk of finishing off Vic since she knew I'd be coming down the steps pretty quickly. She was used to taking her victims unaware and at close range; she might get lucky with the .32 if I came at her, or she might not.

Then there were the dogs.

As I turned the corner at the landing, my radio crackled. "Walt, it's Ruby."

I pulled the radio up as I aimed the Colt at large into the darkened basement. " . . . Kinda busy here."

Static. "Walt, Santiago is here and says he's got more information on Felix Polk."

"Put him on."

Static. "Boss, the name Polk didn't come up as an inmate in Huntsville so I did a search for a Felix P and found a Felix Poulson who did time for killing a garage owner in San Antonio." It was silent for a moment. "Gotta be the same guy, Boss. His next hit was the stretch in San Quentin for kidnapping a woman in Utah and killing her— same name, Felix Poulson."

Where had I heard that name before? I keyed the mic again. "Is there any mention of next-of-kin contact?"

Static. "Kayla."

I flipped the lights on and looked around with the radio over my mouth. "Have we got people coming?"

Static. "Yes. Everybody's on their way."

"Morris is in the bedroom upstairs, and Vic is on the floor in the kitchen."

Static. "What happened to Vic?"

"Fortunately, she was assaulted with a frying pan."

Static. "Fortunately?"

I keyed the mic again. "It was a hell of a sight better than the .32 Gina used on her great-uncle-in-law."

I clipped the radio to my belt and continued to check the basement. There was no one there—man, woman, or beast. I watched the air blow the blue plastic that covered the opening in the old house's foundation back toward me along with the cold from the other end.

The four-by-four attached to the bottom of the tarp was kicked sideways, and I was pretty sure it was where she and the dogs had gone. It was the only way out to the tow trucks that were the only other working vehicles.

I moved to the opening and shifted the wood on the floor to the opposite side. It was dark in the tunnel, and I reached up to the right where I could feel the junction box and switch.

I flipped it and absolutely nothing happened.

"Damn."

I pulled my Maglite from my belt and directed it into the tunnel; the batteries were starting to fade, I'd been using it so much lately.

Poulson. Where had I heard that name?

The weak beam of the flashlight only penetrated the gloom of the tunnel for so far, and the only things I could see were a few cardboard boxes, a stack of mulch, and another of fertilizer. Saizarbitoria had done a pretty good job of cleaning out the place; it was such a shame that it had turned out to be his swan song.

I started into the jagged opening and had gone about a

dozen steps when I felt the air pressure in the confined space change. The cold was like a wall, and I could feel it increase as I stood there. I listened carefully but could only hear a scrambling noise.

It was about then that I heard the breathing of something at the end of the tunnel, something running. I raised the flashlight again and could plainly see a single set of golden eyes moving fast and headed my way.

16

At least it was only one set of eyes.

Something in me hesitated as I brought the large-frame Colt up; I remembered how Butch had licked my hand. Maybe it was the ranch boy in me, maybe it was just being stupid, but I wasn't willing to kill the less ferocious of the dogs.

If he got to me and there was no choice, well, then there was no choice.

But what if it wasn't Butch?

A lot of this stuff was passing through my mind in the few seconds it took the dog to race down the tunnel. I had learned how to handle a dog in a death struggle in the Corps. In boot they'd given us a chance against a few extremely well-trained German shepherds; an eight-man squad, and we'd all lost badly.

Hypothetically, the trick was to feed the dog your passive forearm, then wrap your other around its neck and push, effectively breaking the dog's neck. The instructor said that it usually worked, unless the dog was large and powerful, in which case his jaws could break the proffered arm, making it doubly difficult to concentrate on step two. He also said that if the dog was trained properly it would leap for the arm but then at the last instant go underneath and clamp its jaws around your throat.

A recruit had asked what you did at that point, and the instructor said he'd heard that if you stick a finger in the attacking dog's anus, the animal would break off the attack. Intrasquad consensus was that you'd have just as good a chance if you stuck the digit up your own asshole.

I set my feet and kept the butt of the .45 ready to bring down on the dog's head.

I could see him plainly now, but it was impossible to tell which one it was. He looked like he meant business though. braced my legs for the impact and then suddenly remembered the only other weapon I had at hand—my voice.

Just as he was shortening his stride to time a leap, I yelled "Butch, bad dog! Down!"

It was as if someone had cut off the fuel, and he landed at my feet a little clumsily. His head was between his paws a he looked up at me with the glow of the flashlight in his eyes He wagged his tail in supplication, just a bit, and then wa motionless.

"Good boy." His head rose. "C'mere." He stood and turned, sitting his behind on my boots. "Good boy, good boy. I ruffled his ears, stroking the silky hair at the back of his neck and remembered the biscuits that Larry had given me at the drive-through. I pulled one out and gave it to him. That left me with another biscuit for Sundance, an item likely to be a helpful as an accordion on an elk hunt.

With the experiences of the last few months, I had to re

member to carry an entire assortment of animal treats with me. "Good boy, good boy."

I started down the tunnel again, this time with a wagging companion. I didn't think I could get him to stay, so I let him tag along, figuring that I could close the door at the end of the tunnel to keep him from joining Sundance if Gina put him on me.

When I got to the end, I could see that the snow had crept in the doorway and held the door open a few inches. I looked down at my companion, still wagging. "This is as far as you go, buddy."

I buttoned my sheepskin coat, flipped up the collar, and pulled down my hat. I wedged the door back far enough to get a leg through and just hoped that Gina wasn't waiting on the other side with the .32 pistol. It was dark, and the darting snowflakes stung.

I dropped my face down into my coat and tried not to think about how my skin already stung, my foot already hurt, and about the bite wound on my right cheek. Butch had tried to follow after me, but I brushed him back with my boot and shoved the cellar door closed. I again figured if he got together with Sundance and Gina, he was more likely to run with the pack.

I turned into the night and wondered where my pack was.

Visibility was no more than twenty feet. I looked around for prints, but the gusts had filled anything that was out here. The wind was coming straight out of the North Pole, and there were no stars or moon.

I looked toward the ridge in hopes of seeing something

that might indicate that she'd gone that way, but there was nothing but drifts, running like shallow sea waves toward the southeast. I looked toward the gated walkway that led to the quarry, but there was nothing there either.

She had to be after the tow trucks. They were solid and had four-wheel drive and weren't blocked in by my three quarter-ton. Had to be.

I postholed my way toward the junkyard below, aware that if I went in the wrong direction, I could take a seventy five-foot header. The wind had scoured the edge of the cliff and the pathway became more evident as I got to the gate which was swinging freely in the wind. I could see boot prints now and figured I should move as quickly as I could, since there was no way Gina would stay out in this weather any longer than absolutely needed. If she was going for the tow trucks, she'd be going for them fast.

It was easier going downhill, and the wind wasn't as bad inside the quarry. The snow had been accumulating with a vengeance and was about two feet deep in the junkyard itself but at least the visibility had improved to the point where I could now see about thirty feet, which was the length of one of those behemoths they made back in the forties and fifties.

It was easy to feel small and alone in the muffled quiet of the snow amid all that dead hardware.

It was hard enough for me with my long legs to move quickly in the deep drifts, and I wondered about the desperation that must have forced Gina to try. I thought I saw something ahead and stopped by a '66 Belvedere with a Buic stacked on top of it and a Ford sedan on top of that. It was only when the ricochet of a .32 slug caromed off the quarter panel of the Plymouth that I became really sure.

I jumped back to the rear of the coupe with all the agility of a circus bear and peered around the taillight. "Gina, it's the sheriff. There isn't anywhere to go. I've got people on the way and they're going to block off the gate, so you better just give it up now!" I hoped the part about the people was true.

My answer was another round from the .32, which disappeared somewhere behind me, and the barking of the dog.

I figured I'd flank her and continue down the next row and try and cut her off before she got to the trucks. I high-stepped to my right and hoped she and the dog hadn't had the same idea as I made my way along the other side of the car tower. I tried to remember how many rows there were before the main thoroughfare that held the office and the straight shot to the gate and was thinking three before I hit the turn of the century in motor vehicle manufacture and crossed the road.

I hurried through the seventies and the eighties, and was just making it to the nineties when I thought I saw something ahead again.

It was smaller than me and, more important, it wasn't standing upright.

I stood there breathing heavily, most of my energy drained from slogging through the snow, and waited. That primordial stem at the back of my brain shot a jolt through me, the same jolt that it'd sent through my ancestors' brains for a couple hundred thousand years, the jolt that told you something was coming for you and you were too far from the safety of the trees.

He knew where I was but was waiting to see if I knew where he was.

The hackles rose between his shoulders, and the sound that resounded there had nothing to do with civilization. He walked on his paws with the shape of his own savagery: suspicious, hostile, and deadly, with yellow eyes as still as a snake's.

"Easy."

He didn't hesitate for an instant, and it was almost as if my speaking to him had weakened my position on the food chain. My voice went out into the distance like a match dropped in the snow.

I could easily see the great, gapping jaws now and the saliva dripping from his lips. He lumbered in the snow on the first few steps but that almost instantly changed into a gallop. He launched like a torpedo, and I had that sickening feeling that there wasn't going to be any way to circumvent this. The dog's mouth was like a tunnel full of teeth, and he was fast. I had dissuaded Butch but knew the results were going to be different this time.

Sundance didn't waver, didn't misdirect, but came straight at my throat. The beast forced me backward in the snow, and we both rolled ass over elbows. His mouth slammed shut, but the majority of the bite went into my heavy sheepskin coat, and I flipped him over my head, the momentum forcing his jaws loose as he continued to bite at me with bone-crushing force.

I flailed with the .45, but one of the bites hit my wrist.

rolled over and flopped forward, desperately grabbing for my dropped sidearm. It was snow-caked, and I reached for it, but my hand refused to operate. The bite had either broken the bone or hit the pressure points in my hand enough so that the thing was useless.

The monster had turned now and was rising from the snow with his black lips pulled back and his ears lying flat. I could see the muscles ripple under the heavy coat, and the determination in the jaundiced eyes that weren't likely to be fooled again.

I scrambled my left hand across my body, but there was no way I'd make it.

He leapt, and I have to admit at that moment I was stunned by the grace of the animal; the way the broad chest and magnificent head looked in that final moment of attack. Maybe I'd get the Colt up against him before it was all over but probably not.

It was then that something hit me square in the back, forcing my face into the snow and knocking the wind from me. All I could think was that Butch must've gotten free from the tunnel and had decided to join the fun.

My hand finally closed on the Colt but the dog on top of me was gone, almost as if he'd used me as a launching pad.

Only it wasn't Butch.

I raised my head and tried to focus. The two of them rolled like a giant, fur-covered wheel into the open well of a junked, snow-covered GMC pickup. The collision caused the snow to fall off the vehicle like a miniature avalanche, but neither of them was giving quarter. Sundance crunched down on the back of Dog's heavy neck, but Dog lurched forward, slamming him into the fender of the truck. Sundance redoubled his efforts, but Dog's wide head rammed him, flipping him sideways and backward. Sundance was faster, but Dog's muscle mass gave him the advantage in close contact.

My dog stood there in the center of the pathway between us, the hackles raised on his swirling red, brown, and blond back that surged with a tide of muscle. His muzzle was wider than the wolf's, mastifflike, with teeth like the edge of a front end loader.

Sundance started to move left, still intent on getting hold of me, but Dog shifted his weight, and I watched the spittle drip between his splayed legs. There was blood in the strings, but he showed no sign of weakening.

I had to give the wolf credit for concentration; even faced with Dog, he was still focused on me as his victim. I brought the .45 around with my left hand, fumbling to get it aimed, but my movement distracted Dog. That was all the wolf needed. He sprang forward but was struck sideways when he passed as Dog closed his massive muzzle on one of Sundance's forelegs, and I could hear the sickening crunch from a car length away.

The damage was done, and he fell away with a squealing yelp. Dog stood his ground and watched as the other dog struggled up on three legs to pace right. Dog pivoted to follow.

Sundance stopped pacing and growled, but Dog countered by digging his claws into the ice and snow in a false charge. The wolf backed off, and just like that, the fight was gone from him.

The .45 trembled in my hand. I lowered it and pushed up on my hands and knees.

I stayed there for a few moments, trying to get my adrenaline level back to approaching human. I cleared my throat and caught my balance with a hand extended to the nearest junker.

I struggled up beside Dog. "Jeez . . ." I could feel the bile in my throat and choked back the nausea. My balance was still a little off, and I put a hand on the door of another rusted hulk, took a few more breaths, and got my voice back to a squeak. "What took you so long?"

He didn't turn to look at me, but his head cocked as if I were calling to him from another world—I guess, in a way, I was. He raised his bloodied muzzle but kept his eyes on Sundance. "Good boy." I breathed out a great sigh. "Good boy."

He was bleeding from his jaw, and his ear looked torn, but he wouldn't turn. I took a few more deep breaths and whispered the only word I could think of saying. "Stay."

I swear he glanced up at me with the expression of "What the hell else do you think I'm going to do?" I smiled and kicked off after the only prey left, confident that Dog had my back.

My right hand was still inoperable; it didn't hurt, but it wouldn't work from the wrist down and only flopped when I rotated my arm. I checked the Colt to see that the breech was still pulled and the safety off, which it was.

In the distance I could hear a motor turning over, the starter grinding in the cold, running the battery down. I continued through the snow and could finally see the row of tow trucks, but I couldn't tell which one was producing the noise.

I stepped from the row as one of the tow-truck engines caught and fogged a blackened exhaust onto the snow. It was the one closest, and I raised the .45 in my left hand. "Sheriff's Department, freeze!"

My voice might've carried to the end of my arm.

I cleared my throat and tried again. "Sheriff, freeze!"

Maybe two arms' length.

I bellowed out with all I had as I staggered forward, the Colt leading the way. "Sheriff!"

I could see Gina, frantically trying to get the tow truck in gear with both hands, and then could hear the horrendous noise as the gears caught and the big vehicle leapt forward in granny—a good one mile an hour.

The Fords I remembered from that period had floor shifters like Arthur's sword in a stone and, once you got them in the lower-case gears, they didn't come out. The hubs were locked, and the heavily knobbed snow tires dug like the steel wheels of a locomotive.

We were now set for the slowest chase in high plains history.

Brandishing my sidearm in a highly dramatic fashion, I limped forward, only slightly faster than the approaching truck. "Gina, shut that thing down! Now!"

The truck continued to forge on toward me, the tow-lift cables swinging behind it in the falling snow. The grille guard on the front was homemade and consisted of four-inch pipe and steel grating, honeycombed across the front, with a large opening so that the hood could be raised.

I had limited ability with my left hand but figured I could

hit the radiator, so I raised the barrel of the Colt and fired. The thing spewed a blast of steam and dribbled a sickly green onto the packed ice and snow, but it kept coming at me.

I could see Gina better now, and it looked as if she was intent on upping the stakes. Her hand came forward, and she pushed the pistol toward the glass.

"Gina, don't! That .32 won't—"

The double crack of the firing pistol and the bullet's collision with the heavy glass sounded as one, and then I could hear the round, which was incapable of breaking the windshield, ripping through the cab. Undeterred, she fired again, spreading the spiderweb of breaking glass. This time the ricochet must've found Gina. She fell against the steering wheel, and the tow truck lurched in my direction.

"Oh, hell."

I scrambled backward, started to slip, but then caught my balance as I tried to get next to the relative safety of the stacked cars. The Ford was bearing down and it occurred to me that as slow as the tow truck was, I was slower.

I made a calculated decision and changed direction—it wasn't like the thing was going to kill me with speed. I tried to make it to one side, but I slipped again and had no choice but to climb onto the grille guard.

I hitched a leg up and rolled myself onto the hood as the truck slammed into the nearest stack of cars, moving them sideways for about four feet. I looked in the cab, but Gina was still slumped against the wheel.

I heard a groan of metal as the vehicle slowly moved the stack of cars clockwise, its wheels spinning on the packed snow like Mexican fireworks. Something caught my eye, and I looked up to see a Subaru sedan teetering at the top of the stack.

"You have got to be kidding."

I threw myself to the left as the car slid a little toward me and then toppled over from twelve feet above, top down.

I slid completely into the open space between the hood and the grille guard as the Subaru crashed onto the tow truck like some giant samurai trying to stomp me to death. The majority of the car hit the cab of the Ford but then pivoted on its top and slid down toward me as I tried to make myself as svelte as possible in the space between the grille and the guard.

The Subaru slipped to the side and fell away as the tow truck continued on its merry path of destruction, driving us back in time down the aisle of cars through the nineties, the eighties and, finally, the seventies. Towers of cars kept falling but the granny gear was bound and nonetheless determined.

We had to be approaching the sixties where Dog held Sundance at a stalemate, and I hoped that they'd have the common sense to run for their lives. All I could do was lie there behind the grille guard and hope it held up against whatever we ran into, which at the moment looked like a particularly solid stack of vehicles that included a defunct ice-cream truck, a Buick station wagon, and a powder blue International Scout.

I had plenty of time to contemplate the impending collision as the tow truck ground on, but the vehicle that arrested my thoughts was the Scout on top. There was something about that particular model of car.

And there was something else, something important

That was the way my mind had been working as of late; I'd think of something important but neglect to write it down, and then the only thing I could remember the next day was that it was, indeed, something important.

I looked up at the black sky and watched as the flakes of snow swirled and danced down out of it, but my eyes slipped to the faded, dry pigment of the Scout. The color reminded me of the summer sky, and I thought about the warmth of the sun's cascading rays, about waves of grass stalks, and women in cotton dresses.

The Ford crashed into the stack of vehicles like a wrecking ball, bucking and kicking until the International slipped sideways from the top of the crushed station wagon. It fell onto the hood of the tow truck and the upper edge of the massive grille guard—powder blue, just as if the hoped-for summer sky were falling.

EPILOGUE

I had been trying to keep my head down for the last three days; not that I hadn't had to do that before, being married once and having a lawyer for a daughter, but this was for medical purposes.

I had a round, donut-shaped pillow that I used to rest my face, which Ruby had acquired when she'd had a bout with hemorrhoids; this provided no end of levity for the staff of the Absaroka County Sheriff's Department.

"It seems appropriate; I mean, he is the biggest pain in the ass we have on duty."

The eye doctor whom Andy Hall had sent me to in Billings had opted for the pneumatic retinopexy, during which an air bubble was injected into my eye that pushed the rip in my retina back so that a laser could seal the tear. Consequently, I had to stay in one or two positions for the next few weeks so that the air bubble continued to push the retina and wouldn't cause cataracts or high pressure in my eye.

"Just what he needs is more hot air."

They also said I wasn't allowed to fly anywhere, which

was the one thing I was thinking about, if for no other reason than to escape the grief I was getting. I had about six weeks of medical leave saved up, but I'd gotten bored at home after two days and had decided to come into the office and just rest my head on my desk and try to assist Henry in getting my daughter's wedding plans cemented.

"I don't think most people have noticed any difference in your performance."

I wasn't supposed to, but I raised my head and looked at Vic. "You're in a good mood."

"I bought a house today."

The Bear was studying me, but I ignored him. "Where?"

"The one I was looking at, the one on Kisling."

I lowered my head onto the pillow to further avoid Henry's gaze, but it did little to avoid his voice. "I thought that one got sold."

"The other buyer couldn't get a mortgage, so the realtor called me, and I got it for the asking price. Then John Muecke at the bank called and financed it, so I didn't even have to borrow the money."

"Wow, imagine that."

I knew that he was actually talking to me and, if he didn't cut it out, I was going to be forced to throw my circular pillow at him. I cleared my throat and spoke into the surface of my desk as I reached down and petted Dog, who was sleeping on my boots. I changed the subject and not too gracefully. "So, did the ballistics on Gina's gun match up with Ozzie?"

It was quiet. "Did you hear me? I said I just bought a house."

"I did. Congratulations."

There was a longer pause, and her voice changed. "Yeah, the .32 was a dead match, and so was the equestrian needle she used to kill Geo that we found in with her stuff. As near as we can figure, she changed the clock in Duane's room to throw him off and even wore his boots out into the junkyard when she killed Geo. She must have worn the same boots when she killed Ozzie."

I was going to be in trouble for changing the subject, but trouble was the better alternative to her finding out the truth. "Who's transporting Gina?"

She continued talking in a strained tone of voice. "Me."

"Don't you need to get going?"

"I guess so." Quiet again. "David Nickerson got her patched up. She's milking it for all it's worth, but in twenty minutes she's headed for the more luxurious female facilities in Casper where she'll await trial." There was a rustling of papers. "I've got the faxes from San Quentin. The PO says that during Polk's—"

Henry interrupted. "Are we calling him Polk or Poulson?"

"We'll just call him Polk." Vic sighed. "Polk's only contact after he was in San Quentin was with his old buddies from the Aryan Brotherhood, who told him that they knew the whereabouts of his granddaughter. Of course, they knew that she was dead and had gotten Gina to be the substitute. She's got a history with The Order, a motorcycle gang associated with the AB. If I was going to place a bet, I'd say that this was to be Felix's blood in, blood out, and Gina was supposed to watch over the operation for the guys inside. Polk would be allowed o go into semiretirement as long as he kept providing product or the Brotherhood."

The Bear folded his arms and covered half his face with a hand. "So they were not really related."

"Nope." Vic shifted in the chair by my desk. "Polk had a daughter, but she died of an apparent suicide two years before he got out, and the real granddaughter died in a car accident shortly after that. Polk never knew about the granddaughter, and as near as we can tell, Gina started writing to him to establish some sort of bullshit family bond. Polk was about to go rogue, and the whole fake granddaughter thing was a way to keep tabs on him." She rustled some papers, and I assumed she was reading from a report. "The PO says he disappeared about ten months after release, which would've placed him here about seven months ago and that coincides with Gina's contact with the Stewarts."

I ignored the temptation to raise my head. "Did she really meet Duane in Mexico?"

She took a deep breath and sighed. "She might've met him in a Mexican restaurant, but that's about as far south as that goes. She's a poster child for fucked-up—in and out of foster homes, finally living on the streets, and prostitution. Then she got hung up with this motorcycle gang. The only way a female gets anything in that gang is by putting out sex, information, drugs, and all of the above."

"How's Duane doing?"

The desk jostled, and I was pretty sure she was now resting her boots on the edge. "Who the fuck knows? He's back at the big house."

"He knows he's got a sentencing tomorrow."

"Yeah. Vern says he's going to do some time and maybe some community service. I guess the judge figures a dead grandfather is enough of a burden."

Henry wanted a ruling on the paternity issue. "So, Duane is the father after all?"

"Nope."

I listened as Henry's chair squealed. "No?"

"She's not pregnant."

I raised my head to join the conversation. "She's not?"

"Betty Dobbs was a little disappointed; I think the old broad was planning on adopting the little bugger." She sighed. "Ozzie ran the business into the ground, but Betty's got her own money and will be all right. I heard the whole development sold to investors."

"How is Morris?"

"He's recovered, and from what we've heard he's taken his brother's place and was out on the roof this morning."

I thought about it some more and lowered my head; it felt like I had been staring at the surface of my desk for months, not just days. "And the marijuana?"

"Well, Gina and Polk were the long-term deal, but Gina saw a short-term scam in Ozzie. She had a lot to lose, but she had a lot to gain pitting both against each other. As for Geo, I guess he was getting a little too close for comfort on the ganja deal, and she figured she needed him out of the way. She must've seen him heading back with Betty and thought it was an opportunity to get him after he dropped her off. When she overheard the argument between Geo and Ozzie and saw the fight, it must've seemed fuckin' perfect."

Henry interrupted. "So, Ozzie called Polk at the Chicken Shack and then Polk called Gina to tell her to get rid of Ozzie?"

"Yeah, if Gina hadn't gotten greedy they might've pulled it off."

The intercom on my phone buzzed, and I hit the button. "Yep?"

Ruby's voice sounded tinny in the plastic-ribbed speaker. "Mike Thomas just called the Fire Department and said there's a chimney fire out on TK Road. They want to know if we want to send someone along."

Vic was the first to answer. "Why would we want to do that?"

"It's the Stewart place."

My head came up, and the three of us stared at each other as Vic smiled. "Must have been the kerosene. Fuck it, let it burn." There was a pause as she stood. "I have to go take a prisoner to Casper." She didn't move and continued to glare at me. "By the way, I let Dog out at the junkyard—I figured he could find you faster than I could. Oh, and when I have my housewarming party? He's invited but you're not." With that final salvo, she turned and left.

I allowed my head to stay up so that I could watch her shapely derriere with one eye as she departed my office. There was another welcomed half-sight there in the doorway.

I hadn't heard from him in almost a week, but Ruby said

he'd been in a couple of times to check on me. Neither of us said anything for a moment, and I was pretty sure he was looking at my damaged eye.

"How are you feeling, troop?" The Basquo looked more rested, and I was glad to see a little bit of that wayward spark in his eyes again. There wasn't much of it, but enough to give me hope. "Sorry, but I've got to keep my head down." I spoke into the surface of my desk again. "That was some pretty fine detective work, figuring out that Polk was Poulson."

I listened to the chair creak as he sat in the spot Vic had vacated. "You seem kinda shorthanded."

"We are."

"Um . . . I was wondering if I could have my star back?"

I smiled; it wasn't like anybody was going to see it. "Yep, and you can have your gun back too, as soon as Joe Meyer finishes the investigation in Cheyenne." In all actuality, the state AG had already told me he figured Saizarbitoria's case was a walk-through and that I could reinstate him anytime I wanted. "How's the family?"

"Good." I listened as he took a deep breath. "We're good. Antonio's sleeping more, so we're actually getting some rest."

He said his son's name this time, and I continued to grin at the surface of my desk. I reached into one of my drawers, which made Dog move just a little, and thumped the Beretta, still in the duty holster with the Basquo's star attached, onto my desk alongside the back of my head. "Here." I raised said head and glanced at him. "Please go make sure the Stewart place doesn't burn down."

He laughed, picked up his goods, and departed.

I began lowering my head back onto the pillow, but the little red light on my phone began buzzing and blinking again. I punched the button, my blind hand educated by practice. "Yep?"

Ruby's voice rang through the tiny speaker. "I've got Comox, Vancouver Island, on line one."

"Got it."

I started to punch the button, but she continued speaking. "Also, I thought I should point out that Felix Polk's thumb is still in the commissary refrigerator."

"Do me a favor and ship it up to Billings with the rest of him."

"Also? John Muecke wants to know why you had him transfer funds to buy a house over on Kisling just so you could sell it through the bank."

I thought about my Valentine's gift that hadn't come with any card.

"Tell him to mind his own business." I raised my head a little and looked at Henry. "What?"

He smiled. "Nothing."

I punched line one and the speakerphone button. "Mr. Cook?"

The connection wasn't great. "Kingfisher Lodge."

"Is this Pat Cook?"

"Speaking."

He sounded old. "Mr. Cook, this is Sheriff Walt Longmire, and I've been trying to track you for a few days."

The line was quiet for a moment. "Concerning?"

"Well, I'm the sheriff of Absaroka here in Wyoming." It was silent as I studied the phone and pulled the base in closer. "Mr. Cook, were you a deputy with our sheriff's department in 1970 when Lucian Connally was sheriff?" He didn't say anything, but I could hear him breathing on the other end. "I know that it wasn't a particularly pleasant experience for you."

"What is this about?"

"Pat, do you remember a man by the name of Fred Poulson?"

Another pause, but his voice became stronger. "It'd be a hard name for me to forget."

"I'd imagine so." I rested my forehead in the palm of my hand and ignored the pain in my eye socket. My other hand drifted down and petted Dog—I was careful to avoid the taped up ear. "I just thought I would give you a call that might help you to sleep a little better at night. . . ."

I glanced at the Cheyenne Nation with my one eye, and things didn't look half-bad.

Craig Johnson's seventh novel featuring
Sheriff Walt Longmire is now available
in Viking hardcover.

Read on for the first chapter of

HELL IS EMPTY

ISBN 978-0670-02277-9

1

"Didn't your mother ever tell you not to talk with your mouth full?"

I tried to focus on one of my favorite skies—the silver-dollar one with the peach-colored banding that seriates into a paler frosty blue the old-timers said was an omen of bad times ahead—as I stuffed a third of a bacon cheeseburger into Marcel Popp's mouth in an attempt to silence the most recent of his promises that he was, indeed, going to kill me.

At last count he'd made this statement twenty-seven times to me, eight to other members of the Absaroka County Sheriff's Department, and seventeen to Santiago "Sancho" Saizarbitoria, who was dragging a few french fries through his ketchup as his eyes stayed trained on a paperback in his left hand.

I looked at Sancho. "That was twenty-eight."

The sun reflected through the western window and struck my face like a ray gun. I was tempted to close my eyes and soak in the warmth of the early afternoon, but I couldn't afford the luxury. I hadn't allowed any silverware at the table and Marcel Popp was manacled, but I still warned him that if he bit either Sancho or me he'd go without food.

The Basquo tilted his head from the book. "Do dirty looks count?"

Popp glanced at Santiago, who was watching the othe two convicts quietly eating their lunches, and we could onl guess what his words would've been as he chewed.

"No." I placed the rest of the convict's burger on his plat and looked back out the window as the sunshine took anothe dying shot at my face.

Sancho and I had been amusing ourselves by keeping score, and even though the Basquo was down by eleven, he had made a fourth-quarter comeback with a tirade he'd received a we'd unloaded the transported prisoners at South Fork Lodg in the heart of the Bighorn Mountains. The Basquo'd apol ogized for handling Marcel's head into the top of the doo while getting him out of the vehicle; I still wasn't sure if it had been entirely innocent.

I glanced at Santiago and then risked closing my eyes fo just a second. Even with present company, I had enjoyed m own Absaroka burger and fries. South Fork was my favorit of the lodges, with the best menu and a river-stone fireplac in the dining room that owners Holli and Wayne Jones kep roaring when the temperature was under fifty degrees. It wa a year-round, full-service lodge nestled away in one of th southside canyons, with snowmobiling, cross-country skiing horseback riding, trout fishing, and hunting in season.

It was early May, and the summer crowds hadn't arrive yet. With the outside temperature in the high thirties not in cluding windchill, I was afraid we still had a few shots of win ter left.

Despite the weather, there was a comfortable, close qual-
ty to the lodge, and I fantasized about reserving one of the
ustic cabins by the partially ice-covered creek and calling
Victoria Moretti, another of my deputies, to see what she was up
o this weekend. Vic had just bought a new house, and she'd
nvited me and my best friend, Henry Standing Bear, over for
linner tonight. I was still thinking about the cabin when Popp
poke again.

"I'm going to kill every single one of you motherfuckers."

It was a general statement, but he'd been looking at me.
Twenty-nine."

Currently, Marcel wasn't a happy camper. I hadn't released
ither him or the other two murderers from their traveling
hains in order to eat. Marcel had already killed two Win-
emucca, Nevada, city policemen and a South Dakota high-
vay patrolman in an attempt to escape a year back. That and
is limited vocabulary had endeared him to the entire Absa-
oka County staff. We would be just as happy to be rid of him
vhen we met up with the Big Horn and Washakie counties'
heriff's departments, the FBI, and the Ameri-Trans van near
Meadowlark Lodge in less than an hour.

Ameri-Trans was a private firm that contracted with law
nforcement to transport prisoners, but they had no contract
vith us; I didn't like the fact that they had a record high per-
entage of escapees and wouldn't allow them in my juris-
iction, so we'd made a little jaunt into the mountains this
fternoon with the prisoners.

I'd asked the FBI agent in charge over the phone what
ll this was about but had been told that the details would be

made clear when we delivered the convicts to the multiagenc
task force that awaited us a little farther up the road. I didn
like his answer, but for now that was my problem.

I glanced at Raynaud Shade, the prisoner who worried m
most, the one who continued to look at his plate as he chewed.
didn't know why the Crow-adopted Canadian Indian was bein
transported but would be just as glad when he was no longe
my responsibility. He hardly ever spoke, but in my estimation
was the quiet ones you really had to worry about. I'd been di
tracted by my thoughts for only a second, but when I paid atter
tion again his pale eyes were studying me from under the dar
hair. He had this unnerving ability that whenever you refocuse
your eyes on him, he was there with you—like a cat in a cage.

"I'm going to kill you, you little Basque prick. I'm gonn
kill your big boss here—I'm gonna fuckin' kill all of you."

I picked up the rest of the burger and pushed anothe
third into Marcel's mouth.

Sancho stuffed the paperback under his arm, looked a
the stack of books at his elbow, and smiled a wayward, electri
smile that made the women in the county give him that se
ond look, or even a third. "That was a triple."

"Almost an in-the-park home run." I frowned at him. "Tha
was one for you, one for me, and a general score we can share.

"C'mon."

I tallied it up. "Thirty to nineteen."

He sighed and resumed reading Dante's *Inferno* as I reache
over and slid *Les Misérables* off the top of the pile to reveal *L*
Trois Mousquetaires—both in the original French. The Basqu
regretting a stint in higher education devoted almost exclusivel
to criminal justice, was attempting to fill in some of the literar

gaps. We had all made lists for him, including *Bury My Heart at Wounded Knee* from Henry and of all things, *Concrete Charlie: The Story of Philadelphia Football Legend Chuck Bednarik* from Vic, but my dispatcher Ruby's list, which included *Crime and Punishment* and *The Pilgrim's Progress* as well as the *Inferno*, had been the most daunting, so the Basquo had started with it. I, taking pity on the poor kid, had included *To Kill a Mockingbird*, *The Grapes of Wrath*, and the aforesaid *Musketeers*.

"How's it going, troop?"

He peeled a thumb against the sides of the prodigious paperbacks, especially *Inferno*. "Slow."

"Hey, I am God-damned starving here."

Popp was a monster, just the kind of obstacle you didn't want to meet in a dark or otherwise illuminated alley. Roughly my size, he was already in shape when he'd gone into the South Dakota Maximum Security Facility in Sioux Falls, and four hours of weight lifting a day over the last year hadn't allowed him to exactly winnow away.

"And fucking dying of thirst, you assholes."

Or improved his vocabulary.

Hector Otero, the third of our terrible trio, smiled at the latest of Popp's outbursts, and I wondered what wrong turns had resulted in the scam artist killing two people on Houston's south side. The ever-smiling Latino had been shocked when Santiago had spoken to him in fluent Spanish. I'd understood only a percentage of the conversation, but the Basquo had rolled his eyes afterward, putting the street hood's intelligence in question. "Who wrote that anyway?"

Sancho regarded the Latino with one eye. "What?"

The gangbanger seemed actually interested, his eyes like

drips of crude oil flicking between Sancho and me. "That book, that Dante's *Inferno*; who wrote that?"

The Basquo and I traded a look, and I waited to see how my deputy was going to play it.

"Hector, do you know who's buried in Grant's Tomb?"

"Nope."

Saizarbitoria went back to his Penguin Classic. "Didn't think so. Just be glad we're letting you eat at the big-person table."

Otero, aware that he was being made the butt of a joke, clicked his eyes to me so I'd know that he wasn't up to anything and then raised in his chair just enough to see the other titles in Saizarbitoria's pile. "Yeah, well, at least I'm not reading a book by Alexander Dumb-ass."

Hector was grinning when Raynaud Shade sucked the air out of the room.

"Shut up, Hector."

If anybody had ever said that to Hector Otero in the outside world, they might've gotten more than a couple of ounces of lead in response, but not Shade. The smaller man looked at the Indian but said nothing.

When I looked at Shade, he was staring at me again.

His features were flat, his nose spread across his face like a battering ram had been used one time too many, the bones of his brow and cheeks prominent. He was an average height but his chest, shoulders, and bull neck let you know that if something were to start, Raynaud Shade would get his share. You wouldn't have thought him capable at twenty-seven of the rap sheet he carried—but when you looked into his outlandish eyes, it was all there. His irises were the same washed-out blue as the winter Wyoming sky and just as cold.

At least one was. Raynaud's left eye was a replacement, and whoever had done the work had failed to capture the exact color. The shade, no pun intended, was an elusive one reflecting an altitude where humanity could not survive.

I'd read about him—he must have been the one the Feds were really interested in. He was on the express back to Draper, Utah, to either a lethal injection or a firing squad, which meant that he was a dead man walking and, as long as he walked in my county, he would walk in chains.

He looked at me through the hood his dark hair formed and spoke in an empty, halting voice. "Thank you."

It was the sixth time he'd communicated since we'd been responsible for him, coming up on seventy-two hours. "For?"

His eye stayed with mine for a second—it was as if he was half paying attention—then panned around the café like a searchlight. "For allowing us to eat in a restaurant." He smiled as though he didn't know how, and I figured it was the only one he had—the one with a lot of teeth and no warmth. "I imagine this will be my last time to do something normal."

He spoke in the cadence of the Yukon Territory where he'd been born, and his voice carried—one of those you could hear from a hundred feet away even when he was whispering. His eye went back to his plate, and his hair fell forward, again covering his face. "I gotta go to the john."

I studied him. "In a minute."

He nodded and raised his cuffed hands, putting the fingertips on the table at its edge, his thumbs underneath. I watched as the fingers bent backward with the pressure of his grip.

"Me too, I gotta take a fucking piss."

Popp made a clicking noise as he spoke, and I could tell he

was thinking of spitting again. He'd spit on Sancho as we wer
unloading him, at which point I'd grabbed him by the back o
the neck and pulled his face in close to mine, making it clea
that if he spat again he'd go without lunch. My fingerprint
were still on his neck; I was feeling bad about that.

"I've been here before."

I turned back to Shade. "Excuse me?"

"First kill outside of my family."

He said it like they didn't count.

"I gave one of his bones to two other men who sent i
back to me in the mail in an attempt to get some money I hav
put away—that's why they're meeting us."

He had finished his meal and carefully pushed his plat
back a couple of inches, his thumbs still under the table, hi
hair still covering his face. "There is an FBI psychologist tha
I've been seeing; her name is Pfaff. I told her about where th
body is buried." He was suddenly silent, aware that everyon
had been listening to him, but then stared directly at me. '
just thought you might be curious."

The waitress interrupted the little breakthrough an
squelched my hopes of extending Shade's confession. "Woul
you like some more coffee, Sheriff?"

It took me a second to come back; Shade's dead eye wa
like that—it drew you into the cold.

"Yes, ma'am."

I caught her looking at the convicts and figured it was t
be expected. If they're lucky, most people in the private secto
never get to meet someone like Marcel Popp, Hector Oterc
or especially Raynaud Shade, but with our little road show o
recidivism, prurient curiosity was to be expected.

She poured in a distracted manner. "Do you get the check?"

"Yes, ma'am." I looked at her. "I don't know you, do I?"

Her eyes slid away. "No, I'm new."

"Hi, New. I'm Walt Longmire."

I held out my hand, and she took it as she held the coffee urn out of the way. "Beatrice, Beatrice Linwood."

I listened to the way she rounded her vowels. "Minnesota?"

She nodded without enthusiasm and took a second to respond. "Yah, Wacouta."

I smiled. "Well, you don't have to be ashamed about it. What's that near?"

"Red Wing."

"Where they make the work boots?"

"Yah."

I sipped my coffee in appreciation and studied her for a moment; midforties, she was too thin and a little mousy, but it was a nice smile. Something else there, though, something that reminded me of my late wife. Her hair was thin, and she looked like she might've undergone some form of chemotherapy recently.

"What brings you out this way this time of year?"

She shrugged and pushed her glasses back onto the bridge of her nose, and I noticed her rubbing her finger where a wedding ring might've once been.

"Snowmobiles."

I should've figured. Most of the flatlanders got tired of doing a hundred miles an hour on the ice of the ten thousand lakes and eventually wanted to try their hand at the mountain trails. A lot of them ended up buried in the snow or running into trees. I'd tried the power sport once with the Ferg, my

part-time deputy, but didn't like the noise or the sensation tha
my crotch was on fire.

"Holli and Wayne treating you well?"

She glanced toward the opening where the smiling head o
flamboyant chef Alfredo Coda had appeared from the kitchen
and then turned back to me. "Yah, they've all been great."

"I don't mean to break up old home week, but could I ge
something to fucking eat and drink?"

I tipped my fawn-colored hat back and looked at Marcel
but Saizarbitoria was faster. Holding a portion of *The Divin*
Comedy in one hand and picking up the remainder of the pris
oner's burger in the other, he gave him the last bite. I notice
Sancho was even less gentle than I'd been, and his voice was
little irritated. "Anything to shut you up."

I reached over to take the coffeepot from Beatrice s
that she wouldn't have to get in arm's reach of the prisoners
"Here, I'll take that."

She pulled away, just slightly. "No, I'll get it."

I took the coffeepot anyway and tested the temperature
"That's all right." To a desperate man, anything was a weapon.
poured a round for the chain gang and one for the Basquo. "Can'
be too careful."

She smiled up at me. "They don't look all that danger
ous."

"Well." I stood and returned the pot to her. "I'll take tha
check now."

She put it facedown alongside my empty plate.

"Shade? Let's go." I glanced at Sancho, making sure w
made eye contact, and left him with the other two.

The convict stood and then rounded the table toward me

glanced at Saizarbitoria one more time. He rested the paperback on the table and nodded. I took Shade's arm, and he began a shuffling, manacled gait past the front counter, through the gift shop, and around the corner to the communal sink and the two doors that led to the bathrooms.

Shade paused. "Do you need to come in with me?"

I glanced into the small stall that said BUCKS and noted the only egress was a seven-inch vent in the ceiling. "Not unless you're planning on turning into a field mouse and crawling up that pipe."

"No." He stared at me. "Not a mouse."

"Leave the door ajar."

He did as I asked, and as he busied himself I remembered how he had stumbled in the dining room as we'd gone past the last table where they had been rolling silverware, bumping it with his hip and pausing for only an instant.

There were small alarms going off in my head as he came out a few moments later, turned his back to me, and began washing his hands. After a few seconds he raised his head, and the eye studied me in the mirror. "I'm sorry if I seem preoccupied, but it is difficult to see you."

Aware of his disability, I nodded as he lifted his cuffed hands with the traveling chains that led to the manacles at his feet and tore a paper towel from the dispenser. "It's the snow." He tossed the towel into a trash can in the corner and stepped toward me. "It's difficult to see you because of the snow; surely I'm not the first one to tell you that?"

I stared back at him and dropped my hand to the Colt at my hip. "Snow."

His face was impassive, and he gestured with one hand,

the other along for the ride. "There is the outline of you, bu inside is only snow—like an old TV."

I watched as the one hand dragged the other over h shoulder. "You mean static?"

"Yes, but not exactly like that. It's as if you carry the snov within you." The pupil in the live eye stretched open while th dead one remained still. "When did this happen?"

I stood there for a long moment, studying him and tryin to get a read on whether it was an act or if he was truly insane I'd been around crazy people before, but none with the ded cated malice that this man seemed to exude. "We should g back to the others."

He leaned in and whispered as his hands dropped an shifted to his side. "I didn't have to go to the bathroor but wanted to speak to you alone about the snow and th voices."

I didn't say anything, and he stepped in closer.

"You see them and hear them, too."

I countered and casually brought the large-frame Colt u holding it loose at my hip. "Shade, you wouldn't have palme the steak knife from that table in the dining room?"

He said nothing, but the one eye slit. There was a sligl twitch as his motor response was to try for it, but then h smiled with his wide, even-set teeth and brought the knife ou wrapped inside a fist.

I turned so that he could see that the Colt was cocked an the safety was off. "Give it to me."

He held back and regarded me for a long moment, lettin the words settle between us like ash. "You don't believe tha they are near, do you?"

I didn't move, didn't even breathe. "Give me the knife."

His other hand folded around it in a two-fisted grip, the blade pointed directly toward me. "The Seldom Seen; they are with you, but you pretend that they aren't."

I still didn't move.

"When did they first become known to you?" I could feel my breath becoming short as he continued. "They spoke to me infrequently after my first kill, but now it's constant—they talk to me night and day, many voices as one." He shifted his shoulders the way you would if you were preparing to move. "Many voices as one."

I raised the Colt and pointed it at the center of his chest.

"You have also killed, and they speak with you—we have something in common, Sheriff."

I raised the sight to his head. "The knife."

"We are pawns to these spirits, souls they play with for their own satisfaction like hand games." He didn't move, and we both knew that the next threatening shift, no matter how slight, would result in his death. He continued to show me his teeth. "It will be interesting to see how they respond to your disbelief, who it is that they will send for you."

The tension went out of his body as he lowered the knife, and he drew back. Keeping the .45 trained on his face, I reached over with my other hand and took the knife, handle out.

Handle out—I'd never seen him flip it.

I got my breath back and thought about the ghosts slamming about in the particular machine in front of me as I reholstered my sidearm and put the knife in my back pocket. "Let's go."

I guided him back through the gift shop, past the counter where Beatrice Linwood watched us.

Shade said nothing more as I seated him at the table, bu
he looked back up at me and stared as if we had shared some
thing important. I stood there thinking about what he had
said, then straightened and found my deputy studying me.

"You all right?"

It took a second for me to respond. "Yep." I glanced back a
Shade and shot another look at Sancho, who closed his book
again, gave me an almost imperceptible nod, and turned to look
at the prisoners like a red-tailed hawk regarded field mice. I picked
up the check and crossed the twelve steps back to the cash regis
ter, peeled off three twenties, and asked Beatrice for a receipt.

She held the money and glanced back as Holli entered be
hind her through the swinging door that led from the kitchen
The owner/operator paused at the register and looked past
me toward the seated men. "What did they do?"

I thought about whether I really wanted to tell her, finall
deciding that if she didn't want to know, she wouldn't have asked
"They're murderers, all of them." I waited a moment to see i
the two women wanted me to continue, and they did. "The
little guy with all the tattoos, his name is Hector Otero. He's a
credit card hustler and gangbanger from Houston. The big guy
with the mouth is Marcel Popp, a methadonian who . . ."

Holli looked puzzled. "A Methodist?"

I cleared my throat. "Sorry, it's kind of an inside joke—
heroin users who use methadone clinics to get high."

Beatrice stiffened a little. "I don't think that's very funny."

I thought of telling her about the dead officers and Popp'
girlfriend, whom he'd strangled to death with an electrica
cord, and how none of them had thought their situation ver
humorous, either.

I looked at the woman behind the counter. "Yes, ma'am."

As I turned to go, her whisper came after me. "And that ne?"

I stopped and stuffed a portion of the change into a tip ır and the receipt into my wallet without looking back at her. Beatrice, you don't want to know."

A PENGUIN READERS GUIDE TO

JUNKYARD DOGS

Craig Johnson

AN INTRODUCTION TO
Junkyard Dogs

Walt Longmire is tired. "It had been the kind of winter that tested the souls of even the hardiest" (p. 1), and the Sherriff of Wyoming's Absaroka County is feeling the accumulated weight of nearly thirty years on the job—plus the complications of his quasi-romance with Deputy Vic Moretti. Walt has little time for introspection, however, when the town junkman is dragged two-plus miles over frozen roads tied to the back of his family's 1968 Oldsmobile Toronado. Fortunately, seventy-two-year-old Geo Stewart is seemingly indestructible and survives his icy escapade. But, as the Stewart clan's unwieldy saga begins to unfold, the whole department finds itself caught up in a case that strains their already frayed nerves to the breaking point.

Walt's other deputy, Santiago "Sancho" Saizarbitoria, is grappling with his mortality after "having a serrated kitchen knife filleting one of his kidneys" (p. 25). To make things worse, Sancho's reentry to police work is complicated by the recent birth of his first child. He's ready to call it quits, but Walt is determined to keep him on the job, or at least cure him of his

3

"bullet fever" (p. 48) first. So when Geo and his grandson, Duane, find a recently severed thumb at the dump, Walt puts Sancho on the case.

While recovering the thumb, Walt and Sancho witness a stand-off between Geo and Ozzie Dobbs, a local real estate developer. For years, Ozzie has been working to build Redhills Rancho Arroyo—a spread of "five-acre ranchettes with four-million-dollar mansions alongside a golf course" (p. 27). The only fly in the ointment is the fact that the development's splendid views are marred by the junkyard—which Geo refuses to sell. But the lawmen are stopped in their tracks by the prolonged kiss exchanged—out of Ozzie's sight—between the junkman and Ozzie's exceedingly lovely and genteel mother, Betty.

His professional duties momentarily on the back burner, Walt returns to his mounting personal troubles. Vic longs to own a home that doesn't rest on wheels, and she's upping the hostility toward Walt for his inability to commit. Meanwhile, his grown daughter, Cady, a Philadelphia-based lawyer, is planning her wedding—to Michael Moretti, Vic's younger brother. Beset with headaches brought on by a neglected eye injury, Walt fantasizes about retiring to "Hatch, New Mexico . . . [and] a little adobe house . . . with chilies hanging in the window" (p. 97).

All too soon, a very real dead body jolts the honorable sheriff out of his daydreams to uncover a tangled web of illicit drugs and even more illicit family relations. With the mother of all snowstorms on the way—and stonewalled by Duane, Duane's wife Gina, and a pair of the meanest mutts in the West—Walt must draw on all his resources to stop a killer. Filled with humor, pathos, and unforgettable Western imagery,

Craig Johnson's *Junkyard Dogs* is another page-turning adventure in the series that's made Walt Longmire a beloved mystery favorite.

ABOUT CRAIG JOHNSON

Craig Johnson is the author of six Walt Longmire mysteries. He lives in Ucross, Wyoming, population twenty-five.

A CONVERSATION WITH CRAIG JOHNSON

Junkyard Dogs *shows a more sober and reflective Walt than previous novels. Was this intentional?*

The town of Durant is hunkered down for a winter storm, and for all the severity of the weather and isolation it might as well be on the moon. Winter tends to bring out the morose in my sadder but wiser sheriff; I looked at the book as my "winter of our discontent." It deals with the more venal aspects of human nature and that has a tendency in law enforcement to wear you down in the day-to-day, which might be what you're responding to. In direct opposition to this is that I think this is also the most humorous book I've written.

Parental anxiety (e.g. Walt/Cady, Betty/Ozzie, and Sancho/ Antonio) seems to be a central theme of this novel. What inspired this?

Nobody pushes your buttons (both good and bad) like family, and with the claustrophobic aspects of the book, I thought it just fit. The microcosm of community is family, so it was the next logical step in going inward. In a lot of ways that's what the book is about; the things that people do to each other and just how far they'll go. What starts out as a neighborly squabble erupts into a full-blown range war.

This is Walt's sixth outing. What do you do to stay fresh over so many novels?

Tony Hillerman once told me that—at the risk of sounding like an old sports analogy—you've got to play 'em one at a time. Each book is an entity unto itself and you have to treat it with that respect, not try and get it to fit some artificial formula you've cooked up or that might've been successful for you before. Each of the books deals with a social problem as a catalyst such as the one for this one—the economy of the new West. It might be dangerous rolling the dice on each book, but I'd rather offend the readers that way than by writing the same book all the time.

You've incorporated the country's current economic woes into the story. Have you felt its repercussions even in your town of twenty-five residents?

There's always a cushion in rural living, but times are hard for a lot of people and I think it's important to reflect the world n which the characters live accurately. The financial limitations hat Walt faces as a small, rural police force are more of an dvantage to the writing than a hindrance. Walt can't always get n his cell phone or computer and look for answers, so instead e falls back on old-style policing, which lends itself to the xploration of character and humanity. That stuff is always going o be more interesting than gadgets.

Sometimes the setting of a novel can be so vivid that it's like nother character. In Junkyard Dogs, *one could say that about the veather. Is it really that much of a presence? Do you, like Walt, antasize about retiring to New Mexico?*

You know, there was a point last spring where I tractored the ix-foot drifts on my ranch road four times in two weeks, and hat got old. I live in Walt's surroundings and I think that's an dvantage in the writing. I'll let you in on a dirty little secret of nine, a way that I'm very different from Walt—I love cold. I uilt my ranch in northern Wyoming for a reason. If I'd wanted o, I could've built it in New Mexico or Arizona but I like he winter; it keeps you tough. Walt fantasizes about warmer climates, but I don't think he'd last here—as much as he'd enjoy he great Mexican food, he needs the high plains.

In one passage, the emergency room doctor tells Walt that Geo's "hair has grown through his long underwear" (p. 16). Is this, or any of the other colorful stories in the novel, based in real life?

You caught that, huh? It's true. They brought a neighbor of mine in after he cracked a few ribs and discovered that indeed, his hair had grown through his long underwear. There are so many weird and wonderful things about where I live, and it's just too much of a temptation to place them in the novels; most of the time when somebody confronts me about something ridiculous in my books it's actually a true story.

Your last novel, The Dark Horse, *featured a highly intelligent horse and a woman who felt more connected to horses than humans. Here, the junkyard dogs, Butch and Sundance, have very distinct personalities and loyalties. Do you believe that animals are capable of good and evil?*

I think we can discern their actions as good or evil, but that's just us. There was a character in my last novel who stated my feelings on the subject best, "Animals is some of the finest people I know." In many ways, the defense for Butch and Sundance is very similar to the ones we have for ourselves—just doing their job. Thankfully, Dog was just doing his . . .

Some might think that big-time drug dealing is an urban problem. Would this be an incorrect assumption?

Yes. For production purposes, these individuals need privacy and there's a lot of open country out there. This isn't exactly a news flash with the number of methamphetamine and marijuana busts that have been made across the country in very rural areas.

Previously you've said that outrage over social inequities inspires your work. Is that the case in this novel?

Not much question about that, is there? If you look at the differences between Red Hills Arroyo and the Stewart compound the differences become pretty evident. A lot of the economy of the West is one of the haves and the have-nots, and I'm not sure it's getting any better. I get outraged pretty easy, and it's great fuel for the writing.

What's next for Craig Johnson and Walt Longmire?

Hell Is Empty is the title of the next book and it comes from Prospero's line in *The Tempest*—"Hell is empty and the devils are all here." Walt is involved in an exhumation in the Bighorn Mountains when a number of individuals escape from a private transportation firm. The novel is a metaphor for *The Inferno*, which Saizarbitoria happens to be reading in an attempt to make up for the lack of liberal arts education in his criminal justice degree. When Walt starts out after these very dangerous individuals, Sancho pokes the paperback into his pack for reading material and the similarities begin to mount. Can anybody remember who Dante's guide through hell was?

QUESTIONS FOR DISCUSSION

1. In what ways is Walt the archetypal Western lawman? In what ways is he different?

2. Why does Gina pretend to be pregnant with Ozzie's baby? What does she hope to gain?

3. Should Betty have told Ozzie about her relationship with Geo? Does a parent owe it to her child—young or grown—to share her romantic status?

4. Is Walt's own reluctance to commit to Vic rooted in their age difference, their working relationship, or in Cady's engagement to Michael? What would you do in Walt's position?

5. Discuss the metaphorical significance of the book's title.

6. Does Walt do the right thing by trying to cure Sancho of his "bullet fever"? Would Sancho's reaction have been the same if he hadn't recently become a father?

7. In this novel, is it more difficult to be a parent, or a child?

Spoiler Warning: Don't read any further if you don't want to know whodunit!

8. An injection of air kills Geo, but one also saves Walt's vision. Are there any other examples of this kind of duality in the novel?

9. Did you feel any sympathy toward white supremacist Felix Polk/Paulson because of his cancer and the fake granddaughter that his so-called pals used to trick him? If so, did you find these feelings troubling?

10. When Walt discovers that Gina is the killer, he seems to want to exculpate her crimes, saying: "She's a poster child for fucked-up—in and out of foster homes, finally living on the streets, and prostitution." (p. 301). What are your thoughts?

For more information about or to order other Penguin
Readers Guides, please e-mail the Penguin Marketing
Department at reading@us.penguingroup.com or write to us at:

Penguin Books Marketing Dept.
Readers Guides
375 Hudson Street
New York, NY 10014-3657

Please allow 4–6 weeks for delivery.
To access Penguin Readers Guides online, visit the
Penguin Group (USA) Inc. Web site at www.penguin.com or
www.vpbookclub.com.

The Dark Horse

Wade Barsad burned his wife's horses in their barn; in retribution, she shot him in the head six times. Suspicious of her guilt, Walt goes undercover and discovers that everyone had a reason for wanting Wade dead.

ISBN 978-0-14-311731-5

Another Man's Moccasins

The body of a Vietnamese woman dumped along the Wyoming interstate opens a baffling case for Sheriff Longmire, whose only suspect is a Crow Indian with a troubled history. But things get even stranger when a photograph turns up in the victim's purse that ties her murder to Longmire's experiences in Vietnam years earlier.

ISBN 978-0-14-311552-6

PENGUIN
BOOKS

AVAILABLE FROM PENGUIN

Death Without Company

When Mari Baroja is found poisoned at the Durant Home for Assisted Living, Sheriff Longmire is drawn into an investigation that delves into fifty years of the woman's mysterious life.

ISBN 978-0-14-303838-2

Kindness Goes Unpunished

Walt's trip to Philadelphia to visit his daughter, Cady, turns into a nightmare when she is the victim of a vicious attack that leaves her near death. Walt is forced to unpack his saddlebag of tricks to mete out some Western-style justice.

ISBN 978-0-14-311313-3

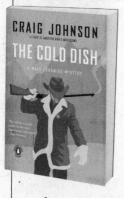

The Cold Dish

Walt Longmire knows he's got trouble when Cody Pritchard is found dead. Two years earlier, Cody and three accomplices had been given suspended sentences for raping a Northern Cheyenne girl. Longmire means to see that revenge, a dish that is best served cold, is never served at all.

ISBN 978-0-14-303642-5

PENGU
BOOK